Ryan Weller Thrillers:

Dark Water

Dark Ship

Dark Horse

Dark Shadows

DARK HORSE

A Ryan Weller Thriller

EVAN GRAVER

THIRD REEF
PUBLISHING LLC

Dark Horse

© 2018, 2019 Evan Graver

www.evangraver.com

All rights reserved. No part of this publication may be reproduced, distributed, or transmitted in any forms or by any means, including photocopying, recording, or other electronic, or mechanical methods, without the prior written permission of the publisher, except in the case of brief quotations embodied in critical reviews and certain noncommercial uses permitted by copyright law.

ISBN-10: 1-7338866-2-1

ISBN-13: 978-1-7338866-2-8

Cover: Wicked Good Book Covers

Editing: Larks and Katydids

Proofreading: Gerald Shaw

This is a work of fiction. Any resemblance to any person, living or dead, business, companies, events, or locales is entirely coincidental.

Printed and bound in the United States of America

First Printed May 2019

Published by Third Reef Publishing, LLC

Hollywood, Florida

www.thirdreefpublishing.com

CHAPTER ONE

R yan Weller climbed out of the water and stood on the deck of the Newton 46 dive boat. He was one of twenty other divers on the cattle run to the wreck of the USS *Spiegel Grove*. He walked forward to the small cabin, unclipped the two forty cubic inch bailout bottles, set them in the tank rack, and finally slipped the rebreather off his shoulders. He eased the device to the deck and checked it over before stowing it under the boat's built-in bench seat.

Next, Ryan peeled off his three-millimeter thick wetsuit. He wore compression shorts underneath and pulled gray boardshorts over them. After he shoved his wetsuit, mask, gloves, fins, boots, computers, and compass into his dive bag, he climbed up to the bridge with a cold bottle of water and stood beside the captain. Stacey Coleman was a short girl with wide hips, small breasts, purple hair, and several piercings in her ears, nose, and lip.

"Have a good dive?"

"Terrific, Stacey. How can they be bad on a day like this?" He spread his hands to encompass what they referred to as Lake Atlantic on days when the ocean was mirror flat, the current nonexistent, and visibility exceeded seventy-five feet.

"Days like this make me wish I was diving instead of driving the boat."

"You driving this afternoon?"

Stacey stuck her lip out in a pout. "Yes, I'm taking forty-five snorkelers to the Christ of the Abyss statue."

"That doesn't sound like fun." He took a long drink of water.

"It's better than sitting in the office. Why aren't you teaching today?"

"I took the day off. Speaking of which, can I borrow your car to run down to Stock Island?"

"You can't borrow Mark's?" Stacey asked, referring to Mark Lester, Ryan's roommate and fellow instructor at the dive facility.

"He's using it today."

Stacey turned up the stereo. Queen's "Fat Bottomed Girls" reverberated off the water. She cocked a hip and grinned lasciviously at Ryan.

He gave a half smile and shook his head. It was a game they played. Neither of them took it seriously enough to move past the overt flirting.

Sweat trickled down Ryan's back as the sun bore down on them. He adjusted his sunglasses, took a swig of water, and absently watched the other divers climb back on the boat. They'd done a double dip, two dives on the *Spiegel* instead of a single dive before moving to another location. The double dip had allowed him to do a longer, forty-minute decompression dive instead of the normal twin twenty-minute dives. He'd entered the water with the other divers on their first dip and surfaced before they'd completed their second.

Ryan had also surfaced because his mind wasn't on the dive. When his mind wandered to other pursuits while he was underwater, it was time to head back to the boat. He had no desire to die from complacency. His thoughts were filled with memories of twenty-five million dollars in gold bars in a sunken ship off the coast of Haiti. Even sitting beside Stacey, he could see in his mind the gleaming gold bricks in the ship's hold.

Queen morphed into Zac Brown. Two or three people began singing along with "Toes." Ryan tapped his foot and hummed the "I got my toes in the water ..." lyrics.

Stacey grabbed a clipboard and headed down the ladder. She began calling names of the divers to ensure everyone was back on the boat. With the roll call complete, she returned to the bridge and cranked up the diesel engine. It snorted eagerly to life. She edged the boat forward, allowing the crewman to release the boat's bridle from the mooring ball.

Ryan finished the water and crushed the bottle flat before screwing the cap back on. He watched Stacey spin the boat's wheel, swinging the bow around to face Key Largo. She shoved the throttle forward and the big boat came up on plane.

Thirty minutes later, Ryan watched the multi-million-dollar houses slide past while they idled up Port Largo channel. Most of the homes were empty this time of year. Some still had hurricane shutters bolted in place, and others had obvious storm damage yet to be repaired. Occasionally, maintenance workers could be seen mowing lawns, trimming bushes, or making improvements.

The boat made the blind left-hand turn, known as "Crash Corner," and continued past marinas, more homes, hotels, and other dive charter services. Stacey spun the

Newton one-hundred-and-eighty degrees and eased it alongside the dive shop's dock. Crewmen tied the lines fast. She cut off the motors, climbed down to the main deck, made a speech to the divers about tipping their guides, and invited them back to dive again.

Ryan carried his gear off the boat and set it on a picnic table. He turned back to the Newton. Stacey and her crew were busy refilling scuba tanks and preparing the boat for the afternoon run.

"Hey, Stacey," Ryan called.

"Yeah?" She glanced up.

"Can I borrow your car?"

She laughed. "You really need to get a life, Ryan."

The tide was out, and the boat was much lower than the dock. He placed his hands on the bridge deck and leaned under it to see her adjusting the fill whip on a tank near the boat's cabin door. "You're right, but I still need to run down to Stock Island."

Stacey climbed the steps off the boat and stopped in front of Ryan. He was six-feet tall and she barely came up to his chest. "You might be all sexy with your sun-bleached brown hair and your green eyes, but this beach bum thing you got going is kind of a turn off."

He grinned. "Thanks."

"It wasn't a compliment."

"I'll take you out to dinner," he offered.

"Are you asking me on a date?"

"No, just to thank you for borrowing the car."

"You're an idiot."

"Most of the time." Ryan shrugged. "Stacey, do you want to go on a date?" He'd avoided getting involved with anyone because the job was only temporary until he figured out how to remove the bounty a Mexican drug lord had put on him, or he decided it was time to go for the gold. The bounty wasn't going away, and it was time to nurse the gold fever.

She rolled her eyes before handing him her car keys. With a smile, she said, "Make sure you fill the tank up."

Ryan took the keys and shoved them in his pocket. "Thanks, Stace."

"Call me if you're going to be too late."

"Yes, ma'am." He snapped to attention and rendered a hand salute.

"Asshole," Stacey muttered, stepping down into the boat.

Ryan gathered his gear, rinsed it in the freshwater buckets, and crammed it into the back of Stacey's Kia Rio. He drove south on Highway 1 to a small apartment complex, parked the car, and carried his equipment inside. After a quick shower, he pulled on cargo shorts, a polo shirt, and deck shoes. He grabbed a sandwich and a Mountain Dew and shoehorned himself back in the car.

CHAPTER TWO

The Overseas Highway had been rated as one of the best drives in North America by multiple bloggers and National Geographic. What had once been the Overseas Railroad, built by Henry Flagler, and operated from 1912 to its partial destruction by the Labor Day Hurricane in 1935, had now become a four-lane highway to bring tourists, industry, and trade to the Florida Keys. Routes had changed and new bridges constructed to handle the increasing traffic traveling through the jewels of the American Caribbean, but the beauty, mystery, and adventure remained.

Ryan always enjoyed the drive. It put him in a tropical frame of mind. Everything from scuba diving to skydiving were at his fingertips. He couldn't help but smile as he passed sunburned tourists, swaying palms, and run-down T-shirt shacks. Old Florida mixing with the new. But today, twenty-five million other things occupied his mind.

Over the last three months, he'd thought a lot about the gold. It called to him. He now understood why thousands of miners braved the frontier and crossed oceans in search of the precious metal, and the opportunities it brought. But it was more than the prospect of striking it rich; it was the excitement of the hunt. Adventure called. He'd spent enough time being idle. He needed to go get it, or someone else would.

As far as Ryan knew, besides himself, there were only a handful of people in the world who knew there was gold on the *Santo Domingo*. Chief among them was Jim Kilroy, the international arms dealer who had agreed to supply Haitian warlord Toussaint Bajeux with a shipload of weapons in exchange for the two pallets of gold.

After Kilroy's deliveryman was killed at a resort in Belize during a raid by Russian hitmen trying to capture Ryan and has partner, Mango, Kilroy had offered the men sanctuary on the *Santo Domingo* in exchange for delivering the weapons. He had also promised to get the two-million-dollar bounty lifted by negotiating with José Luis Orozco, leader of the Aztlán cartel. The bounty was Orozco's retribution for Ryan killing the former cartel leader, Arturo Guerrero.

During the delivery of the weapons, a rival warlord had attacked the *Santo Domingo* with RPGs. The weapons, vehicles, and gold payment had all sunk with the ship. Ryan and Mango had donned rebreathers and sat inside a Humvee until the ship had sunk to the seabed and then swam to shore. They then rescued Greg Olsen, from the hands of a Russian bounty hunter. The trio, along with Toussaint's mistress, Joulie Lafitte, used DWR's Hatteras GT63 sportfisher, *Dark Water*, to escape to the Bahamas to avoid Hurricane Irma.

DWR had declared Ryan and Mango lost at sea, but even with their supposed deaths, Orozco hadn't lifted the bounty. Mango and his wife, Jennifer, had sailed away on their Amazon 44 sailboat, *Alamo*, and Ryan had chosen to hide out in the Florida Keys like many outlaws and pirates before him. He'd worked various jobs to help clean up after Hurricane Irma had destroyed much of the Lower Keys. He'd gutted houses, salvaged boats, and helped remove debris, scraps, abandoned shacks, and rusted appliances. Eventually, he made his way to Key Largo, where he spent most of his time teaching scuba diving and thinking about the gold.

But, like many people who hide in the American Caribbean, Ryan found the pace of life could be just as hectic as living on the mainland with schedules, bills, stop-and-go traffic, and high rent.

Ryan groaned as he slammed on the brakes for the lengthy line of cars that had stopped for a camper turning into Bahia Honda State Park. Several car horns blared to express the displeasure of the waiting drivers. Ryan felt the frustration himself but didn't let it boil over. He took a deep breath and watched the vehicles whiz by in the opposite direction. To his right, a couple rode on bicycles on the repurposed railroad bed known as the Florida Keys Overseas Heritage Trail.

The traffic began to move, and he worked his way west through Big Pine, Middle Torch, Saddle Bunch, and a host of other small keys to reach Stock Island, the next-to-last key before A1A dead-ended in Key West.

Key West had once been the home of great fishing and shrimping fleets. In the name of progress, they were relocated to Stock Island and over the years the fleets had dwindled in proportion to the supply of their catch. Now, these meager fleets were in danger of being pushed out again as more houses, apartment complexes, and businesses encroached on their industrial docks.

Fifth Avenue turned into Fourth Avenue just before it made a forty-five-degree bend to the northeast. At this bend, Ryan turned into a parking lot. The entrance was flanked by vine-covered chain-link fence and a haphazard stack of wooden pallets. Just inside the gate he turned right, and followed the cracked and eroded blacktop, passing between lobster boats backed up to the concrete quay and long stacks of their lobster traps. The road turned into dirt as it ended at another concrete pier.

Ryan parked the Kia in the shade of a satinleaf tree, climbed out, and stretched his legs and back. He took a deep breath of the brine mixed with diesel, fish, and something rotten. He walked to the water and saw a sheen of oil prisming the colors of the rainbow beside a bobbing cigarette butt. Absentmindedly, he patted his cargo pocket. It was empty, and he remembered he hadn't had a cigarette since his last visit to Toussaint Bajeux's home in Haiti, over six months ago.

He lifted his gaze from the polluted water and found the faded red steel hull of a seventy-five-foot trawler, *Peggy Lynn*. This was the boat he'd come to see. He walked across the parking lot, kicking up dust with each step. As he walked, he checked out the converted fishing boat. The tall steel posts of an A-frame mast, sprouting out of the hull and towering above the bridge, had been gusseted and bracketed to increase lift capacity. Thick braided cable ran off a heavy-duty reel, up through the block and tackle, and out along the single boom extending from the A-frame. Cables leading down from the peak of the A-frame supported the boom, allowing it to be raised, lowered, or swung over the sides of the boat. Ryan looked up at the crane's big lifting hook and pictured a cargo net full of gold bars dangling from it.

With the tide in, the boat's railing was slightly higher than the quay. Thick rubber tires bolted to the concrete kept the converted trawler off the dock. More tires hung from chains around the boat's stern.

"Ahoy the boat," Ryan yelled.

A man with a thick head of white hair and a trim white beard stepped out of the bridge. He wore white tennis shoes, stained khaki pants, and a T-shirt with the words *Peggy Lynn* on the left breast pocket, matching the words printed on the boat's bow in block white letters.

"You hollarin' for me?"

"Yes, sir," Ryan said. "Are you Captain Dennis Law?"

"I am." Dennis nodded.

"I'd like to talk to you about a job."

"I'm retired, son."

"That's why I'm here. Everyone else is busy. I need a good salvage vessel to go after a load of cargo in a sunken freighter."

"Them days are long gone. Old *Peggy Lynn* doesn't leave the dock anymore." He patted the ship's handrail. "She's a grand old lady, but her days are numbered. You'll have to find another captain to take you out. I was lucky to get her up in the mangroves and survive the hurricane." He stepped back into the wheelhouse.

"Look, Captain, I need your help." Ryan moved closer to the rail. "This is a big haul. If you won't go as captain, sell me your vessel."

Dennis slowly turned around.

"I'm serious," Ryan said. "I need a working salvage vessel. Yours fits the bill."

Captain Law ran a hand through his hair. "Make some sense, son. This vessel is older than you are. She's seen better days. Besides *Peggy Lynn* is my home."

"Permission to come aboard, sir?"

"Come on." He motioned for Ryan to join him on the bridge.

Ryan climbed aboard, introduced himself, and followed the captain inside.

"Cup of coffee?" Dennis asked.

"Yes, black."

"Good. I don't have anything to put in it unless you want a little whiskey." Dennis held up a pint of Jim Beam.

Ryan shook his head. "I'm good, I like mine black. Like my soul."

The captain laughed. He handed Ryan a cup of steaming black coffee and poured a shot of whiskey into his. "What's this nonsense you're talking about, wanting to buy my boat?"

"I know where there's a lucrative treasure in the hold of a sunken ship."

Dennis sat down in the chair behind the helm and propped his foot on the dash. "How exactly do you know where this ship is, and what's on it?"

"I was on the freighter when she sank. I also helped load the cargo." Ryan sipped at the coffee. It was hot and bitter. He would have to make a change in what grounds they used if they agreed to work together.

Captain Law stared out the front windows of the bridge for several long minutes. Ryan waited patiently for the older man to continue. He took a sip of coffee and then ran a hand through his hair.

"I met my wife before I went to Vietnam," Dennis said quietly. "I spent my whole life fishing, shrimping, and salvaging just to make money to keep her happy. She gave me three children." He turned to face Ryan. "She died four years ago, be five next May. Cancer stole her from me and her babies." He shook his head. "I lost my will to do much of anything when she died. I did some fishing and some salvage work, but my heart wasn't in it. A man's got to have something to live for, you know what I mean?"

"Yes, sir." Ryan glanced down at the framed picture of the couple. Peggy had been a petite blonde with a broad smile.

"What makes you want to salvage this ship?"

"I'd like to tell you about it, Captain, but only if you agree to skipper this vessel."

"And if I say no again?"

"I'll find someone else, and you can go back to wallowing in your pain, sir."

The older man was about to take a sip of coffee. He stopped and looked over the rim. "Blunt, aren't you?"

"I need you, Captain. I need your boat. You need me. You need this job. You have surface supply air?"

"You're being impertinent, son."

"I can get some men to go over your boat, check all the systems, and put on some new gear."

"You got deep pockets?"

"Deep enough, and when we complete this job, neither of us will have to worry about making a living again."

"What are you after?"

"Not until you say yes."

"If I say yes, you'll tell me what you're after and have men fix up my boat?"

Ryan finished his cup of coffee. "Yes, sir."

"This must be important to you."

"It is, Captain." Ryan poured another cup. He figured the liquid could double as paint thinner, or rust remover. "I almost died over this cargo, and I've been declared dead because of it. What we're after is the stuff dreams are made of. Men will be willing to kill, steal, and lie to get their hands on it. Men have already died for it. Are you willing to take that chance, Captain Law?"

"Son, I've been shot by gooks, stabbed by disgruntled crewmen, and suffered more than one broken heart. The only things I've got left in this world are this boat, three kids, and five grandkids, most of which I don't see." Law stood up. "The only thing to drive a man as crazy as you say is gold, or drugs. I don't mess with drugs. So, what are we talking about, son?"

Ryan said, "It's not drugs."

"All right, Mr. Weller," Dennis said, thrusting his hand out. "I'm in."

"Great news, sir."

"How much are we talking about?" Dennis asked.

"There were fifty-two gold bars, each weighing twenty-seven pounds. That's ..."

"One thousand four hundred and four pounds," Dennis finished the sentence.

Ryan paused to look at the old man, his mind obviously clear and sharp despite the two shots of booze Ryan had seen him pour into his coffee. Who knows how many he'd swallowed before he'd arrived?

Dennis continued, "At the current spot price of gold, that's $26,766,540.43."

"How do you know what the price of gold is, Captain?"

Dennis tapped the flat screen computer monitor beside the coffee pot. "I keep an eye on my wife's stocks. She was a frugal woman. I gave her every paycheck. She put it to good use, raised our kids, bought a house, invested in the stock market. When I wanted to buy this boat, I told her I needed to go to the bank and get a loan. She had a sizeable down payment already saved up, like she knew what I wanted before I did."

Ryan laughed. "Leave it to the women to take care of us."

"You got a woman taking care of you?"

"I did, but she didn't like my adventurous life."

Dennis nodded in understanding and sipped his coffee. "Where are we going?"

"Haiti."

Captain Dennis Law shook his head and laughed. "I hope you have some good engineers, son, 'cause we're gonna need 'em."

CHAPTER THREE

Ryan sat at a waterside table at Hogfish Bar and Grill, staring at the sailboats floating along the small wharf. He nursed a margarita and waited for the waitress to deliver a hogfish sandwich smothered in Swiss cheese, onions, and mushrooms on Cuban bread. He had to take Stacey to dinner in a few hours, but he couldn't pass up the chance to eat one of the restaurant's signature sandwiches.

The last time he'd occupied a stool at the famous eatery was last June when he and Emily Hunt had what would become their first date. There weren't many women in Ryan Weller's life whom he really missed. If he counted, there were three—his mother, his high school sweetheart, Sara Sherman, and Emily Hunt.

He tried not to reminisce about their evening at Hogfish, or the night of lovemaking that had followed. She was passionate about many of the same things as he was: sailing, diving, and traveling. But they lived in two different lives. Hers was the starched world of insurance investigation. His was the more fluid world of what? What was his job right now? Scuba instructor? Salvage diver?

Ryan grinned as he thought about what John D. McDonald's fictional character, Travis McGee, told people when they'd asked what his job was. He'd always answer, "Salvage consultant."

He took a sip of the margarita. Beyond the masts of the sailboats, Ryan could see *Peggy Lynn*'s red hue. A slight breeze rustled the palm leaves and a metal clip clanged against a hollow aluminum sailboat mast. It made a rhythmic clinking sound, adding to the engine noises of the steady stream of boats passing in and out of Safe Harbor.

Ryan picked up his cell phone and scrolled to his favorite contacts. He tapped the button over Greg Olsen's name and held the phone to his ear.

"How's the vacation?"

"Pretty good," Ryan answered. "I've got a favor to ask you?"

"Oh, no. How much is this going to cost me?"

"Consider it an investment."

Greg laughed. Ryan pictured his friend and former employer. The two men could have passed for brothers with similar height and builds. Greg's eyes were gray, and his hair was a darker shade of brown. His shoulders and arms had filled out from pushing his wheelchair, and the constant use of his upper body.

Greg had been president of Dark Water Research when he'd recruited Ryan to be the company's Homeland Security liaison. Greg had wanted to be part of the action and tagged along on both of Ryan's assignments and had nearly got himself killed on the last one.

"What kind of investment, Ryan?"

"Why are you so suspicious?"

"Because I think you're about to do something crazy."

"Maybe."

"Details," Greg demanded.

"Remember the ship that sank a few months ago?"

"Uh-huh."

"I want to go after the cargo."

"I'm not authorizing my crews and vessels to get tangled up with a psycho gun dealer."

"I found an old salvage boat and captain. What I need is a few goodies added on and a guy to go through the mechanicals."

Greg let out a deep sigh.

Ryan prodded, "You know what's down there."

"I know the risks, too."

"This is what DWR does, Greg," Ryan said. "Send me a diver if you want."

"I'd rather come myself, but I've been told I can't play hooky anymore."

"This is a dangerous business. I want you to be safe at the office." Ryan glanced up to see the waitress delivering a plateful of sandwich and fries. "Speaking of the office, what are you doing now that Admiral Chatel is running the place?"

Greg yawned. "I'm sitting on my back deck, enjoying the sunshine."

"Are you doing anything at DWR?" Ryan asked. Greg had chosen to step down from his position as president after hiring Kip Chatel, a former executive at Boeing and at one time their commanding officer at Navy Expeditionary Combat Command.

"Yeah, Shelly made me the point of contact for all our operations in Puerto Rico. We've been rebuilding port facilities and upgrading their infrastructure."

"Sounds like you're busier than you want to be," Ryan said with a grin. Shelly wasn't going to let her boyfriend sit around with nothing to do as long as she was DWR's chief operating officer.

"Too busy. But I'm tired of paperwork. Where's this boat you want to fix up?"

Ryan finished chewing his fry. "Safe Harbor on Stock Island. Her name's *Peggy Lynn*."

"What makes you so sure that Jim Kilroy hasn't already recovered the gold?"

"I'm not."

"Lucky for you I know a guy who says there haven't been any salvage boats operating around Cap-Haïtien, or Fort Liberte."

"Really?" Ryan asked. "You have a source in Haiti?"

"Yeah. Billy Parker, the guy who runs the marina where Volk held me hostage, keeps me updated on what's going on."

"You knew I was going after the gold?"

"Ryan," Greg said patronizingly.

Ryan closed his eyes and shook his head. "You've been waiting for this call, haven't you?"

Greg laughed. "From the moment we left Haiti. Send me a list of what you need, and I'll have Chuck fly everything out."

Ryan asked, "Do I need to find a diver, too, or do you have one handy?"

"I should sic Jerry DiMarco on your ass," Greg said. "But he told me he wouldn't mind if you didn't come back from the dead."

"Tell Jerry I miss him too," Ryan said without any warmth in his voice.

Greg laughed. "Okay. I have a guy I'll send along."

"Is he any good?"

Greg snorted. "Send me the list."

Ryan was about to say something when he realized Greg had hung up on him. He pocketed the phone and tucked into his meal.

Twenty minutes later, the waitress brought him the bill and a refill for the cup of coffee he'd ordered halfway through his sandwich. Ryan watched the passing boats as he sipped his drink. The plan was coming together. He couldn't wait to get started. A nervous energy surged through him, and he wanted to jump up and run a marathon just to burn off some steam. A smile crossed his lips. He was going into action, and once he stopped hiding, the bounty hunters and the cartel would come for him. It made him feel alive.

A man walked out of the restaurant and lit a cigarette. He lingered along the dock, admiring the boats. When the smoker came abreast of him, Ryan asked, "Can I bum one of those?"

"Yeah," the man said, digging out the pack. He handed a Marlboro Gold to Ryan and turned away.

"I hate to bug you again, but can I borrow your lighter."

The guy chuckled. "Want me to smoke it for you, too?"

"Nah, I've been trying to quit." Ryan took a deep inhale of smoke and handed the lighter back.

"Aren't we all?"

"Thanks," Ryan said and picked up his coffee cup. The man continued his stroll down the dock.

The first few inhales were good. The rush of nicotine hit his system, and he enjoyed the repetitive action of putting his hand to his mouth. He'd been a two-pack-a-day smoker during his deployments to Iraq and Afghanistan. When he'd returned home, he'd cut back, but still smoked at least half a pack a day. Mango and Emily had been on him to quit, and he would have for her. While she wasn't around

anymore, he had gone cold turkey after his arrival in the
Keys. Right now, he didn't care. She'd tossed him off like
some bad hat, so what difference did it make?

It was the fifth inhale of smoke which made him feel
like he was just going through the motions. His lips were
dry, and his throat and lungs ached. Ryan crushed the butt
out before he was halfway through.

With his tab paid, he walked out of the Hogfish and
found the Kia. He climbed in and started the engine.
Backing out of the spot, he glimpsed two men standing
beside a beat-up pickup truck. One was a muscular African
American with long dreadlocks and a full beard. It was
obvious he spent many hours in the gym. His arms and
chest bulged around the fabric of a black wife beater and his
thick calves indicated he hadn't skipped leg day. The
second man was shorter and of Mexican descent. His black
hair was cut close to his scalp and a ragged goatee hung
from his chin. He wore baggy jeans and a short-sleeved
fishing shirt.

Both men looked straight at Ryan as the nose of the Kia
swung past. When Ryan made eye contact with them, the
Mexican turned away, and Dreadlocks opened the door of
the pickup truck.

Ryan's heart rate increased. *Relax, they're fishermen
sharing a joke at the end of the day, or friends meeting for
dinner.* The conjecture did little to satisfy the adrenaline
rushing through his veins. He had no reason to be suspicious of the men, yet their actions had made them suspicious. If they were friends, why not continue to talk? Why
turn away?

He watched the road behind him, through the rearview
mirror, as he navigated the streets back to A1A. He glanced
at the clock. He was going to get back late, and Stacey

would not be happy about having to wait for supper. He dialed her number and apologized when she came on the line.

"Typical, Ryan," she said. He could hear the frustration in her voice. "Call me when you get to my place."

"Yes, ma'am."

The phone went dead. He dialed another number.

"What's up, bro?" Mango Hulsey asked in typical fashion.

"You ready to get back into the action?"

"No ... why?"

"I'm going after the gold, you in?"

"Hell no."

"Come on, man. I need you."

"Not after the last dive we did together. I'll stay within recreational limits, bro."

Their last dive had been a harrowing experience. They'd sat in a Humvee while the *Santo Domingo* sank. When she came to rest on the ocean floor, the Humvee had rolled over several times and trapped them in its twisted frame. They'd negotiated their way out of the Humvee and the ship's cavernous hold before swimming a mile to shore. The total dive had taken them two hours, and Mango had made it clear that he would not be doing any more technical diving.

"This will be different. We'll be on surface supply."

"He said no, Ryan." Jennifer Hulsey's voice came over the speaker. "He's staying right here with me."

Ryan asked, "How's the trip been so far?"

"Really good," Mango replied. "We're in Guadalupe."

Ryan chuckled. "You haven't made it very far."

"Far enough, bro. We're taking your advice, enjoy the trip and don't rush."

"I'm glad things are going well for you," Ryan said.

"What about you, bro?"

"I was teaching diving in Key Largo. Now I'm going to recover some gold. You sure you don't want in on this, Mango?"

"Look, bro, I had a good time shootin' and lootin' with you, but, bro, I'm out. I can't keep putting myself and Jennifer in harm's way. We have to use fake IDs because we still have a bounty on us. I don't need more bad guys chasing me. You know, bro, as soon as you perform your miraculous resurrection, they'll be dog piling you."

"I understand," Ryan replied glumly, disappointed Mango didn't want to join him. He couldn't blame him though. Their work was dangerous, and both men had come close to losing their lives on the two missions they'd performed for DWR and Homeland.

"Be careful, Ryan."

"I will. Talk to you later."

"Later, bro."

Ryan hung up and tossed the phone on the passenger seat. "Well, crap."

———

THE DIGITAL CLOCK readout on the Kia's dash blinked seven thirty as Ryan pulled the car into the lot at Stacey's apartment complex. He parked and jogged up the stairs to her rental unit. She jerked the door open before he could knock.

"You're late," Stacey said.

"Hey, I called."

"I don't like to be kept waiting."

"Here's your car keys. Sorry I was late. I'll see you

later." Ryan dropped her keys into her hand and started down the stairs.

"You're an insufferable ..."

Ryan paused and looked up at Stacey. "I don't need to be treated like this. I've got enemies who treat me better than you right now."

Stacey raised her eyebrows and pulled the door shut behind her. With an air of exasperation, she said, "Let's go."

"Maybe it's better this way, Stacey. I'm leaving tomorrow, turning in my resignation at the dive shop, and taking off."

She stopped midstride and stared up at him. "Where are you going?"

"Back to my day job. This six-month vacation in the Keys has been nice, but I have a job I need to go back to."

"Where's this job?"

"Texas."

Stacey shook her head. "No way, mister. You're not getting off that easy. You're taking me to dinner. What other lies did you make up to get out of taking me out?" She started for the car again.

"It's not a lie." Ryan ran to catch up, feeling bad that he'd misled her. He put a hand on her shoulder and turned her to face him. "I'm out tomorrow."

"Get in the car, idiot." She pointed at the passenger seat.

Ryan climbed in beside her. Ten minutes later, the car slid to a stop outside Ryan's apartment. Ryan stepped out and was about to close the door.

Stacey asked, "Why now?"

He leaned down to see her. She blew a strand of purple hair out of her face.

"Because I need to," Ryan said.

"Why not stay here?"

"It's not that simple."

"It is, really. If you want to stay, you stay. If you want to go, you go, and it sounds like you're going."

"I'm going."

"What was the point of going to Stock Island?"

He squatted down by the open car door. "Part of getting back on the job."

"Do you dive for a living, or was that a lie?" Stacey asked indignantly. Then softly, she asked, "Was it all a lie?"

"No, it wasn't all a lie. The truth is, I've been hiding out. I screwed up and my boss gave me a vacation. I am a dive instructor. I was in Navy EOD, and I did just break up with my girlfriend."

Stacey looked away, her hand wiggling the gear shifter. "Good luck."

"See you later, Stacey."

"I doubt it." She slipped the transmission into reverse. Ryan stood and closed the door. He shoved his hands in his pockets and watched her drive away.

CHAPTER FOUR

Customers had formed two lines at the dive shop's service counter, waiting to check in and be assigned their boat for the morning dives. Ryan pushed through the crowd, waved at the two women working the counter, and headed for his boss's door. Ron Case had been kind enough to give Ryan a job with the understanding that he was between commercial salvage jobs and needed something to tide him over. Ryan's qualifications as a dive instructor in multiple specialties and as a captain with his 100-ton Coast Guard license made him an easy hire.

The office door, which was normally open, had been partially closed. Ryan stepped to the side to see through a gap between the door and the jamb. A man in his late twenties sat opposite Ron. He had sandy blonde hair over an oval face with a strong chin. He was fit, lean, and looked capable.

Stacey snuck up beside Ryan, then pushed him out of the way so she could see. Without taking her eye from the crack, she whispered, "Who's he? He's hot. Looks like Zac Efron."

"Who?" Ryan asked, surprised she was speaking to him after last night.

She lashed out with her sarcastic whip. "Duh. The movie star."

The guy glanced at Ryan, his blue eyes shining and intense, then back at Ron. "You sure you don't have any work for me. I'm an SSI and a TDI/SDI instructor."

"I'm sorry, Travis," Ron said. "We don't teach with those agencies here. You'd have to go through our instructor crossover class, and we don't have one for another two weeks."

"Can I do something? I came down here to get a job, and I'm striking out all over the place."

"You can keep trying the other dive shops."

Travis stood. "Thanks. Maybe I'll find another commercial job. Any of those around here?"

Ron gave Travis a list of commercial diving companies in the area. Travis folded the paper before sticking it in the back pocket of his well-worn khakis.

Ryan glanced down at the man's feet. They were encased in Doc Martens. He wore a long-sleeved button-down shirt which made Ryan sweat just looking at it. The newcomer was clearly not from Florida or used to the tropical climate.

Travis pulled open the door and walked past Ryan and Stacey, giving them a look of exasperation.

Ryan followed Travis out the door and down the steps to the parking lot. The guy was steadily marching toward a mid-eighties GMC K-1500 sitting on a six-inch suspension lift with thirty-five-inch tires. Bolted to the bed was a chrome light bar adorned with six chrome KC Daylighter off-road lights.

"That's a nice pickup," Ryan said. "Straight out of *Fall Guy*."

"Yeah, thanks," Travis said without stopping.

"You're a commercial diver?"

This time, Travis stopped. He turned around. "You betcha."

"Where'd you work?"

"I worked all over the Great Lakes and did some time in the North Atlantic. I got tired of the cold."

"Are you familiar with surface supply?"

"Helmet, or hookah rig, eh?" Travis asked.

"Helmet," said Ryan.

"I've got a few hours in a Kirby Morgan SuperLite," Travis replied, referring to the yellow hard helmet ubiquitous to commercial divers.

"Who'd you work for?"

"Superior Salvage in Houghton, Michigan. What's with the twenty questions, eh?"

"Just asking." Ryan pointed at the dive shop. "This place is really great if you can get on."

"I can't wait two weeks for the crossover program. I need work now."

Ryan nodded. "I get that. Let me get your number and where you're staying. I know a few guys who do commercial work around here. I'll put in a good word."

"Who are you again?" Travis asked.

"Ryan Weller. I work here." He extended his hand. By way of further explanation, Ryan said, "I heard your conversation with Ron."

"Travis Wisnewski. Some people call me Whiskey." He shook Ryan's hand.

Ryan glanced over at Stacey. She'd followed them to the parking lot and was staring at Travis. Ryan thought he saw drool coming out of the corner of her mouth. He could almost hear her say, "That's some well-aged whiskey."

Stacey shook Travis's hand while she continued to stare. "I'm Stacey Coleman."

"Nice to meet you, Stacey," Travis said, looking her up and down.

"I'll give you a call if I hear of anything," Ryan said to interrupt the silent appraisal both Stacey and Travis were giving each other.

"Thanks," Travis said and climbed into his truck.

Stacey followed Ryan back into the dive shop. "What are you doing here, I thought you were leaving?"

"I'm tendering my resignation."

"Are you going to take Travis with you?"

Ryan stopped at Ron Case's door. "If he wants to go."

CHAPTER FIVE

Ryan left the dive shop and walked to where he'd chained his bicycle to a tree. He unlocked it and swung a leg over the saddle and set off toward A1A. He hadn't seen the need to buy a car and put his name on a title and registration in Florida. It was one of the things keeping him off the radar. He had to use his real name to get a job as a dive instructor and used direct deposit for his paycheck, but anyone searching for him couldn't access his records without a warrant. His name wasn't on the apartment lease. All he had were some clothes and his dive gear. He was a ghost, and it was liberating.

The downside to not having a car was that he would need to bum a ride to get himself and his dive gear to Stock Island. He glanced at his watch. It was too early for a margarita.

He stopped at the Shell station and bought a pack of Camel Blues and a Mountain Dew. He cracked open the soda and took a long swig. He loved the first long, cold drink. The colder, the better. With his thirst quenched, he set his purchases in the cruiser's basket and started for his apartment. The place was a mile down the road and when he got there, he was hot and ready for a shower. He walked through the small breezeway and into the rear courtyard. He knew everyone would be at work, except Mrs. Hillsborough, the owner. She spent most of her time either watching television or taking her white Bichon Frise for long strolls through the island's back streets. Mrs. Hillsborough carried the dog more than the dog walked. Ryan could hear her television blaring a game show, even with the air conditioner running and the windows closed.

Pulling his prepaid smart phone from his pocket, he scrolled through the contacts to find Greg Olsen's number. He hit *send* and tucked the phone between his ear and shoulder while he packed the Camels against his palm and then opened the pack. He got a cigarette sparked up as Greg came on the line.

"This can't be good."

Ryan said, "Don't be jealous because Shelly has you under lock and key."

"Ever time you go down range, I'm jealous."

"Don't be. It's not that exciting, and besides, you didn't have to hire me."

Greg laughed. "My life would be less entertaining without you."

"I'm glad you feel that way," Ryan replied.

"Are you smoking?"

"Maybe."

"I thought you quit."

"I thought you weren't my mother."

"I should call her and have her talk to you."

"Hasn't done any good so far," Ryan admitted.

Greg laughed again. "What do you need, dude?"

"I want you to check out a guy by the name of Travis

Wisnewski. He's a commercial diver from Michigan." Ryan filled Greg in on what he knew about the man.

"All right, as if I don't have enough on my plate already, and Shelly is giving me the stink eye for even talking to you."

Ryan said sweetly, "Give her a kiss for me."

———

THIRTY MINUTES LATER, Ryan had his gear packed into several duffle bags and was double-checking his room for stray items. He'd left the phone on the kitchen counter and heard it ringing as he fished an errant sock out from under the bed. The call went to voicemail before he could get to it. He ignored the fact Greg hadn't left him a message and hit redial.

"What's up?"

"Your dude is a pretty straight arrow. Nothing unusual stands out, no arrests or warrants. I talked to Joe, the guy who owns Superior Salvage, and got a pretty high recommendation. Are you thinking about taking him to Haiti?"

"Yeah, and you won't need to send one of your guys and leave a crew shorthanded."

"Sounds good, but you better lay it on the line for this guy. Tell him what the stakes are because he's not an operator. This isn't pumping concrete for the Mackinac Bridge or welding string in the North Atlantic."

"Yes, Mom."

"Ryan, listen, dude," Greg's voice grew serious and hard. "I know how cavalier you can be about some shit, but you're asking another man to put his life on the line for sins you committed. This ain't a Sunday picnic. This is gold, and bounty hunters. It's the real deal."

"There's danger with every job." Ryan knew Greg was right. Anytime treasure was involved, the stakes were infinitely higher.

Greg and Ryan were more prepared to handle the danger. They'd been in combat and had worked as technicians in the Navy's most rigorous program, Explosive Ordnance Disposal. The initial course was a grueling year of diving, ordnance disposal, parachute training, small unit tactics, hand-to-hand combat, and firearms skills. For ten years, Ryan had been on constant training cycles, staying in peak physical condition while deploying to Iraq, Afghanistan, and other hot spots around the world to disarm and dispose of all manner of explosive devices from car bombs to underwater mines.

Greg changed the subject. "I've almost got the list of stuff we talked about ready to fly. When will you be back in Key West?"

"Tomorrow, if not tonight."

"Call me so I can get Chuck booked. He's been flying crazy hours with all the hurricane backlog we've got going on."

Ryan grinned. "Roger that."

CHAPTER SIX

Ryan sat in the apartment courtyard smoking another cigarette and thinking about the mission's logistics when he heard car doors slam. It wasn't unusual for people to come and go in the neighborhood, but these doors had shut right in front of his four-unit complex. He eased out of his chair and stepped to the breezeway.

His heart skipped a beat when he saw Dreadlocks and the Mexican standing beside the same pickup truck as the night before.

Then a Kia Rio turned into the parking lot.

Shiiiiit! Ryan thought, recognizing Stacey's purple hair.

The two men from the pickup started up the walk toward the apartments.

Ryan took a deep breath to calm the adrenaline mainlining through his system. He'd trained to work through the "fight-or-flight syndrome." These dudes were up to no good and Stacey was about to walk into a street fight.

He watched as she pulled into a parking spot beside the men's truck and opened the door. "Stay in the car!" Ryan shouted.

Stacey continued to get out. The two men turned to look at her. Dreadlocks' face twisted into an evil grin.

"Get back in the car," Ryan commanded.

Stacey stood in the open door, staring at the three men in the breezeway.

"What do you want?" Ryan asked the two men.

"Two million dollars, mon," Dreadlocks said.

"What are you talking about?" Ryan feigned innocence. He was ready for this moment. He'd grown used to the idea there were men hunting him, knowing someone was coming. Here they were, on his doorstep. Everything seemed to move in slow motion. A bird chirped. Shadows played across the wall. Dreadlocks's gold teeth gleamed. Ryan's heart rate had increased, and he blinked long and slow. Oh, this was going to be fun.

"Chu know, *pendejo*," Mexican snapped. He slid his left hand behind his back.

Ryan wanted nothing more than to pull a pistol and plug both men in the head. He'd have done it in the Iraqi desert or the high mountain peaks of Afghanistan without hesitation. They were a threat to his life. Even though he had a Taurus Protector .38 revolver in his pocket, this wasn't a war zone. This was a peaceful apartment complex in Key Largo. Unless this got really messy, he didn't want to go loud.

Dreadlocks glanced back at Stacey. Mexican started to bring his hand forward. Ryan saw the glint of a blade in the man's closed fist. Stepping inside the arc of the knife, Ryan grasped Mexican's wrist with his right hand. Ryan jammed his left palm hard into the man's jaw, forcing his head up and back. Ryan spread his fingers and the tips dug into the Mexican's eye sockets. He let out a muffled scream into Ryan's palm as Ryan applied pressure to his eyes. At the same time, Ryan continued to push the Mexican backward. The shorter man stumbled, and Ryan ran him hard into a wall. Mexican's head hit with a sickening thud, and he went limp.

The knife clattered to the concrete and Ryan kicked it away during his spin to confront Dreadlocks. As he brought his fists up and crouched into a fighting stance, he saw two thin wires arc through the air. One hit the big, black man in the chest, the other in his abdomen. Suddenly, Dreadlocks began to dance and writhe. Electricity crackled in the air. His knees buckled, and he fell face down on the sidewalk.

Stacey held an Axon Taser Pulse in both hands. The gun continued to stun the man for twenty more seconds. She grinned at Ryan. "Mom got it for me last Christmas." She unplugged the wire pack from the front of the gun and dropped it on the ground and shoved the gun into her pocket.

"What's going on?" she asked.

"The reason I'm hiding out here instead of working in Texas."

"Now would be a good time to explain."

"It really would, but let's get my stuff out of the apartment first."

They ran up the stairs and grabbed his gear. Ryan made a second trip, and when he came down the stairs, he grabbed the wire pack and jerked the plugs out the Dreadlocks's chest. He wrapped the wires up and stuffed them into his bag while he slid into the passenger seat. Stacey put the car in reverse and backed out of the parking spot.

"Where to?" she asked.

"You know where Travis is staying?"

"Yeah, it's not too far up-island." She turned north out

of the parking lot and accelerated with traffic. "Tell me what's going on?"

"Those dudes were trying to collect a bounty." He leaned forward to look out the passenger side rearview mirror.

"Are you some kind of criminal?"

"No. I'm wanted by a Mexican drug cartel for killing their leader."

"Holy shit, Ryan!" Stacey stared at him.

"Look at the road," he yelled.

Stacey swerved to miss a slower car.

Ryan glanced at the speedometer. "Slow down. I don't want to get pulled over."

"Are you wanted by the cops, too?" she asked, hunched over the wheel with her hands at ten and two.

"No, just slow down." He kept glancing in the mirror but didn't see anyone following them.

Stacey complied and ten minutes later, she pulled into the crushed shell parking lot of a small hotel. Travis's GMC was sitting near the front entrance.

"Park around the side where the car can't be seen from the road," he instructed.

She obeyed and put the car in park.

"What's going on, for real?" she demanded.

"I want to talk to Travis."

They got out of the car and followed a winding stone path through a small pool courtyard to the back of the hotel where Ryan knocked on Travis's room door.

"Hey, what's up?" Travis asked when he opened the door.

"Can we come in?" Ryan asked.

Travis smiled at Stacey. "Come on."

They crowded into the tiny room. Stacey sat down on

the queen size bed and Travis leaned against the bureau doubling as a tv stand for a small flat screen. Ryan pulled the curtains back and looked out at the courtyard.

Travis asked, "What's this a-boot, guys?"

Stacey screwed up her face. "What's this a boot?"

"A-boot."

"You mean, about?" Stacey corrected.

"What I said, a-boot."

She shook her head. "Where are you from?"

"Da U.P."

"Where the hell is the U.P.?" Stacey asked.

It was Travis's turn to look askance. "The Upper Peninsula."

Ryan laughed. "He's a Yupper, Stacey, from Michigan."

When Ryan saw no one had followed them, he let the drapes fall back into place and took a seat at the little round table. Other than the flat screen, everything in the room was right out of the 1970s. The carpet looked like it could use a good raking.

Travis asked, "Did you come about a job, eh?"

"Yeah, Ryan, tell us what's going on," Stacey insisted.

"Look, this is going to take a few minutes to explain and it will end with a job offer."

"Okay," said Travis.

Ryan asked, "Do you remember the bombings that happened in Austin, Phoenix, and Los Angeles?"

"Yeah, some ISIS guys were behind it," Travis said.

Ryan shook his head. "The ISIS agents were working for Mexican drug cartel kingpin Arturo Guerrero. He wanted to start a war with the United States to take back what they call Aztlán, the desert Southwest."

"What?" Stacey said, confused. "The news said it was ISIS."

"Law enforcement initially thought it was," Ryan confirmed. "But the real guy behind it was Guerrero. I figured it out and went into Mexico to stop him. I ended up killing him. Then their new leader, José Luis Orozco, put a two-million-dollar bounty on me and my partner, and, now, everyone is trying to collect. Until today, I'd been left alone because I'm supposed to be dead. Someone figured out I wasn't."

Stacey screwed up her face. "What do you mean dead?"

"Six months ago," Ryan continued, "and this is where we get to the job, my partner and I were chasing an international weapons dealer. We ended up delivering a shipment of guns and Army vehicles to a Haitian warlord. Before we started unloading the goods, we took payment in the form of twenty-five million dollars in gold bars."

Travis whistled, and Stacey's eyes widened.

"We offloaded some of the gear before the ship was sunk by a rival warlord. My partner and I went down with the ship and swam out on rebreathers. We let everyone think we were dead."

Travis crossed his arms and legs. "Where's your partner?"

Ryan recognized the closed-off, defensive posture the man had adopted. "He's with his wife on an around the world sailing expedition. Which is what I should have done."

"Why didn't you?" asked Travis.

"Because I've got gold fever."

Travis narrowed his eyes, and then his expression relaxed into a smile. "You're going after the gold."

Ryan nodded.

Stacey frowned. "So, these guys are going to keep trying to kill you to collect the bounty?"

Ryan nodded. "Yes."

"Do you have a boat?" asked Travis. "What's the plan?"

"I have a boat in Stock Island. It needs some work, but my benefactor is going to hook us up."

"Who's your benefactor?"

"Dark Water Research."

Travis whistled. "Bringing the big dogs, eh?"

Stacey looked puzzled. "What about the bounty? Are you just going to gloss over that?"

"No," Ryan replied. "I want to get out of here as soon as possible. That means getting to Stock Island and getting the boat ready."

"How are you connected to DWR?" asked Travis. His posture was beginning to relax, but Ryan could tell he wasn't completely on board yet.

"I used to work for the owner."

"Is he getting a cut of the gold?" Travis asked.

"We haven't discussed it."

Travis scratched his chin. "If he's not getting a cut, why's he helping?"

Ryan leaned forward and put his elbows on his knees. He could see out a slit in the curtains to observe the court-yard. "Let's just say Greg Olsen and I have a mutual under-standing."

"DWR has all kinds of divers, what do you need me for, eh?"

"This isn't an official DWR project."

Stacey got off the bed and leaned over Ryan's shoulder. "See anything?"

He shook his head. "No."

"How deep?" Travis asked.

"Three hundred plus feet."

"On surface supply?"

"Yes," Ryan shrugged. "I have some rebreathers as well."

Travis pondered this for a minute. "What's the pay?"

"Five percent of the haul."

Travis pulled out his cell phone and used the calculator to figure out his cut. "If I'm risking my life to recover gold and have to put up with a bunch of bounty hunters, then it'd better be a bigger number."

Ryan stared out the window.

Stacey asked, "Ten percent?"

Ryan closed his eyes and pictured the gold. Ten percent wasn't bad. It was fair, but if everyone received ten percent, then his share was getting smaller by the hire.

"I'll do this," Travis said, rubbing his chin, pinching his cleft between his thumb and index finger. "Ten percent of what we haul. If we don't haul anything, I get paid thirty dollars an hour for every hour I'm on the salvage boat."

"Fair enough," Ryan said.

Travis's next question was one Ryan had been pondering himself. "What about line handlers?"

Ryan turned away from his window vigil and faced Travis. "Me and the captain."

"What about her, eh?" Travis pointed his chin at Stacey. "She coming along?"

Ryan said, "She drives a boat at the dive shop."

A look of disappointment clouded Travis's face. "That's a shame."

Stacey chirped up, "Oh, I'll go. I can go. Can I go, Ryan?"

"Can you tend lines?" Travis asked.

With too much enthusiasm, and while leering at Travis, Stacey said, "I can tend anything you want."

Ryan shook his head. "Stacey, please, stop drooling."

Travis winked exaggeratedly at her and clicked his tongue.

Stacey flushed across her neck and cheeks, turning her tan a crimson red.

"I'll go if the purple-haired, crazy chick comes."

Ryan furrowed his brow. "Really?"

"Yeah." Travis shrugged while grinning at Stacey. "I dig the purple hair."

Ryan gave Stacey a hard look. "If you want to come, you'll be placing yourself in the same danger as everyone else."

Stacey nodded. "I know, Ryan. I had to Taser some guy to save your ass already."

Ryan started to chuckle, remembering when Mango had said something similar after he'd used a sniper rifle to kill a man about to shoot Ryan.

Stacey crossed her arms and narrowed her eyes. "What's so funny?"

"Nothing." Ryan stood. "We need to get going. It's a long drive to Key West."

Travis said, "I haven't made it that far south, yet."

Stacey grinned and touched Travis's arm. "I'll take you out on Duval Street."

"I'm ready to give 'er tar paper."

Ryan and Stacey both look dubiously at their new friend.

"So," Stacey demanded, "what does, tar papering mean?"

"Give 'er tar paper," Travis corrected. "It's like Larry the Cable Guy saying, 'Git-R-Done.'"

Stacey smiled seductively at Travis. "I'm ready to tar paper a few drinks in Key West with you."

"Easy, Stace," Ryan said. "We've got a lot of work to do."

"Let's get started," Travis said.

"Do you have room to haul my gear?" Ryan asked. "I don't have much, and I don't have a car."

"I've got some room," Travis said. "Let's load it up, eh?"

"You sure you're not from Canada, eh?" Ryan asked with a grin.

Travis held up his middle finger and said emphatically, "I am *not* from Canada."

Stacey ran a hand through her hair. "How soon are you leaving, Ryan? I have a bunch of stuff in my apartment and I'm not sure how long it will take me to move it, or where to move it to."

"You don't have to move. This job won't take more than a couple of weeks and you can be back here driving a boat and teaching diving in no time."

Stacey crossed her arms and glared at him. "What if I don't want to come back?"

Ryan threw her words back at her. "It's simple, either you want to go, or you don't. What's it going to be?"

"I'm going."

"Pack light," Ryan told her. "There's not much room on the boat and bring your dive gear."

"Give me a couple of hours," Stacey pleaded.

Ryan checked his watch. "We'll put my gear in the back of Travis's truck and he can get started to Stock Island while we load you up."

Travis picked up Stacey's keys from the bed. He tossed them to Ryan. "You drive her roller skate down, and I'll help her pack."

Ryan shook his head and rolled his eyes. "Fine."

CHAPTER SEVEN

J im Kilroy picked up his ringing satellite phone and looked at the caller ID. It was Damian Reid, the muscular Jamaican he'd sent to Key Largo to watch Ryan Weller. "Give me some good news, Damian."

"He killed Jorge."

Kilroy's anger boiled in his chest. Through clenched teeth, he demanded, "What do you mean he killed Jorge?"

"We approached him at his apartment. Jorge pulled a knife, mon. Weller slammed him into da wall. Broke someting in his head."

"What were you doing, Damian, standing around with your thumb up your ass?"

"No, sir," Damian said sheepishly. "A woman shot me with da Taser."

Kilroy paced the length of the deck of his converted Alaskan crab boat, *Northwest Passage*. His voice was low and full of menace. "I told you not to approach him. I told you to observe him and tell me what he was doing. You have no idea how hard it was to find this guy. You acted like a fool and scared him off."

"No, suh, I know where he be goin'. I be followin' him right now."

"And where pray tell is he going?" Kilroy demanded.

"Back to da Stock Island, mon."

Kilroy stopped pacing and straightened up. "Why?"

"Da boat I told you about, suh," Damian said. "I left someone to watch it. Da captain be taking on a mate and supplies. They be readyin' for a voyage."

"Where are they going?"

"I don't know, Mista Kilroy."

"Damnit, Damian, find out." Kilroy punched the *end* button and very much wanted to send the phone sailing through the air and into the water. Instead, he pocketed it and slammed his palm against the hull of the Yellowfin center console nestled in blocks on *Northwest Passage*'s deck.

As soon as he'd heard Toussaint Bajeux had died in a boat explosion, Kilroy knew Mango Hulsey and Ryan Weller had survived the sinking of the *Santo Domingo*. His hunt for them began in earnest after Hurricane Irma had subsided, and he'd called every government contact he had.

He had men staking out the DWR compound and watching Greg Olsen's home, hoping they would eventually show up at one of the locations. Mango Hulsey's sailboat, *Alamo*, was gone from the DWR docks by the time Kilroy's spies had arrived. Kilroy had men at his Caribbean resorts watching for either the boat, or Mango and his wife, Jennifer.

But finding Ryan had been a complete accident. Jim's wife, Karen, had flown to Miami to inspect their boutique hotel on South Beach. On a whim, she decided to go scuba diving in Key Largo. After her dives, she'd stopped to have dinner and spotted Ryan at a restaurant with several other people. Karen had followed one of the women from Ryan's table into the bathroom and feigned interest in him.

The woman had been slightly drunk and bubbled out information like she and Karen were best friends. Karen learned Ryan was a dive instructor at a local facility. The woman had a crush on the handsome instructor. Karen had laughed as she told her husband about the girl's use of air quotes around, "doesn't sleep with his coworkers."

Kilroy had been ecstatic and sent Damian and Jorge to Key Largo. He wanted them to follow Ryan, who would lead them to Mango. Then he would force them to use Dark Water Research's equipment to recover his gold. If they didn't want to play ball with him, he could turn them over to José Luis Orozco and collect the two-million-dollar bounty.

Taking a deep breath to calm himself, Kilroy jogged up the stairs to the bridge and used the computer to access a map of the Caribbean. Right now, they were off the coast of Colombia while he searched for a freighter to replace the *Santo Domingo*. He missed the loyalty of the sunken freighter's dead captain and first mate. But money would buy more loyalty, and Jim Kilroy had plenty of money.

After consulting the map, he called Damian back. "You told me Weller met with a boat captain, what kind of a boat is it?"

"An old fishin' boat. Look like it's been converted to a salvage vessel."

"Who else is on the boat?"

"Just da captain and da mate. Dey both be old men."

"Who else does Weller have with him? Have you seen the guy with an artificial leg?"

"No, suh. No Mango Hulsey. He has a woman and a man. Don't know who dey be."

"Okay, Damian. Stay with them."

"Yes, suh."

Kilroy hung up the phone and stepped out of the bridge. If Ryan was putting together a crew on a salvage vessel, he was going after the gold for himself. It made things much easier for Kilroy. All he had to do was sit back and wait for them to bring up the gold, then take it from them.

He leaned against the railing and watched a rubber Zodiac approach at a high speed. The driver's blonde hair streamed out behind her and the man in the front kept a white-knuckled grip on the boat's lifeline as the small craft bounced and skipped across the water. At the last moment, the driver shoved the tiller over and chopped the throttle. The Zodiac dropped off plane and settled into the water right beside *Northwest Passage*.

"Hey, honey!" Karen called as she caught a rope he tossed down.

"How was the diving?"

"It was wonderful. I love this part of the Caribbean."

"I've got some bad news."

"What?" she asked, busying herself with handing up diving gear.

"As soon as we have the Zodiac onboard, we're heading for Haiti."

"What for?"

"Ryan Weller is going there."

Karen looked up from the boat, shading her eyes with her hand. She smiled. Kilroy wondered if it was a smile to cover her sadness at leaving Colombia or her anticipation of seeing Ryan again. Jealousy and anger surged through Kilroy at the thought of Ryan even being near his wife. It was a strange feeling he couldn't explain, but it strengthened his resolve to force Ryan Weller to recover his gold and then to end the insufferable bastard's life.

CHAPTER EIGHT

Ryan was glad to get out of the Kia, which he'd decided should be Killed in Action to match the military's acronym. He stretched his arms and legs and jogged in place for thirty seconds. If the Kia was KIA, then he was DOA, Dead on Arrival. Travis and Stacey were climbing out of the GMC when Captain Dennis Law came down the gangplank to meet them.

"Welcome back," Dennis said, extending his hand.

Ryan grasped it. "Thanks, Captain."

"Who do you have here?" Dennis asked, indicating Travis and Stacey.

Ryan made the introductions. "We would have been here sooner, but it took Stacey a long time to pack." He'd followed them to her apartment and tried to hurry them along, but she had kicked him out and Ryan had waited in the car. When Stacey and Travis had finally come out, they were both flushed from physical activity and it wasn't hard to guess what they'd done.

"I've got a mate aboard already, miss," Dennis said. "You don't by chance cook do ya?"

Stacey gave the older man a quizzical expression and shook her head.

"She'd burn water, Captain," Ryan said. He slung a pack over his shoulder and grabbed the rebreather. He headed up the gangway and nearly collided with an old man with wispy white hair under a black-knit watch cap.

"Watch where ya be goin', sonny." He spat a stream of tobacco juice over the rail. A brown streak from the corner of his mouth to his chin marred a scraggly, white beard.

"My apologies, sir."

"Don't call me, sir, I work for a living."

"Leave the boy alone, Emery," Dennis said. "He's the new boss."

"Pardon me, there, sonny," Emery touched his cap with a knurled finger.

Ryan grinned. "No worries, Emery."

"Just cause you the boss don't mean you can call me by my Christian name, boy."

"What should I call you?" Ryan asked.

"Well, boy, you can call me Mr. Ducane." A broad smile crept across the wizened man's face.

"Stop giving him a ration," Dennis chided.

"I think we should just call him Grandpa," Stacey said.

"Lookie here, a little girl with a sassy mouth."

Dennis said, "Stop harassing the help, Emery,"

"Where are we going to bunk, Grandpa?" Ryan flashed Emery a grin.

Emery turned and led the way below deck. He mumbled, "Ya can sleep in the bleedin' bilge."

Ryan dropped his gear in one of the small bunkrooms. He turned to ask Travis if he wanted the second bunk, but Travis was in the room across the passageway with Stacey. They had their arms around each other and their tongues down each other's throats. Ryan shook his head and headed out to grab more gear from the car. It took him two more trips and a half an hour to get everything stowed the way he wanted, then he made his way topside to find Dennis.

The captain and Emery were standing behind the bridge structure, looking at a round, metal tank approximately ten feet long and six feet high. Mounted to the side of the tank were a series of large face gauges above a tangle of pipes, levers, valves, and smaller gauges. Ryan walked to the end and stuck his head through the open hatch. He'd been in quite a few recompression chambers, but this was the smallest, accommodating only two people. There was an airlock on the side for passing in food and drink and thin padding over steel benches. Gray oxygen masks lay on the seats. He pulled his head out and looked over at Dennis. "Nice piece of history you've got here."

"She may be old, but she'll do. I've kept her serviced. Got records all the way back to the day I bought her from the Navy yard in ninety-eight."

"You was a whippersnapper back then, sonny," Emery said to Ryan.

"Where'd you dig up this fossil, Captain?" asked Ryan, indicating the first mate.

"I've known Emery most of my life," Dennis said. "He's been crewing for me off and on for the better part of thirty years."

"I hope he does something other than harass the help," Travis said, coming up beside Ryan.

"Don't worry," Dennis said. "Emery can outcook most people. Plus, he can dive, work tender, and drive the boat."

Emory aimed his beard at Ryan. "What are you bringing to the party, whippersnapper?"

Ryan folded his arms and leaned against the chamber.

"I bring the financing, the coordinates for the dive site, and I'm a diver and tender as well." He nodded at Travis. "Travis is a commercial diver, he knows surface supply and can act as a tender."

"What about the girl?" Dennis almost whispered.

"She's certified to drive a one-hundred-ton vessel and she'll learn to tender. She's a dive instructor as well."

"Fine and dandy." Emery spit over the rail.

"Your health going to hold out for this trip, Grandpa?" Travis asked.

"Boy, you better mind your elders," Emery snapped. Turning to Ryan, he said, "I hear we're going to Haiti."

Ryan looked hard at the old man. This was a battle of wills. The younger generation against the older, and the sooner they settled down and began working as a crew, the better off they would be. "Don't be spreading it around."

"I know how to keep my mouth shut, boy. I've been chasing treasure in these waters for damned near fifty years."

Ryan asked Dennis, "Did you tell him what's at stake?"

Dennis said quietly, "I told him we were going to Haiti on a salvage mission."

"Looks more like a circus," Emery said, staring at Stacey, who was coming up the gangway with her duffle bag.

"Look," Ryan said. "We can stand here and bicker and banter all day, but we've got work to do. I don't want this shit floating around when we've got a man at three hundred feet."

"Yes, sir," Emery replied, pulling his cap off his head. His unruly hair stuck out at all angles.

Dennis nodded, and Travis said, "Yeah, I'm good as long as Grandpa is, eh?"

Emery held up a bony fist. "I oughta take you over my knee."

"Dammit, Travis, knock it off," Ryan said.

Travis laughed. "Emery, I like you. You remind me of my grandpa, and I call you that as a sign of respect."

Emery nodded and pulled his watch cap back on. "I'm honored, son."

Ryan pulled out a cigarette.

"If you light that thing by my recompression chamber, I will take you over my knee," Emery declared.

Ryan paused and knitted his brow.

Emery pointed. "Don't tell me you can't see them no smokin' signs by the oxygen tanks."

Ryan turned and looked at the row of tall, green cylinders chained and bolted between the recompression chamber and the back of the bridge. A large No Smoking sign hung above them.

"You want to smoke, do it on the fan tail." Emery pointed at the back of the boat.

"Fan tail," Ryan mused. "Now I'm certain you were in the Navy."

Emery nodded. "Got out as a senior chief bosun's mate after twenty-five years."

Ryan looked over the boat's rear rail at the thick tires hanging by chains. They were cracked and faded, some missing their tread, and the chains were rusty. He lit his cigarette. "You didn't happen to meet a guy by the name of Henry O'Shannassy?"

"What'd he do?" Emery asked.

"He was a senior chief back in the day. Spent most of his time as a diver; runs a marina in North Carolina now."

Emery shook his head. "Can't say that I knew him."

Ryan took a deep drag from his Camel. He needed to

quit again. His lungs didn't ache quite as bad when he wasn't huffing carbon monoxide.

"What's the plan?" Dennis asked, leaning against the rail. Stacey and Travis joined the three men.

"I have a plane load of gear coming in from Dark Water Research," Ryan said. "They're also sending one of their mechanics to go over all your systems and gear." Dennis started to speak, but Ryan cut him off, glancing around the long-neglected boat. "I can see that everything is in perfect condition, but let's let him do his job. We have a long voyage to a foreign port where we don't know how much support we'll have in getting spare parts, or even diesel. We may have to go in and out of the Dominican Republic just to get fuel."

Dennis scratched his beard and looked annoyed. "I know you're trying to be sarcastic about my boat, but she's in good shape."

"We agreed," Ryan said.

Dennis scratched his chin then grudgingly said, "Yeah, we did."

Travis nudged the diving compressor with his toe. "When was the last time you changed oil in this thing?"

Dennis scratched his beard again.

Emery said, "I just changed it." He asked Dennis, "When did we do that job for Key West Public Works?"

"Two years ago," Dennis replied.

Emery's face slackened. "Two years?" He scratched his head. "Guess I am gettin' old."

"No worries, Grandpa," Travis said. "I'll get started on it. What does she take?"

Emery held up a finger. "That, I can help with. Come on, whippersnapper." He led Travis toward the bridge.

"I kept records of all the maintenance we did on the

gear," Dennis said. "And you're right. We should go through everything to make sure it's in working order. It's been awhile since we were an operating salvage unit."

Ryan stubbed out his cigarette, field stripped the butt, and shoved the trash in his pocket. He glanced up to see a truck drive through the marina gate. It was the same battered pickup from the Hogfish's parking lot and his apartment complex. He swore.

"What's the problem?" Dennis asked, gazing in the same direction.

Ryan nodded toward the truck. "Do you recognize the guy in that pickup?"

Dennis said, "Never seen him before. Why?"

They watched the truck kick up dust as it drove east to the end of the quay and made a U-turn. The driver didn't get out, but Ryan saw the glint of sun off glass as the man put binoculars, or a rifle scope, to his eye.

"Let's go up to the bridge." Ryan nudged the captain forward.

"What's going on?" Dennis asked.

"A good question," Ryan said. "Right now, we need to get under cover." If the man was staring at them through a high-powered scope, Ryan wanted to be behind something that could deflect the bullet from the gun the scope was mounted on.

"Under cover?" Dennis said.

"You ever work a salvage case where someone wanted to take away what you were bringing up?"

"A few times," Dennis replied, stepping into the bridge.

Ryan followed and snatched up the binoculars from the console. He trained them on the truck. Dreadlocks stared back at him through his own binoculars. Ryan felt a sense of relief that it wasn't a gun scope, and a little let down at the same time. His heart rate slowed, and he took a deep breath to help ward off the adrenaline pounding through his veins.

"Who's in the truck?" Dennis asked.

"That's the same truck from your apartment," Stacey said, moving past Ryan to look out the window. She grabbed the binoculars from his hand and staring through them, said, "Holy cow, that's the dude I tasered."

CHAPTER NINE

Captain Dennis Law leaned forward and took the field glasses from Stacey. "What do you mean tasered?" he asked, fitting them to his eyes.

"That dude was attacking Ryan at his apartment in Key Largo," Stacey said. "I lit him up with my Taser."

Dennis set the binoculars down and stepped to the coffee maker. He poured a cup and added a splash of Jim Bean. "This is a story I'd like to hear."

Ryan explained the situation with the bounty, Jim Kilroy, and the Haitian gold.

Dennis scratched his beard. After a few moments of silence, he said, "That's a real pickle."

Stacey had been watching the pickup. "What are we going to do with that guy?"

Ryan glanced out the window and then back at Stacey. "Feel like lighting him up again?"

She grinned and waggled her eyebrows. "You sure know how to talk sweet to me."

Dennis snorted, and Ryan grinned.

"Better not be anyone sweet talking my girl, eh?"

Travis said, stepping onto the bridge. "I need to run into town and get some oil and parts for the compressor." He moved over to the window. "What are you all staring at, eh?"

"Dreadlocks is back," Stacey said.

"Who's Dreadlocks?" Emery asked.

"Just a guy who's been following me around," Ryan replied. He lifted a cup of coffee to his lips and took a sip. They really needed to get some new beans. "What are you brewing in this thing?"

"Some blend from Publix," Dennis said. "I don't pay attention."

Ryan said, "It sucks."

Dennis shook his head. "You're footing the bill, boss, get us something better. I'm on a fixed income, remember?"

"You can't taste it through all the Jim Bean," Emery said.

"Look, old man," Dennis began.

"Don't you sass me, whippersnapper." Emery shook his finger at the captain.

"Don't ride me, Grandpa."

"Somebody's got to," Emery said quietly.

"When are you going to town?" Ryan asked.

"Now," Travis said. "I've got the oil draining, and it'll need a couple of changes. There was some water in it."

"Water?" Dennis asked in surprise.

"Guess Ryan wasn't being so sarcastic after all," Travis said.

"Go get the oil." Ryan pulled a DWR credit card out of his wallet and handed it to Travis. "Get whatever else you need."

Travis's face lit up in a broad smile. "That's an open invitation. Come on, Stacey."

"We've got a little job to do before Stacey leaves," Ryan said.

Travis cocked his head.

Ryan nodded toward the truck. "I'm going to distract Dreadlocks, and Stacey is going to Taser him again."

"What for?" Emery asked.

"I want to talk to him, and I want him under control when I do it."

Stacey grinned and pumped her fists. "Twice in one day."

Ryan instructed the group on how he wanted things to go down. Then he walked off the pier and headed for the front gate. He stopped to light a cigarette. Travis barreled past him in his big GMC Sierra with Stacey in the passenger seat. Ryan continued inspecting the lobster and fishing boats as he walked along the docks.

At the front gate, Travis stopped, and Stacey hopped out. Ryan knew she would be hidden from Dreadlocks's view by a screen of trees and brush as she came up on the blind side of the pickup while Ryan kept Dreadlocks distracted.

Ryan smoked two cigarettes by the time he got near the pickup. Dreadlocks had slouched down in the seat and was trying to hide. Ryan walked to the back of the old truck and stopped at the tailgate. It opened with a squeal of protest. The passenger side support cable had snapped in two, and the tailgate hung lower on that side. Ryan hefted his leg up and set his right butt cheek on the corner of the tailgate and pulled out his cigarettes. He had one in his lips and was bringing the lighter up when Dreadlocks stepped out of the truck.

"What you doin', mon?"

"Just wanted to have a chat with you?"

"No, mon, ya not sit on another mon's truck without der permission."

Ryan let out a long stream of smoke. "I used to think like that. Mine, his, yours. What we have, mon, it belongs to de gods, mon."

"Dis truck don't belong to no gods, mon. It belong to me." He pointed a finger at his chest. Suddenly, his eyes widened and his whole body stiffened. Ryan watched with indifference as electricity coursed through Dreadlocks. He rose to his tiptoes and then fell over on the ground. He curled into a ball as the Taser continued to crackle, releasing voltage into his twitching form.

When the gun finished its thirty-second discharge, Stacey unplugged the cartridge and tossed it onto the ground. The prongs were still lodged in Dreadlocks's back.

Ryan took another long draw on the cigarette and then stubbed it out on the bed of the truck. He tossed the butt into the pile of trash behind the truck cab and squatted beside the black man on the ground. He pulled the man's arms out straight and rolled him onto his stomach. He pulled the Taser leads out of his back and tossed them in the truck bed. Next, he fished through the man's pockets, removing a billfold, a tactical folding knife, and a Hi-Point C9. The 9mm semi-automatic pistol had a reputation for jamming and some said the best way to use the gun was just to throw it at the enemy. He shoved it into his cargo pocket anyway. Better to be safe than leave the gun and have Dreadlocks use it on him later. Inside the billfold, he found a Florida driver's license for Damian Reid.

Damian moaned and started to roll onto his side. Stacey held the Taser near his head and depressed the trigger. Electricity sizzled between the contacts at the end of the muzzle. "Want me to hit him again?"

"No," Ryan said. He tossed the wallet in the dirt by the truck's back wheel. He pushed Damian with his foot. "Sit up."

"Shit, mon," Damian moaned, rolling onto his back. He sat up and laboriously scooted back against the truck's rear tire. His face was ashen, and his pupils were dilated.

Ryan took the Taser from Stacey and squatted beside Damian. "Who do you work for?"

"I don't have to tell you nothing, mon."

"You're right. You don't." Ryan hit the button on the Taser while holding it so Damian could see the blue tongues of electricity arcing between contacts. "Three times in one day might damage your brain. Then again, I doubt if you have that much to start with."

"Yeah, okay, mon." Damian leaned away from the Taser. "I work for Jim Kilroy."

Ryan nodded. "When did you talk to him last?"

"This morning, after you killed Jorge."

Stacey gasped, but Ryan moved past it without blinking. He'd killed men before, and Jorge was in self-defense. "Did you leave him in the breezeway at the apartment?"

"Yeah, mon, some old lady came out and began screaming at me."

Again, Ryan nodded. If Mrs. Hillsborough had seen Damian run away from the crime scene, it would put suspicion on him and not Ryan, even though Ryan had also disappeared at the same time. If Ryan wasn't wanted by the cops for questioning, he would be surprised.

"You got a phone number for Killer Roy?" Ryan asked, using a nickname Greg Olsen had come up with during a conversation with the gun dealer.

Damian tried to laugh. It came out in a hoarse cough. "It's in the truck. I have a sat phone."

Stacey rummaged through the cab and came back with an Iridium Extreme. Ryan recognized it as the same model he'd used when on the EOD teams. She handed it to him, and he scrolled through the call log to find Kilroy's number. "Tell Kilroy you've been made and ask him if he wants you to go to Haiti with us."

Damian stared up at him with a questioning look.

"You told him we were working on the boat, right?"

"Yeah."

Ryan closed his eyes for a brief second. He was trying to remain calm. All hope of getting out of town unnoticed was now gone. "He knows we're going to Haiti, and he knows why."

"He's going there too, mon."

"Yeah, I bet he is." Ryan finished thumbing Kilroy's number into his smart phone and then tossed the sat phone in the dirt beside Damian's leg.

CHAPTER TEN

Greg Olsen slid down the stairs of the Beechcraft King Air B200C on his butt and hands while Chuck Newland held Greg's legs up. At the bottom of the steps, Greg transferred into his wheelchair.

"That wore me out just watching," Chuck said, pushing his white Stetson back on his head.

"I'm wore out from doing it," Greg complained.

"Well, boss, you're an inspiration."

Hostility tinged Greg's voice. "Don't ever say that again."

"Yes, sir."

"Ryan should be here any minute." Greg looked at his watch.

"If I know your boy, he'll be late."

Greg put his hands on his wheels and lifted his butt off the cushion to readjust his weight. "He's probably on island time after living in the Keys."

A third man came down the steps and sat on the bottom one. He was tall and rangy with a mop of brown hair under a faded, burnt orange University of Texas Longhorns ballcap. He wore blue coveralls with the name Don stenciled over the left breast pocket and on the back the red DWR with a white slash ran through the letters from the top left to the bottom right to simulate a diver down flag. In his early twenties, Don Williams was one of the finest mechanics in DWR's stable. His IQ had tested near genius level and he had a degree in mechanical engineering from the University of Texas. He and Greg often argued about who had the better football program, Texas or Greg's alma mater, Texas A&M.

"Ryan's always on island time." Chuck grinned, remembering the last time he was in Key West with Ryan Weller. They were investigating stolen sailboats with Ryan's ex-girlfriend and insurance investigator, Emily Hunt. Ryan had decided to use scuba gear to look at two of the deliberately sunken boats. It was two fun-filled days of beautiful women, fast boats, and pub crawling on Duval Street. Chuck was hoping to squeeze in a little romancing on this trip as well because the last woman he'd met on Duval had invited him to call whenever he was back on the island. He touched the phone in his breast pocket.

"Forget it, Chuck," Greg said, as if reading the pilot's mind.

"Not even a parting gift?" Chuck whined.

"Just a paycheck," Greg said.

A brown, jacked-up GMC pickup slid to a stop beside the airplane. The passenger door opened, and Ryan hopped out. "Hey, bros!" He buddy-hugged Chuck and Greg. Introductions of Travis, Stacey, and Don were made before they began transferring gear from the Beechcraft to the GMC.

When they were done, the back of the truck was piled high. Travis and Stacey headed for the docks while Greg wheeled himself with Ryan and Don to the airport parking lot where the Kia was parked. They wedged themselves and the wheelchair into the tiny car and headed for the boat. As they rounded the north end of the island on Roosevelt Boulevard, the Beechcraft roared overhead on its way back to Texas City.

Greg shook his head. "You corrupted that man, Ryan. He heard he was coming to Key West to drop off some gear and all he could talk about was the fun he'd had here with you."

"You should have let him stay. We could have had a party. Besides, how's the crooner getting home?"

"Crooner?" Greg asked.

"Yeah, the Gentle Giant." Ryan motioned to the mechanic in the backseat beside the wheelchair. Don had a grin on his face.

Greg turned to look at Ryan and then back at Don. "What are you talking about?"

Ryan asked, "You've never heard of Don Williams before?"

Greg said, "Just the one in the backseat."

"'I Believe in You.' 'Tulsa Time.' 'Good Ole Boys Like Me.' Any of them ring a bell?"

Stupefied, Greg asked, "What genre is that?"

With a snort, Ryan said, "Those are the real country-western songs."

Don began to hum a few bars of "Tulsa Time."

"I thought that was Eric Clapton," said Greg.

"Heck no," Ryan said. "Come on, bro, Eric Clapton did a cover."

"What's with the bro?" Greg asked. "You've been hanging around Mango too long."

Ryan laughed. "Wait until you hear Travis start talking like a Canadian, eh?"

"He's from Michigan," Greg said. "I did his background check." He grabbed the door handle to keep himself from sliding around when Ryan made the turn off A1A and entered the industrial side of paradise.

Ryan smirked. "The UP, man, he's practically Canadian."

"He would have been if we hadn't won the War of 1812," Don pointed out.

"A music and a history lesson in one car ride," Ryan said gleefully.

"Shut up," Greg moaned. "Next you'll be spouting some Travis McGeeism."

Ryan held up a finger, as if to pontificate. "We are in the Keys."

Greg rolled his eyes and truly hoped his friend didn't start quoting from one of the twenty-one novels written about the fictional character who'd lived on a barge-type houseboat at slip F18 Bahia Mar, Fort Lauderdale, Florida. Ryan had toted the dogeared paperbacks around the world. Greg had read a few of them, but they weren't his cup of coffee. He mentally chastised himself for knowing as much about Travis McGee as he did, and that was Ryan's fault.

"Anyway," asked Ryan, "how's Don getting back home?"

Greg smiled with relief when Ryan slowed the car. Both were highly trained drivers and had been to several schools to hone their skills, but he felt more in control when he was behind the wheel. "I was going to have Chuck come get us when we're done. Have a sendoff party for you."

"Mighty nice of you," Ryan said, pulling into the marina parking lot. He stopped beside the GMC, which Travis had backed up to the gangway. Travis, Dennis, Stacey, and Emery were forming a bucket brigade to get the gear onto the boat. Ryan sent Don to help while he assembled Greg's wheelchair and got his boss out of the car.

After the gear was aboard, Dennis swung the crane boom over the side and rigged a sling under Greg's wheelchair to lift him onto the boat. Greg could only move around the stern area where the original deck opened to allow access to the fish storage lockers. Dennis had modified the locker doors to make them smaller and installed short benches for gearing up divers in the center of the vessel between the recompression chamber and the diesel-driven Bauer surface supply air compressor. Aft of that was the open stern where Greg was free to roam. When Emery lifted one of the cargo doors, his free real estate became much smaller. Emery and Dennis rigged a canvas tarp over the crane boom to provide shade for the workers.

Don immediately began examining the boat's twin-diesel drive engines. He found one to be in serviceable condition. The second required the replacement of several injectors, and a bad alternator. Don climbed out of the engine bay and went aft to where Greg sat. "Boss, the whole shootin' match ought to be hauled out and junked. Them diesels are old enough to have great- grandbabies."

"Can you get them up and running? We don't have time to do a complete refit."

Don nodded, wiping his clean hands on a white rag. "Yeah, I'll make them work." With Emery's help, Don changed the oils, filters, and drive belts, cleaned the separators, checked thru-hull fittings, and installed a backup bilge pump. Don had brought many of the parts with him on the airplane after Ryan had called Greg and told him what engines were in *Peggy Lynn*.

Greg helped Travis take the Bauer apart, clean, and service it before hooking it to his Kirby Morgan SuperLite and testing it. After Travis had stowed his helmet, Greg pointed to a trio of matching helmets in yellow plastic cases. "Grab one of those and check it out."

Travis hoisted a helmet from its box and examined it. It looked like the standard SuperLite 37 except for a small pair of glasses mounted against the inside of the face plate. "What's that?" he asked.

"Something new DWR, the Navy, and a few other companies are experimenting with. They call it Diver Augmented Visual Display. The DAVD is basically a virtual reality program that can be seen through the glasses. It allows the diver to see blueprint diagrams, exploded parts views, and 3D terrain maps."

"Holy cow, that's awesome!" Travis exclaimed. "That will make diving in zero viz even easier if you have an idea of what you're looking at and where you're going."

"Our thoughts exactly," Greg said. "I've got a software program for you guys to install in the new computer system. I also brought three new sets of hoses and dive lines with integrated fiber optics for communications, camera, and DAVD display feeds."

"When Ryan said you were going to hook him up, I had no idea how cool it would be."

"I brought a few other goodies." Greg pointed to a rectangular wooden crate. Over his shoulder he yelled, "Hey, Ryan, come here."

Ryan climbed out of the hold where he'd been working on the second Bauer compressor used to fill scuba tanks with compressed air, nitrox, and trimix needed for diving and working in deep water. "What's up?"

"I was just telling Travis about the DAVD in the Super-Lite. I showed the system to you before you started your hunt for Kilroy."

"Oh, yeah," Ryan said. "Putting the research into Dark Water Research."

"I brought some other toys." He wheeled to the wooden crate and motioned for them to remove the top. Ryan grabbed a crowbar and popped off the lid. Nestled in foam were several odd-looking firearms. Greg explained, "Back in the 1990s, the Russians built a gun to fire bolts underwater. It was a little unwieldy. I put some of our engineers on it and we came up with a better design."

Travis lifted one of the rifles out of the crate. Greg took it from him. "This shoots a six-inch-long by 5.56-millimeter bolt. The bolt has retractable fletches to help guide it both under and above water. We rifled the barrel where the Russians used a smooth bore. Theirs wouldn't shoot below a hundred and thirty feet. Ours will fire up to seven hundred feet underwater."

"What do we need this for?" Travis asked, shouldering another one of the bolt guns.

Greg shrugged. "Just following the Boy Scout motto."

"Always be prepared." Ryan said. He knelt by the box and lifted out a bang stick, a fiberglass pole with a small head that held a .357 cartridge and discharged when it was shoved against a fish, normally a shark. There were also Hawaiian sling spearguns and small pneumatic pistol spearguns. "What do you think we're going to be doing, having an underwater battle like *Thunderball*?

Greg shrugged. "You never know what tool you'll need until you're on the X."

They repacked the crate and stored it below. Greg had also brought Ryan one of his favorite Walther PPQ nine-millimeter pistols and two H&K MP5s with suppressors. Ryan stowed the Walther in his personal kit and Dennis hid the machine pistols in one of several smuggler's holds he'd built throughout the ship.

———

WHILE THEY WORKED on the ship's systems, they kept Stacey busy running errands. She was thankful to get back to the boat after her last trip to purchase new Furuno radar, sonar, GPS, and autopilot systems. The sun was beginning to set. From the bridge, she saw Ryan and Greg smoking cigarettes on the stern. Ryan was talking animatedly with his hands, describing something to his friend. She crept out of the wheelhouse to eavesdrop. Ryan was telling about her tasering Damian Reid on Key Largo.

"And Stacey just shoots the dude like it's an everyday thing," Ryan said, mimicking her holding the gun.

"It is an everyday thing," she said with a grin. "I have to keep you in line."

Greg burst out laughing. "I like this girl."

Ryan stuck his lower lip out in a fake pout. "Don't get too attached. She dropped me like a bad habit when she saw Travis."

"I don't blame her," Greg said. "I've seen you in action."

Ryan held up a fist and used his other hand to mimic turning a crank. The fake crank slowly raised his middle finger.

"Let's go get some supper at the Hogfish," Dennis said, coming out of the crew area in a fresh pair of khakis and a clean T-shirt. "I hear the boss is buying."

Greg shook his head and rolled his eyes. "Everyone's got their hand out."

Stacey held up the company credit card she'd been using on her errands. "Don't worry, I'll pay."

CHAPTER ELEVEN

Ryan spent most of the next morning scraping barnacles off the salvage boat's hull to save fuel and reduce drag. While he was underwater, he checked the propellers and prop shafts.

Emery, Travis, and Dennis continued to work on the engines and systems while Stacey helped Don integrate the new Furuno electronics into *Peggy Lynn*'s console. He also connected the towed side scan sonar array to a new computer hard drive and flat screen monitors.

In the afternoon, Ryan and Travis mounted the sonar array cable reel to the rear of the vessel and designed an extension to the crane boom to keep the cable from drooping and wrapping around the props. Ryan enjoyed the work and collaboration. It was something he missed from the EOD teams. Pressure situations brought out the best in the men, and they became highly innovative at solving crisis situations.

Greg spent his time on the phone or working on his computer under the satinleaf tree. Ryan took a break and walked over to talk to him.

"I called Billy Parker, my contact in Haiti," Greg said. "He's keeping an eye out for *Northwest Passage*."

"Remind me who he is again," Ryan said, squatting beside the tree with a cigarette in one hand and a sweating bottle of Stella Artois in the other.

"He's the guy who runs a marina in Cap-Haïtien."

"I never met him," Ryan said.

"He said the place didn't fair too bad during the hurricane. He also said a friend of yours showed back up."

Ryan looked up. "A friend?"

"Joulie Lafitte."

"What's she doing back in Haiti? I thought she was getting asylum here."

Greg shrugged. "Billy said she's running Toussaint's old gang and took over the crew who blew up the *Domingo*. They were a little light on leadership after you machine-gunned their boat."

Ryan and Mango had manned the fifty-caliber machine gun mounted near the bow of the sinking *Santo Domingo* and used it to shoot and sink the attacking fishing vessel. Ryan had also tried to kill Toussaint Bajeux with it.

Ryan put his cigarette to his lips and took a long drag. Joulie was back in Haiti. Did that mean she was going to want a cut of the gold if she found out they were salvaging it?

"You got Landis on speed dial?" Ryan asked.

"Yeah, I do." Greg hit the button to call Floyd Landis at the Houston branch office of the Department of Homeland Security.

The older man growled into the phone, "What do you want, Greg?"

"Why is Joulie Lafitte back in Haiti?" Ryan asked.

"She chose to go back on her own."

Ryan and Greg glanced at each other before Ryan asked, "Why'd she do that?"

Landis let out a long sigh. "In this current political climate, it has become inappropriate to extend asylum to Haitian citizens. Those who are in the US are afraid they'll be sent back and are fleeing to Canada. Rather than go to Canada, she chose to go back to Haiti."

"Did your intelligence tell you that she's picked up where Toussaint left off?" asked Greg.

Ryan lit another cigarette while Landis pondered this question.

Instead of answering, Landis asked one of his own. "What are you two doing together?"

Ryan said, "We're working a business deal."

"Okay, I'll bite. What is it?"

"Better you don't know," Ryan said.

In the silence, they could hear Landis clicking his pen in and out. He blew out another deep breath. "Greg, do you know why we stopped working jointly?"

"I've got a pretty good idea." He glanced at Ryan.

"Your dad didn't operate like this. Everything he did was above board an—"

Greg hit the *end* button. "How dare that asshole talk about my dad."

"I went rogue, right?" Ryan asked. "My op to takedown Killer Roy was unsanctioned, and I delivered weapons to a warlord in Haiti."

"Something like that."

Greg's phone rang. "It's Landis." He tapped the button to take the call.

"Don't you ever hang—"

Greg hit the *end* button again.

The phone immediately rang, and Greg answered.

"You're just as cavalier as your buddy, Ryan," Landis fumed. "If you lose government contracts it won't be my fault."

"Other than owning the controlling interest in DWR, I have nothing to do with its daily operations, Floyd." Greg winked at Ryan. Both knew Landis hated to be called by his first name. It reminded him of Floyd the Barber in the *Andy Griffith Show*.

"Are you going to Haiti?" Landis asked, more under control.

"Yes," Ryan said.

Another long sigh and pen clicking filled the air. "Just be careful. Greg, you're like your dad in a lot of ways and I know you both operate above board. Ryan, while I know your heart is in the right place, I've been ordered to keep my distance from you if I want to collect my pension, but if there's anything I can do for you, please call me. You have my personal cell number."

"Thanks, but we just wanted some information about Joulie," Greg said.

"She's united two warring gangs and now controls almost half of the country. She did it with the Humvees, MRAPs, and guns you unloaded before the *Santo Domingo* sank."

Ryan asked, "What else is she doing?"

"I don't know," Landis said. "Haiti isn't my department. I only know about the unification of the gangs because her name came up in an interagency meeting. Ryan, before she went back, she asked me where you were. I told her that I had no clue."

Puzzled, Ryan asked, "Why'd she want to see me?"

"She didn't say."

Ryan took a draw on his cigarette. He wouldn't mind seeing her again.

When Ryan didn't say anything more, Greg said, "Thanks. I'll call you if we need any help."

"Good luck, guys."

Greg ended the call. "That adds a wrinkle to things."

Ryan nodded. "Hope she doesn't want a cut."

"I'm sure everyone and their brother will know exactly what's going on when you drop anchor over the *Santo Domingo* and send a diver down."

"No kidding," Ryan said.

CHAPTER TWELVE

The promised party with Chuck didn't pan out as they'd planned. His busy flight schedule meant he couldn't return to Key West for two more days. Days Ryan wanted to use to get to Haiti. Greg waited in a hotel and Don accompanied the crew across the Gulf Stream to Andros Island. He wanted to ensure all his new systems were up and running. Things went smoothly, and Ryan insisted Don go further down the Bahamas, so they could test the surface supplied diving gear and the towed sonar array.

From Andros, they worked their way south. At eight knots they weren't going anywhere fast. Their maximum speed was just over twelve knots and the old boat started to protest when she approached double digits. Ryan had complained about the fuel bill at Andros Town, and Dennis was happy to oblige his old gal and his boss by keeping her below her normal cruising speed to conserve fuel.

Ryan figured Kilroy wouldn't have their exact location, unless Dreadlocks had gotten a tracking device on board the

Peggy Lynn, and that would buy him some free time to enjoy the trip down. He was wrong.

Once they started down the island chain, he became anxious. He was ready to be back in the action and to find the gold. To help alleviate the tension, he had them tow the sonar array through the deeper water between islands. He wanted them to be well-versed on the equipment by the time they reached Haiti. Staring at a television screen was monotonous for a man who had once lived like an action sports star, jumping out of planes, scuba diving, traveling across the globe, blowing up mines, deactivating bombs, and shooting bad guys. He'd had teammates who, in their down time, were professional BASE jumpers, raced dirt bikes, ran triathlons, or rock climbed competitively.

"Hey, Ryan, get your ass up here," Stacey yelled from the bridge.

He jerked his gaze upward from his spot on the stern, stubbed out his cigarette and ran up the stairs. "What?"

"We found a shipwreck." Stacey pointed to the screen. Don was using a computer tool to take measurements and then used them to render a three-dimensional model. In the meantime, Captain Dennis had slowed the boat to make a wide turn for a second pass over the wreck.

"Why are we wasting time on this?" Ryan asked.

Travis looked up, puzzled. "I thought you wanted to try out some of the gear?"

Ryan glanced at the model Don was generating. According to the projection, the boat was an old shrimper. Not surprising for these waters. "Yeah, let's do it. Dennis, make another sweep and then come back around to anchor. Travis and I will take turns on the surface supply."

"You know me and Captain Dennis have been using that gear for years," Emery said.

"Do you want to dive, Grandpa?" Travis asked.

"It's been awhile since I've been in the water, whipper-snapper. I'd like to give it a go."

"What about you, Captain?" Ryan asked.

"I'm good," Dennis replied from behind his cup of coffee. Ryan had noticed the man had laid off the whiskey since they'd been underway.

Ryan asked, "When was the last time you dove?"

"Been a few years," Dennis said.

"Wouldn't hurt to do a refresher dive. We'll probably need a standby diver."

Dennis gazed out the window while guiding the *Peggy Lynn* across the wreck site again. Ryan noticed Dennis had made a mark on the GPS plotter.

"Passing over now," Dennis said.

Everyone except Dennis stared at the flat screen and the sonar's waterfall display. They saw the dark outline of the ship against the sea bottom, the laser scanner adding additional details to the previously generated 3D model of the vessel lying on her port side.

After the sonar had passed over the sunken boat, Don shut off the system and activated the drum winch to reel in the towed array. Ryan went aft to monitor the progress of the winch and to hoist the array aboard. When the nose of the array broke the surface, Ryan motioned for Dennis to put the engines in neutral, and the big salvage boat drifted while Ryan and Travis craned the torpedo-shaped sonar gear back aboard and settled it into its cradle.

"What do you think we'll find?" Travis asked.

Ryan said, "Probably some old, piece of crap that sank fifty years ago."

Travis shook his head. "Are you always so cynical?"

"No." Ryan leaned both hands against the sonar array,

another piece of gear tested and improved by DWR. "I'm a pretty positive guy. I'm just ready to get to Haiti and get on with the mission."

Travis said, "I understand that."

Peggy Lynn's engines shuddered as Dennis brought her to a stop over the wreck.

Ryan straightened. "Our lives depend on this equipment. Let's make sure it works to standards."

"I agree." Travis turned and pulled off his sweaty T-shirt. His back and chest were white as a sheet, but his arms had been bronzed by the sun in a classic farmer's tan.

Ryan started to laugh.

"What's so funny?"

"Nothing," Ryan said, trying to keep the smile off his face.

Forty minutes later, Travis wore his wetsuit and had his helmet locked in place. The compressor was humming, and all their topside checks were complete. Ryan hooked up the Launch and Recovery System basket—a large stainless-steel platform used to lift and lower the divers—to the crane boom. Travis stepped onto the LARS, and Ryan used the crane to lift him over the rail and lower him to the sea floor below. Stacey stood by the thick umbilical cord connecting the diver to the compressor and his topside control. Emery sat on the bench in his faded ratty wetsuit, which he refused to give up for a new one. His helmet was beside him, ready to dive in case of an emergency. Ryan didn't see any reason for Travis, experienced as he was, to run into difficulty at one hundred and fifteen feet.

Once the LARS was on the sand beside the wreck, Ryan retreated to the bridge to watch the video feeds with Dennis and Don. In the clear water, the camera footage made it look like they were standing beside Travis as he walked around the wreck. The boat showed no signs of damage to the hull to provide a clue to the cause of her sinking. There was damage to the bridge, hoist masts, and lifelines. Some were completely missing, and others dangled precariously. Ryan watched silently, knowing he didn't need to warn Travis about the dangers of becoming entangled in the wreck.

"Not much outside," Travis said after making a full circle of the wreck. He turned to watch a school of fish that had taken up refuge on the artificial reef. A good-sized black grouper slid out from one of the hold doors. "Where's the spear gun?"

"Take a look inside," Ryan said into the microphone.

"Roger that." Travis stepped over the bow railing and used a piece of twisted metal to boost himself up to see in the bridge window. The camera bounced around as Travis jerked back and dropped to the sand. "What the hell?"

"Dead bodies?" Ryan asked.

"I guess so," Travis said. "I've never seen anything like it."

"You okay?" Stacey asked through her radio connection at the gas blending station.

Travis sounded a little heated. "I'm fine."

Ryan said, "Take a look inside the hold."

Travis moved slowly around to the ship's stern. The port side cargo door lay open on the sand. Travis clicked on his helmet-mounted lights and shone the twin beams into the hold. Ryan stood with his arms crossed while he watched the scene play out. Something nagged him about the glimpse of the bridge. The quick look he'd had was of two dead guys in what looked like blue coveralls.

"Holy balls," Travis said.

Ryan focused his attention back on the screen. Highlighted in the cones of light were four shrink-wrapped pallets still strapped to the deck. Red, waterproof packages strained the insides of the shrink wrap as gravity pulled them toward the seabed. Only the cargo straps kept them from toppling over. Each red package held a kilo of cocaine.

"Travis, get out of there. Now," Ryan commanded into the radio. He took his finger off the radio switch and said, "Don, back up the video to the bridge."

Don rotated a round controller to back the footage up.

"Stop. Freeze it."

Don had to jump the video back and forth a few times to get it exactly where Ryan wanted him to stop. Ryan bent close to the screen and stared at the image. "Erase all of this and overwrite it."

"Why?"

"Just do it," Ryan said, running out of the bridge and leaping down the steps to the deck. "Stace, get lover boy on the LARS. We need to get out of here."

"What? Why?"

"Just do it!" He stripped off his shirt and strapped a weight belt with four pounds of weight and a wicked-looking dive knife on it around his waist. Next, he grabbed a mask and squirted baby shampoo mixed with water from a spray bottle into it. Stacey had Travis on the LARS. Ryan rinsed his mask in a small bucket and pulled it over his face before jerking on his fins. He grabbed a pole spear. The whole time he'd been working, he was taking deep breaths to purge his body of carbon dioxide.

CHAPTER THIRTEEN

Travis Wisnewski heard a splash and twisted his head to look above him. The SuperLite's faceplate didn't offer a great view upward. "What's going on?"

"Ryan just dove over the side." Stacey's voice came through the fiber optics without the standard tininess of the old coaxial lines.

"What for?" Travis asked.

"I have no idea," Stacey replied, a hint of exasperation in her voice. "He just insisted you get out of the water and jumped over."

Travis swiveled around and finally spotted Ryan descending through the water column. He was kicking for the bridge of the sunken ship, his powerful back, leg, and arm muscles standing out like cords under his skin. Travis watched as Ryan thrust his upper body through the front bridge window. A few seconds later, he used a back kick and a push-off to make his exit. Travis saw Ryan shove something into the cargo pocket of his shorts. Several powerful kicks later, Ryan was at the rear of the ship.

The black grouper edged out of its hole. Travis saw

Ryan slide his hand up the shaft of the pole spear, stretching the black rubber band tight. The grouper stared dumbly at the undersea invader yet did not turn away as he had from Travis. With no bubbles to scare the fish, the grouper mistook Ryan as a fellow sea dweller. Ryan extended his arm, the spearpoint just above the fish's gills. He released his hand, and the spear drove straight through the grouper's tender flesh. Immediately, the fish began twisting and plunging, trying to rid itself of the spear.

The LARS lifted Travis higher when his one-minute deep stop at fifty-eight feet ended. Ryan was still struggling with the fish. Travis asked Stacey, "How long has he been in the water?"

"I didn't start counting," Stacey said. Then, she said, "Grandpa says a minute and twenty seconds."

Travis looked at his watch, mentally marking the spot on the bezel where the second hand had just been. He kept one eye on the sweep hand and the other on Ryan. He estimated the fish was close to three feet in length and nearly fifteen pounds. Ryan grabbed the pole spear in two hands. One near the fish and the other near the base. He started toward the surface, kicking as hard as he could.

Gripping the curved bar of the LARS basket, Travis watched Ryan swim past. Ryan gave him a wide grin, bubbles escaping through his teeth. Red blood streaming from the grouper appeared green in the water. The cage stopped, and Travis looked at his computer. Fifteen feet for three minutes, then he was done. Ryan climbed up the stern using the old tires and Travis was left sitting in the cage, alone. He peered down at the sunken vessel. *What was so important that Ryan didn't take the time to strap on a tank?*

By the time Travis stepped out of the basket and onto the deck of the *Peggy Lynn*, Captain Dennis had the engines started and Grandpa was out of his wetsuit and dive gear. He wore a black Speedo over his wrinkled and sun-burned flesh. His slight paunch and prominent bones gave him a fragile look. White hair matted his chest, lower back, head, and legs.

Normally, Travis relished the first deep breath of fresh air after taking off his hat. The sun on his face and the wind against his wet body always served to remind him he'd survived another dive. But, as soon as his helmet was off, Travis barked at Ryan, "What did you see on the bridge?"

———

RYAN TOOK Travis's helmet and set it in its plastic case. He stood back up and turned to face Travis. "Nothing. I thought I saw something, but my eyes were playing tricks on me."

"Bullshit, man," Travis said, stepping out of the basket. "I saw you put something in your pocket."

"You saw me spearing a fish." Ryan stared right into Travis's eyes.

Travis squared his shoulders and stared back. "I saw you go into the bridge. What did you take?"

Ryan stepped closer, bringing them nose-to-nose. Travis's blood pressure rose, and the adrenaline kicked in. Anger boiled just beneath his skin. He felt prickly all over. "What did you take?"

Through clenched teeth, Ryan said, "I didn't take anything."

"Bull! Shit!" Travis cried. "Empty your pockets."

In a menacing voice, Ryan said, "I am your boss. You answer to me. I'm telling you I didn't take anything out of the bridge, and if I did it wouldn't concern you one damned bit."

Anger swelled inside of Travis. "You're lying, and I don't give a damn if you are the boss. I signed up to go after gold and now we're meddling in drugs?"

"You're the one who wanted to test the gear, remember?" Ryan said, not backing down. "Your girlfriend spotted this wreck, and you dove it. How am I to blame?"

"You picked the route," Stacey said quietly.

"I've got a fish to clean," Ryan said, not moving from his toe-to-toe standoff with Travis. Travis could feel Ryan's anger pulsing off him even as his own anger clouded his judgment.

"You picked the route," Travis said, trying to keep an even tone to his voice. "You knew where that boat was and now, we're recovering cocaine."

"We are not recovering cocaine," Ryan growled. "You want a conspiracy theory, try the grassy knoll. Dennis and I agreed on the route. We're going to Haiti."

Travis's gaze moved past Ryan to Emery, who was coming out of the bridge. The old man stopped at the top of the steps. "Captain says to knock it off."

Shifting his gaze back to Ryan, Travis whispered. "I saw you put something in your pocket, asshole. Boss or not, I don't like people lying to me."

Ryan backed away and picked up the grouper. "Stop being so butthurt and clean up the gear."

Travis's blood boiled again, and he clenched his fists. He stepped forward, pulling an arm back to deliver a blow.

"Stop!" Stacey pleaded, lunging toward her boyfriend.

Travis looked at her and put his arm down, suddenly ashamed of his poor behavior. He began to strip off his buoyancy compensating vest, weight belt, harness, and wetsuit. Once free of his gear, Travis sat down on the bench. Stacey scooted in beside him.

"What was that about?" she asked quietly.

"I don't know." Travis leaned forward, placing his elbows on his knees. "I saw him go into the bridge through the front window and come back out. He put something into his cargo pocket. It was small, whatever it was. Then he shot the grouper."

"Why challenge him about it?" Stacey asked.

"Because we're supposed to trust each other. If I can't trust him to keep his word, then I don't think I can trust him to work topside. What if he plans to get rid of us after we help him get the gold?"

"Ryan? Kill us?" She shook her head.

"We have to keep an eye on him."

CHAPTER FOURTEEN

Stacey climbed up to the bridge. Don was sitting at the computer. She sat down beside him, leaned in close, and whispered, "Do you still have the footage from Travis's dive?"

"Ryan told me to erase it."

"Did you?"

He snuck a quick glance at Stacey. Her eyes were big and pleading.

"I deleted all the dive until Travis was on the basket."

Excitement tinged her low voice, making it husky. "Did you see Ryan's dive?"

"I watched it."

"Did he go into the bridge?"

Don nodded slowly, as if unwilling to continue the conversation.

"And?" she pressed, glancing at Dennis to see if he was eavesdropping. The captain was busy retrieving the anchor, the loud rattle of the chain into the locker and the knock of the diesel engines covered their whispering. "Did he take anything?"

"It's hard to tell," Don said. "If he did, it wasn't very big."

"Did he put something in his cargo pocket?" She swiveled in her chair and mimicked sliding her hand into a cargo pocket on a pair of shorts.

"Maybe. The camera wasn't very clear."

"This is important, Donny."

He nodded. "We could hear them arguing all the way in here. Dennis sent Emery to tell them to shut up."

Stacey's shoulders slumped, and she pursed her lips. "Do you have anything from the dive?"

"No, I erased it all and quit recording after he told me to delete it."

"Thanks, Donny." Stacey stood and walked outside. Travis sat on the stern in the sunshine with his shirt off. "Are you trying to signal surrender or act as our dive flag?"

Travis glanced down at his white chest and deeply tanned arms. "Just getting some sun."

"Donny says he may have seen Ryan put something in his pocket. He wasn't sure, and he quit recording right before Ryan dove overboard."

Travis pursed his lips and shook his head. "Something isn't right."

"What did you see on the bridge?"

"Some dead guys. Stacey, it was gruesome. I don't want to talk about it."

"I know, baby, but if you tell me what you saw, maybe we can figure out what he took."

He nodded and took a deep breath. "There were two guys on the bridge. Both of them were white and puffy, like they'd been in the water a long time." He shuddered. "The fish had eaten away their lips and eyes and earlobes. It was like looking at a grinning death's head."

Stacey's stomach turned. For her, diving had been about guiding people on reefs and watching the pretty fish dart in and out of the coral. She'd shot a few fish and caught some lobsters, but that was it. She'd never seen anything as disturbing as what Travis was describing.

And then there was Ryan. She'd never seen him act that way. She thought she had a pretty good handle on who he was, and she'd tasered the same guy twice for him.

"Are you listening?" Travis asked.

"Yes," she replied, unsure if lunch would stay down. She stared at the horizon, trying to use the old seasickness cure to remedy the nausea.

"They were wearing blue coveralls. Their skin was bloated around the fabric." He shook again, like a dog trying to dry off. "Stacey. Stacey."

A chill coursed through her body and she wrapped her arms around her torso. His voice drew her back from her thoughts. "Travis, what would be so small that he could just shove it in his pocket?"

"I've been thinking about it, but I don't know."

"Something he took from the bridge," Stacey mused. "His pocket wasn't full when he got on the boat and he didn't take anything out of them. I saw him the whole time."

"He didn't go below?"

"No." She shook her head.

"Even when you were swinging me up?"

"He helped. He ran the crane."

"Damnit," Travis muttered. "What's he holding back?"

Stacey ran her fingers through her purple hair, scratching at the back of her head and neck.

Don walked up and sat down on the stern. He tugged his DWR trucker's cap down tighter on his head to prevent it from blowing overboard. "I was thinking about what we were talking about earlier."

Stacey and Travis waited expectantly.

"Ryan had me back the footage up, so he could see something on the bridge. When I found it, he leaned in close to the screen then told me to erase everything. I erased the tape, but I forgot I took a screenshot of whatever he was looking at. It's still on the computer."

"Really!" Stacey cried.

"Keep your voice down, babe," Travis cautioned.

"When can we look at this picture?" she asked, excitement still tinging her voice.

"I'll come topside when you have the zero two to zero six watch."

Stacey nodded and smiled. "I can't wait." She wanted to pump her fists and do a little dance. They were going to figure out what Mr. Sneaky Pants was up to.

"Can't wait for what?" Ryan asked before lighting a cigarette. His fondness of smoking was beginning to grate on her. She'd found him rugged and handsome in a mysterious sort of way when they'd worked together at the dive shop, but now he was just annoying. Still cute, but annoying.

She wheeled to face him. "For you to stop sneaking up on me."

He grinned one of his trademark smiles and her defenses started to melt.

"I just came out here to tell you supper was ready." He sat on the rail beside Travis. "How'd the rig work?"

He doesn't even care that they were about to trade punches a few minutes ago!

To her surprise, Travis was just as friendly. "It worked

great. I like those new hats DWR gave us. The DAVD display is really cool."

"Glad things are working well. Is there anything we need to adjust before we get to Haiti and start diving the deep stuff?"

"Not that I can think of?" Travis replied.

Ryan looked up at Stacey. She crossed her arms and glared at him. He cocked his head. "What about you, Stace, everything okay with topside control?"

"You mean other than you acting like a complete asshat?"

"Dinner's ready." He stood and took a long pull on his cigarette. "Grouper, rice, and the last of the vegetables we picked up in Andros." Then he walked up the starboard side of the vessel.

It angered her that he didn't show any emotion at her outburst.

"Sorry, guys, but I'm hungry," Don said. "I'm going to get something to eat."

"Me, too." Travis patted his belly.

A sudden surge of sexual craving flushed hot across her skin when she glanced at Travis's washboard stomach.

"Go on, guys," Stacey said. "I'll be down in a few minutes." When they were gone, she stood staring at the western horizon. The sun was still several hours away from setting, yet it was already coloring the bank of cumulous clouds in golden hues.

"What's going on?" she asked herself. She had fallen for Travis like a rock off a bridge, but she was beginning to doubt the wisdom of coming on this trip.

IT WAS DARK AT 0500. Without the glow of the red gauge

lights and the wash of light coming from the instrument screens, Stacey wouldn't have been able to see a thing. They were running in deep water and in a few hours, would cross the Windward Passage between Hispaniola and Cuba.

The strait was known for its hazardous conditions, even in good weather. The Passage was one of the major shipping lanes between the Atlantic and the Caribbean, and several massive freighters or crude oil tankers were always visible. As a marine geologist, Stacey had studied this region of undersea topography. The ocean floor dropped several thousand feet into the Cayman Trough, the deepest point of the Caribbean Sea. The Trough was also the tectonic boundary between the North American Plate and the Caribbean Plate. Cuba, Jamaica, the Cayman Islands, and Hispaniola were the results of activity along those plates.

Stacey poured a cup of coffee and sipped it while she checked *Peggy Lynn*'s systems. Everything was functioning normally. She tapped the fuel gauge. The needle didn't move from its half-tank position. Dennis had told her earlier that they had enough fuel to get them to Luperón in the Dominican Republic. There was nothing on the radar, even zoomed out to its maximum range, which was limited to five to seven miles because of mast height and the curvature of the earth.

She sat down at the computer, scrolled through her emails, and looked at some social media sites to see what her friends were doing.

A soft, "Hey," startled her.

"Jeez, Trav, you scared the crap out of me."

He laughed.

"It's not funny, jerk."

He kissed her, and asked, "Did you find anything?"

"No."

"You won't find it looking at Facebook," Don said.

"Where did you come from," Stacey blurted.

"Uh," Don said. "I was right behind Travis."

"Both of you need to stop sneaking around in the dark!"

"Okay, come on, Don, let's go back to bed." Travis turned to go back down the ladder.

"Get your ass back here, mister," Stacey hissed.

Don took Stacey's place in the chair and closed out her internet browser. He quickly opened the folder where he'd hidden the image and a watery blue screenshot filled the monitor.

"What was Ryan looking at?" Travis asked, bending close to the screen.

Stacey put her mug down on the instrument console and came back to the desk. She took Travis's place, pushing her face close to the screen. Travis stood watch, scanning the dark sea for ships and other hazards.

Don replied, "I have no idea."

All three leaned close to the computer and stared at the screen. They jumped when they heard a lighter wheel scraping across flint. A flame illuminated Ryan's face and the smell of cigarette smoke filled the bridge.

"What are you looking at?" Ryan asked.

Stacey backed away from the computer and turned to look out the bridge windows. She picked up a pair of binoculars and pretended to study something far off.

Sullenly, Travis said, "Nothing."

Don scrambled to click the window closed.

"No, let's see it," Ryan said, stepping into the bridge.

"Dennis is going to be pissed if he smells smoke in here," Stacey said, not moving the binoculars.

"Let him," Ryan said. "It's the least of my worries, right now."

"What *are* you worried about?" Stacey asked, turning to face him.

"Yeah, what's going on, Ryan?" Don asked.

"Let's see the picture."

Don reopened the picture.

Ryan bent down to look at the screen. "See anything interesting about those dead guys?"

"Other than they've been eaten by the fish?" Travis asked.

"Yeah, that's pretty common," Ryan said. "They eat the soft parts first and then the crabs and the other scavengers move in to work on the rest."

Stacey made a gagging noise. "That's disgusting."

"Anything else?" Ryan asked.

Don spoke for the group. "Not that we can see."

Stacey watched the men through the reflection of the bridge windows. *Peggy Lynn*'s autopilot kept the boat on course. All Stacey had to do was monitor the systems and make sure they didn't run into anything.

Ryan pointed at the screen. "See that?"

Travis and Don leaned in.

"What?" Stacey asked.

"On the side of the coveralls," Ryan said.

Travis was the first to speak. "It's a patch."

Don zoomed in. They could see part of the circular patch.

"What is that?" Don asked, adjusting the computer program to bring out the colors and shapes. A blurry image of what looked like part of the United States and Mexico filled the screen. The map had been shaded with gray, tan, and red.

"Don't bother," Ryan said, straightening up. He took a deep inhale from his cigarette.

"Get that cancer stick off my bridge," Captain Dennis thundered.

Ryan backed up two paces to the hatch and stepped outside.

"What's going on up here?" Dennis asked. "A person can't get any sleep with you people blundering around above decks."

Stacey said, "Ryan was just about to tell us what he almost got into a fistfight with Travis about."

"Dadgummit," Emery said. "Can't you people let a man sleep in peace?" He rubbed his eyes with the backs of his hands.

"Well, Ryan, what is it?" Dennis asked. He poured a cup of coffee and sat in his captain's seat.

"I didn't want to upset anyone, and I didn't think it would be this big of a deal." Ryan leaned on the hatch combing, using one foot to keep the hatch open. The wind carried his cigarette smoke out to sea. He took another long draw. "I told you about the Aztlán cartel and their pirates," he said, fishing in his cargo pocket. He held up the patch he'd pulled off the dead man's coveralls. "This is the same patch the pirates wore. It represents Aztlán."

Stacey kept her eyes on the horizon, constantly scanning the line demarking the sky and water. It was lit by a smattering of brilliant stars.

"I saw the patch on the dead guys and kinda freaked out. I probably should have told you straight away. Finding a boat full of cocaine belonging to the same cartel who has a hit on me is purely coincidental. I had to see for myself, and spearing the grouper was a good way to cover what I was doing."

"Except Travis saw you," Stacey said.

"Yeah," Ryan replied, drawing out the word.

Travis had reverted to his defensive posture of arms and legs crossed. "What now?"

"We keep going for the gold," Ryan said. "I don't care about a bunch of cocaine at the bottom of the ocean." He tapped the patch against his hand thoughtfully. "Knowing where that boat is might give me some leverage over the cartel."

Dennis said, "I told you from the beginning, I'm not getting involved in drugs."

"We're not, Captain," Ryan said. "I was just thinking out loud."

Stacey glanced around the bridge at the grim faces and tense bodies. "How long 'til we get to Luperón?"

"Another day," Dennis said.

"Good, everyone get some rest," Ryan said. "We're going to need it."

CHAPTER FIFTEEN

L uperón was a welcomed sight. The small village provided them with diesel fuel, fresh fruits and vegetables, booze, and small restaurants. More importantly, it allowed the crew to spread out and relax. Dennis, Don, and Emery checked over *Peggy Lynn*'s systems. Stacey and Travis rented a hotel room near the water and didn't come out for two days. Ryan spent the time looking at charts of the Haitian coast and pinpointing where he wanted to start their search. He had a general idea where the ship had sunk based on landmarks, heading, and speed.

With the boat fueled and ready, they left the Dominican Republic and steamed northwest. They stayed well beyond the three-mile limit and waited for night to fall. Their job would be a little harder in the darkness, but once they had the towed array launched, they would blend in with the other fishing vessels.

The tiny crew gathered on deck to watch the sunset, their bellies full of fresh fish Emery had caught on a trolling line earlier in the day.

"Do you think we'll find it?" Stacey asked.

"Pretty sure we will," Ryan said. "Dennis and I mapped out a grid and it should take us over the area where the ship went down."

They lapsed back into silence. Everyone on board had already spent days staring at video screens, checking readings, and monitoring the ship's position relative to the search grid. They understood the tedious grind that lay before them. By eleven o'clock, the sonar array was well behind the ship on its tether. They agreed to take turns at the screen to ensure no one became fatigued and missed their target.

Frustration had set in by the time the sun rose. Ryan had expected to see the wreck quickly and had only laid out a small search grid. After running the original pattern, Dennis had begun to expand it.

Ryan sat on the stern rail and lit a cigarette. He watched the cable stretch and bow with the movement of the ship; the first rays of sunlight caught the water dripping from it. He inhaled and held the smoke in his lungs before letting it out through his nose, feeling the nicotine try to fight his body's need for sleep. He was tired, and that exacerbated his irritability. The wreck wasn't where he expected it to be.

He looked up when Don approached, carrying a map.

"Stupid thing couldn't have just disappeared," Ryan snapped.

"I have a theory," Don said.

"Yeah?" Ryan took another drag.

"After we worked through your original grid, I called DWR and had my friend, Ashlee, run a computer model based on all the information we've gathered. She pinpointed the wreck close to where you said it would be based on old satellite photos. While she was looking at those photos, she noticed all the clouds. She decided to input the known wind and current data gathered during Hurricane Irma. Her model says the hurricane probably moved the ship."

"To where?"

"That's the bad news," Don said.

With a weary sigh, Ryan said, "Give it to me."

Don held out the map and pointed to a spot in the ocean. "There's a massive ledge to the north of us that drops off a couple thousand feet."

"Shit."

"According to Ashlee's model, that's where the storm probably moved the *Santo Domingo*."

"Well, let's go look for her." Ryan stood and stubbed out his cigarette. He flipped it into an old coffee can Emery had set out for him.

They hiked up to the bridge and spread the map out on the console. Dennis joined them, leaving Stacey and Travis at the sonar monitor.

"Tell us what you want to do now, boss," Dennis said.

Ryan put his search grid over the chart. "Let's keep running this same sweep. Instead of a box, let's just push each leg north. That will bring us closer to this ledge, and if we can't find her, we'll assume Mother Nature had other plans."

"Roger that," Dennis said.

Stacey turned in her chair and hooked an arm over the back. "I once stared at a sonar screen for a whole month. I realized I needed a new job, but that's another story. We'll find her."

"What makes you so positive?" Ryan asked.

"You said she was there, and she will be." Stacey turned back around.

Ryan raised an eyebrow.

DON AND RYAN stared at the computer screen. Even though Ryan had snatched a few hours of sleep between watches, his eyes were dry and his brain foggy with the need for sleep. Ryan thought about putting some of Dennis's Jim Bean in his coffee but knew it would only make him more tired. When Greg had delivered their supplies to Stock Island, he'd brought a case of Black Rifle Company's Silencer Smooth coffee. If they didn't find the *Santo Domingo* soon, Ryan feared they'd run out of the good stuff. Of course, they could get fresh beans right from the docks in Haiti.

Ryan sipped his hot brew. He always joked about how his coffee was like his soul, and right now it was cloaked in black. This whole trip could be for nothing if the hurricane had swept the ship over the edge of the cliff. It would be impossible to get the gold if it was thousands of feet down in a trench.

He stared at the sonar's waterfall as it crawled down the screen. He took another sip and watched a black shape materialize out of the gloom. He almost spit out his coffee as he cried, "Turn the laser on!"

Don flipped on the laser. "Holy cow, is that it?"

"It has to be, based on the size and position," Ryan said.

Dennis peered over their shoulders. "If that ain't it, we're out of luck, boys. The next pass will take us out past the ledge."

The laser began painting a three-dimensional model of the *Santo Domingo* in the corner of the computer screen as *Peggy Lynn* continued along her eastern track. Once the wreck was no longer visible on the monitor, Ryan ordered

Dennis to turn around and make another pass. Dennis shut off the autopilot and began a long turn.

"What's going on?" Travis asked as he and Stacey crowded onto the bridge.

"We found it," Don said.

"Hell, yes," Travis shouted.

Stacey let out a whoop of joy, throwing both hands in the air and shaking her hips. Her purple hair danced while she sang, "I told you we'd find it. I told you. I told you. I told you."

The sonar passed over the ship again. The laser scan filled in more details. Dennis kept the wheel straight and steady as they battled through the waves. "Make another pass," Ryan ordered.

Dennis turned *Peggy Lynn* and brought her over top of the *Santo Domingo* on a north/south course. After another trio of passes, each from a different approach, the image of the submerged ship was as complete as they could make it. Don fiddled with the image while Ryan and Travis reeled in the sonar fish.

By the time they returned to the bridge, Don had the 3D image complete, and he'd overlaid the ship's schematics on top. "Ashlee sent me the old blueprints."

"Where'd she find those?" Ryan asked, pouring another steaming cup of coffee. He was about wiped out from the lack of sleep. His muscles felt slack and his mind numb. All he wanted was to crawl into his bunk. He was in no shape to do any diving, but he wanted to.

"I'm not sure, and sometimes it's better not to ask," Don responded.

Ryan nodded. He needed to have Greg give Ashlee a bonus. Turning to the captain, he said, "Mr. Law, take us back to Luperón."

Dennis made a few calculations. "That's ten hours away. Round trip will waste a day. We've found the wreck. You need to dive it."

The captain was the master of the vessel and had the final say when it came to its operation.

Ryan asked, "What do you recommend?"

"Emery, Don, Stacey, and I will take turns at the wheel. You and Travis get some sleep. You'll need it for the dive. We have enough fuel and food to last another week if all we do is stabilize for dives and then run for the coast."

"Okay," Ryan agreed, and sipped his coffee. "I'll make the first dive. Travis will be standby. Grandpa will be back-up tender to Stacey if things go pear-shaped. Is everyone good with that?"

CHAPTER SIXTEEN

R yan twisted the demand valve on his helmet and flushed out the water that had seeped in through a small leak in the neck dam, the watertight seal around his neck. He hated having water on his face when he was diving. For as long as he could remember, his natural reflex was to breathe through his nose as soon as his mask came off. He'd almost inhaled water on numerous occasions and had a mini panic attack every time he even thought about taking his mask off underwater. He'd spent hours swimming without it during his Navy scuba diving training, and he'd had to fight the instinct through every minute of it.

If the leak got worse, he could leave the demand valve open to pressurize the helmet and keep flushing out the water. Still, the thought of being trapped inside the Kirby Morgan while it slowly flooded was the stuff of nightmares.

He dropped steadily through the gloom. Even though there was easily eighty feet of visibility, there was nothing to see but the dark shadows at the periphery of those eighty feet. The DAVD display gave him the approximate layout of the wreck and where he was in relationship to it. He glanced at his dive computer. The digital depth readout counted down like a New Year's Eve clock and he was dropping like the ball. The lead weights around his waist sucked him down as fast as the crew could unwind the air hoses and safety line.

Sinking into the gloom was unnatural. He remembered the first time he'd jumped off a boat into the ocean and stared into the vast blue. His breath had caught in his chest and he'd had to force himself to breathe. The decreasing visibility made the darkness press in on him. A shadow flashed at the edge of his visibility. *Was that a shark?*

At two hundred and eighty feet, he got his first glimpse of the *Santo Domingo*. She was still lying on her starboard side, but her bow now faced almost due north instead of east as she'd originally sunk. When he and Mango had swum out of her hold, there was a tugboat and barges beside the cargo ship. The tugboat was a hundred yards west of the ship now, the barges had disappeared. The crane gantry had also been ripped away. Tangles of cables draped over the hold and trailed along the sea floor.

He glanced left and right, scanning the dark water for any threats. He loved wreck diving, but every time he dove alone on a wreck, Ryan sensed an eerie presence. Out there, beyond the limits of his vision, were creatures that could kill him. The wreck had its own hazards, and on this one, there were people who had died. Davy Jones had claimed them as bounty, and their ghastly bodies would sway in the currents like lifeless ghosts. Ryan prayed he wouldn't encounter any bodies and shuddered to think of what they looked like after months in the water.

He kept his head on a swivel while the ground continued to rush up at him. "Slow down," he said, and the tension in his umbilical slowed his descent rate.

Silt bloomed off the ocean floor as he sank several inches into the mud and ooze. He stood there staring up at the massive ship. This was the deepest wreck he'd ever dove, at three hundred and fifty feet.

It could be his last if the ship moved just right. The sonar had been correct, and now that he could see it with his own eyes, there was no denying the truth. The rear edge of the five-story superstructure rested in the dirt at the edge of the cliff and the stern projected over it. If the ship moved several feet, its weight would tip it over the edge, and it would plunge into the wild darkness below.

Ryan took a deep breath and slowly exhaled.

"Holy crap, that's scary," Stacey said. Ryan knew she was staring at his helmet camera footage. Emery had chosen to run the topside station. He was proficient at the gas switches they would need to do.

"One wrong move and this whole thing is going over," Ryan said. His thought turned to the explosively formed penetrator bombs he'd built and installed on the ship to prevent Toussaint from getting the weapons. They were still there, wired to her forward keel, one on each side, to send a slug blasting out of a pipe to rip out her guts. They weren't needed, thanks to rival gang leader Wilky Ador's RPG attack. If the EFPs detonated now, the whole ship would slide off the edge. He hadn't told anyone about the EFPs, and he wasn't worried about the C_4 detonating. It was one of the most stable explosives in the world, and the remote detonation system he'd rigged would have shorted out in the water. He'd thrown away the key fob-sized remote when he'd gotten to shore.

He stopped to stare up at the Humvees and MRAPs still held to the deck by their tie-down chains. They could fall at any moment. The ones that had fallen were in a jumbled heap against the starboard hull. A Humvee sat on its wheels on the ocean floor just outside the ship's hold. It looked like he could get in it and drive away. Ryan walked to the back of the up-armored vehicle, the muck tugging at his boots.

His breathing was normal, and he felt good, but he had to hurry. His time was limited here, and he wasn't looking forward to the three hours of decompression stops for twenty minutes of bottom time.

"Coming hot," Travis said in his ear.

"Roger that." Ryan turned and stared up. He saw the cluster of tanks dropping toward the bottom.

Their landing stirred up a cloud of silt, which bloomed several feet into the water column and hung there. Ryan looked back at his steps and saw a silt cloud around each footprint leading out of a larger cloud where he'd landed. Both the footsteps and the clouds were slowly dissipating with the slight current.

Ryan moved into the silt bloom, unclipped the tanks, carried them two at a time to the back of the Humvee, and slid them inside. Each bottle had been clearly labeled with bright stickers indicating which gas blend the bottle held. Several contained 11/70, their bottom gas; eleven percent air, seventy percent helium, and nine percent nitrogen. If the surface supply system stopped functioning, they would have plenty of extra gas on the bottom, including the normal bailout bottle each diver carried on his back. Other bottles contained what they referred to as travel mix, the gas they would breathe on their ascent to the surface. There wasn't enough gas to allow them to do the full in-water decompression schedule. They would surface and go straight to the chamber, where they would be able to do the full measure of stops. This would keep the nitrogen trapped in their body tissues from escaping into their bloodstream and causing decompression sickness, what everyone called, "the bends."

Again, he felt as if someone or something were watching him. He glanced around for signs of life but saw none. Then he checked his dive computer. Ten minutes left.

Carefully, he edged under the serpentine crane cables and into the hold. He stepped onto the hull and used the bumper of a Humvee to climb up onto an MRAP, which lay on its side. He tried to figure out which Humvee he and Mango had ridden in while the ship was sinking. The vehicles had moved so much in the storm's turbulence that he couldn't tell. He clicked on a light and swept it around the hull. The narrow beam barely penetrated the darkness of the hull's interior. Ryan grinned, fantasizing that he was holding a light saber as he slashed it across the pile of vehicles.

He stopped wasting time and slowly moved the light along the hull and under the wreckage, searching for the two strong boxes. One, he recalled, had come open during the initial wreck. He'd seen the bars lying on the deck, gleaming gold in the weak light as he and Mango had exited the ship to begin their swim to shore. That was the wonderful thing about gold; no matter how long it was immersed in salt water, it never lost its shine.

There were complications with the open box of gold. If the storm had moved tons of steel freighter, tugboats, barges, and vehicles, then the gold could be scattered all over the ship's hold, or even flung over the cliff into the abyss to never be recovered. He prayed that wasn't the case and the gold bars were still clustered around the strong box. It could take years to find the individual gold bars amid the chaos inside the wreck.

Ryan stopped the sweep of the light, jerking it back to focus just behind the tire of an MRAP standing on its nose. The massive high-wheel base vehicle leaned against the rear of another MRAP, which lay on its side. The opening between the two massive trucks formed a V, like a teepee, with the giant tire as the circular entrance. A gold bar peeked out from under the vehicles. He scrambled across the wreckage, leaping in the weightlessness across the gaps between trucks.

"What's going on?" Stacey demanded. "You gotta go slow."

"Just a second." Ryan bent and reached behind the truck. His fingertips barely brushed the gold bar. "Shit."

"What?" Stacey asked again.

"Hold on!" Ryan inverted himself, so he could see under the truck. Water rushed across his faceplate and sloshed into his nose. He coughed and spat. Then his discomfort was forgotten as his eyes widened, and he laughed. He heard Stacey suck in a deep breath. The camera was seeing the same thing he was, a broken strong box with gold bars spilling out. They gleamed and sparkled in the beams of the dancing light.

Emery put a stop to the jubilation. "Time's up, Ryan."

Ryan glanced at his computer and muttered, "Damnit!"

He lay on his belly and thrust his arm under the tire. His shoulder butted against the rubber, preventing him from reaching further. Ryan patted the ground until his fingers wrapped around the closest gold bar, and he started to laugh. He dragged it to him and held it up, surprised by the weight of the small brick.

"Let's go, Ryan," Emery commanded.

Ryan heard Dennis whisper, "Sweet Mary and Joseph."

"I'm coming." Ryan stuffed the gold into the pocket of

his BCD and made his way out of the wreck. He'd found the first strong box. Travis's objective would be to locate the second one, and then they would devise a plan to recover the whole lot.

Once clear of the wreck, Ryan stepped into the LARS basket which the crew had sent down after dropping the tanks, and tugged hard on his tending lines four times in addition to using the radio to say he was ready to ascend. He watched the crane cable draw tight, and slowly he lifted off the sea floor. He cracked the demand valve again to clear the water. They'd already calculated the decompression stops and the gas changes needed before the dive. Emery would use the gas control panel to change the mixtures with each stop. The initial stop was for ten minutes at one hundred and seventy-five feet. Ryan was thankful he could rest in the basket as the stops became longer the closer he got to the surface.

With thirty-five minutes of decompression left, Ryan was ready to be out of the water. The helmet was making him claustrophobic and even with the drysuit on, he was getting cold. The water drained his body heat faster than he could produce it. A shiver racked up and down his spine. He closed his eyes and took measured breaths to calm himself. Three-second inhale, four-second exhale, pause at the top and bottom. Three in, pause, four out, pause. He began to relax, and the memory of the gold bar in his hand filled his vision.

Then his body tensed. He cocked his head and listened to a low buzzing sound. It grew louder with each passing second. Ryan knew the sound well; it was the churning of propellers on a rapidly approaching boat.

In the clear water, he could see the bottom of *Peggy Lynn* and he kept swiveling his head to see if the other boat would pass near them. The sound came from all directions. The boat's driver cut the throttles and the buzzing slowed. A hull drifted out of the haze, materializing as a white fiberglass V with twin sterndrives.

"What's going on up there?" Ryan asked.

"We've got visitors," Emery rasped.

In the background of Emery's transmission, Ryan could hear Captain Dennis and Stacey shouting at the other boat to keep clear. By law, the boat had to stay at least one hundred feet from any vessel displaying the international blue-and-white diver down flag.

Ryan tracked the newcomer as it circled around to the far side of *Peggy Lynn*. It came alongside the salvage boat just for an instant and then idled away. When it was just out of the range of Ryan's visibility, he heard the boat's captain throw the throttles forward, and the boat rocketed away.

"What the hell's going on?" Ryan demanded.

There was a click as the topside communication system came on and dead air for ten seconds. Then a familiar voice came through the speaker.

CHAPTER SEVENTEEN

Joulie Lafitte's voice filled the small helmet. "Did you find my gold?"

My gold? Ryan thought.

"Hello? Are you listening?" Her annoyed voice filled his helmet. Six months ago, he'd held her shaking body after she'd tried to shoot the Russian bounty hunter, Volk, and seen the puddle of vomit coating the handgun she'd used. Now, she was a warlord demanding her gold be returned.

"I'm here," Ryan said, "and no, I didn't find *your* gold."

"Did you see the gold?" Joulie asked.

"No," he replied flatly. Ryan knew he would eventually have to talk to her. She controlled the gang activity along the northern coast and she'd probably known what was happening the moment *Peggy Lynn* had entered Haitian waters.

"Come up here so I can speak to you face to face," Joulie demanded.

"I can't." He glanced at his dive computer. "I have another twenty minutes of decompression left."

Ryan heard her shout, "Bring him up here!"

"No," Travis said. "If we don't do all of his deco, he could get the bends. Do you want him to die, eh?"

Ryan heard no response. He glanced at the computer again. If time had passed slowly before, it was standing still now. He closed his eyes and tried to picture what was happening topside. "Talk to me, Trav."

"It's all good. Your lady friend is chatting with Dennis now."

"Any way we can speed this up?" Ryan asked, knowing the answer.

"Sorry," Travis replied. "No can do."

Ryan let out a sigh. "Yeah, I know."

"Boring, eh?"

"Yes."

Travis laughed. "That's why I take a book with me."

"A book?"

"I've got a waterproof one."

Ryan asked, "Why didn't you give it to me?"

"I wanted to see how you handled yourself."

Ryan closed his eyes and leaned his head back in the helmet. He cracked the demand valve and flushed away the water which had risen to his chin. He was more comfortable with it now, but it was something he'd fix when he surfaced. His thoughts moved from the helmet leak back to the woman who'd just arrived on *Peggy Lynn*.

He had met Joulie when Toussaint had demanded Ryan hike to the Citadelle Laferrière, at the top of the three-thousand-foot peak of Bonnet a L'Eveque mountain, for their first meeting. Joulie had stood stoically in the small candlelit room. She wore a purple dress, purple lipstick, and purple eye shadow. The color offset her lustrous mahogany skin and wavy, jet-black hair. Her most startling feature were her bright blue eyes, and they had pleaded with him for help. He could still see the look of revulsion in them when Toussaint touched her. Later, when she had snuck into his room in Toussaint's house to bring him a cell phone, he'd seen those same eyes sparkle and dance in the pale moonlight while she cupped his face in her hand.

Those eyes were the window to her soul, and he'd also seen displeasure and disappointment in them as they waited out the hurricane in the Bahamas. After Landis informed Ryan that Emily had dumped him, Ryan threw himself a pity party and spent most of his time half-drunk with a cigarette dangling from his lips. Joulie had tried to console him and, well, he'd turned her down.

"You ready for some sunshine, eh?" Travis asked.

The LARS basket jerked, and Ryan started upward. He stood and grasped the bar. Water cascaded off his body as he emerged from the sea. When the basket was clear of the water, Emery swung the crane boom inboard and lowered the LARS to the deck. Ryan already had the helmet buckles undone and was pulling it off when the basket touched down. Travis grabbed the helmet and unhooked the hoses before setting it inside its hard-shell plastic box.

Tilting his head back, Ryan drank in the tropical sunshine. It was good to be back on the surface. Travis helped him shed the rest of his gear and strip off the drysuit. Neither made mention of the gold bar.

Before making his way up to the bridge, Ryan hung up his gear and used a hose to rinse it off. Dennis greeted him with a cup of coffee and a tight smile.

Ryan turned to face their visitor. She was still beautiful, and her simple white sundress accented the lush curves of her body. "Hello, Joulie."

"It's good to see you again." She crossed the small

bridge, arms outstretched. He squeezed her in a tight hug. Stacey gave him an evil glare.

"Nice to see you, too." He raised his eyebrows at Stacey to say *what do you care?*"

Joulie stepped out of the embrace. "I came out as soon as I heard you were here."

"How did you know we were here?" Stacey asked, staring angrily at Joulie with her fists on her hips.

Joulie returned the stare. "I've taken over Toussaint's operation in Cap-Haïtien. I hear all the latest gossip." She turned back to Ryan and asked, "Are you done for the day?"

"Yes." He wasn't. He wanted to put Travis in the water.

"Good, you can come with me. We need to discuss a few things."

"Let me get cleaned up." Ryan left the bridge and walked down to the bunkroom. He wanted to get the gold and get out of Haiti. Now that he'd seen her again, he did want to have dinner with her. Emery came out of the galley holding a spatula, his eyes gleaming.

Ryan put a finger to his lips. He whispered, "Loose lips, Grandpa."

Emery nodded.

Ryan whispered again, "Get Travis in the water after I'm gone. Find the other box."

Emery grinned and saluted, spatula still in hand.

Ryan smiled back and went into his bunkroom. He was about to step into the small shower when the door opened. He glanced over his shoulder and saw Joulie standing in the door frame. He grabbed his pants off the bunk to cover himself.

"My driver is coming back," she said. "You may shower at my place."

Ryan stared at her for a moment, uncertain what to do.

He could disarm a bomb in pitch black water with a paper-clip and a hole punch, but women were another story. He shrugged and pulled on his pants. He stuffed a change of clothes into a bag and wondered if he should include his Walther PPQ. He wasn't sure how much he could trust Joulie, or if he could trust her at all. As comforting as it would be to have the reassuring weight of the nine-millimeter riding on his hip, he didn't think it was a bright idea to carry it into Joulie's den of thieves. She was sure to have protection. They would just pat him down and take it away.

He left the gun lying where it was, tucked under the pillow, and slung his backpack onto his shoulder. Joulie's quirky smile never wavered as she watched him pack. She led him topside. He couldn't help but notice how the sundress hugged her curves. Her newfound power and wealth hadn't changed her fashion sense. There was something elegant about the understated way she dressed.

Topside, Joulie's boat had been tied off alongside the salvage vessel. Ryan shook his head and grinned. The woman knew how to accessorize. They stepped down into a garishly painted Cigarette 38 Top Gun. Ryan dropped his bag and kicked it under the passenger seat. They cast off the lines, and the driver eased the racing boat away from *Peggy Lynn*. Once clear, the driver shoved the throttles forward and the slim boat rocketed up onto plane. Ryan stood behind the passenger seat, feet spread wide, knees bent, and he kept a firm grip of the grab bars. The driver kept the bouncing boat in a straight line for Cap-Haïtien.

A wild sense of recklessness came over him. He was on a fast boat with a beautiful woman heading for what, he had no clue. It was like his life was caught in a loop, bad guys, fortunes, women, and the unknown. Maybe he was, as Greg liked to remind him, cavalier. He was supposed to be in charge of the operation, recover the gold, and sail off under the noses of Joulie and Jim Kilroy. Now, he was going to have to negotiate away some of his newfound wealth. Joulie wouldn't let him leave with all the gold. It did come from her people to pay for illicit weapons and she had a right to demand it be returned. It didn't mean he wanted to give it to her.

They passed the commercial quays at full throttle. Cargo ships were unloading at one of Haiti's few full-service ports. The driver reigned in the throttles and the Cigarette came off plane and settled in the water. Ryan recognized the dock they were headed for as the same one Greg's Hatteras GT63, *Dark Water*, had been tied to when Ryan had come to rescue him from the bounty hunter. The old fishing trawler and two-masted yawl were gone and the rickety old dock had been replaced with a newer version, capable of raising and lowering with the tide on tall metal poles sunk into the harbor.

When they came alongside the dock, the driver motioned for Ryan to toss out a set of fenders and be ready to tie off. Ryan did as he was asked and climbed onto the long nose of the go-fast boat with a bow line in hand. The driver expertly brought the boat along the dock, and Ryan stepped to the floating structure and secured the bow line to a cleat. He jogged to the rear and caught the stern line the driver threw to him. When he stood, he was nearly thrown off balance by his backpack smacking him in the chest. The driver grinned.

Joulie stepped up on a seat and Ryan extended his hand to assist her. She placed her hand in his. It was nice to hold her hand even if he was just helping her out of the boat. On the dock, she didn't let it go. She led him toward a small building where they were met by an older man with a shock of white hair and a white beard.

He stroked the beard as he looked Joulie and Ryan up and down. "Afternoon, Miss Joulie."

"Good afternoon, Mr. Parker," she replied.

"This be the gentleman you went to fetch?"

"It is," Joulie said.

The man extended a hand to Ryan and winked. "I'm Billy Parker."

As they shook, Ryan introduced himself. He understood the wink. Billy Parker was Greg Olsen's contact, and Greg must have informed Billy of Ryan's impending arrival.

"Your car is here. I wiped it down as best I could. The water ban is still in effect."

"Thank you, Mr. Parker."

To Ryan, Billy said, "Since the hurricane, the government has banned us from washin' cars."

Ryan nodded. He knew the island had suffered a glancing blow from Irma, setting the region back even further, as it had yet to recover from previous hurricanes and earthquakes.

Joulie got into the driver's seat of a newer model blue Toyota Rav4. Ryan climbed into the passenger side and tossed his bag into the back. "No bodyguards?"

She shook her head. "I don't like to use them. It distances me from the people I'm here to help."

"Why did you come back?" Ryan asked.

She backed around and headed down the single lane road off the small peninsula to the mainland. "I came back for two reasons. One, my country needs help and two, your president has decided to eliminate the asylum for my people, and I didn't want to go to Canada. I explained this to Mr. Landis before I left the States."

"He said you were looking for me."

"I tried to find you but couldn't."

"Why did you want to find me?"

Joulie beamed a bright smile and turned into traffic on Boulevard de Cap-Haïtien. She remained quiet as they passed the massive port. She turned off the main thoroughfare and started up a hill. The neighborhood could have been transplanted from New Orleans, with its the French architecture and large, mature trees. She braked and swung the SUV behind a ten-foot-high wall. Lush trees, flowers, and well-manicured grass surrounded a large house. Once a summer home for Henri Christophe, a key leader in the slave revolt of 1791, which lead to the independence of Haiti from France, it was now one of the oldest hotels in Cap-Haïtien, Hotel *Roi* Christophe—the King Christophe.

A cobblestone driveway curved up to an ornate porch. Joulie parked the Toyota, and a valet came around the hood. Joulie led the way through the lobby, past a horseshoe shaped desk, and down corridors covered in gleaming black-and-white checkerboard tiles. Potted ferns hung from the walls and lined the courtyards. Framed black-and-white photos, showing the history of the ancient structure, adorned the walls.

Several staff members greeted Joulie deferentially as she and Ryan passed and continued up a flight of stairs to the second floor. Wrought iron railings spanned the gap between the balcony's ornamental arches, and patrons lounged in wooden chairs. Arched doorways led into guest rooms, and she took him into her suite at the far end of the hall. Ryan checked the rooms over and glanced out the window at the view of the stone courtyard and swimming pool.

"This place is nice," Ryan said. He swung his backpack

onto a king-sized, four-post bed. Mosquito netting hung from the posts like a shroud.

"It is very nice," Joulie said. "The bathroom is through there." She pointed at another polished, wooden door. "Take a shower and I'll meet you downstairs for a light lunch."

Ryan watched her close the door behind her. He stripped and stepped into the shower where he luxuriated in the hot water. The *Peggy Lynn* had a limited supply, and they took just long enough in the water to rinse the salt from their bodies. He dressed in khaki pants, a blue-and-white cabana shirt, and deck shoes before going downstairs for lunch.

CHAPTER EIGHTEEN

Joulie Lafitte took a seat at her usual table in the hotel's restaurant. It was close enough to the veranda to feel the cool breezes, but private enough for her to conduct business if she chose to. One of the waiters came over, bowed slightly, and asked her what she wanted to eat. Joulie ordered two glasses of ice water, salads, and a fruit platter. Within minutes, the waiter poured water and the glasses were sweated in the heat. She took a long, cool drink, almost finishing the glass. The ride out to the salvage vessel and back had made her thirsty for both water and gold.

She had tried to contact Ryan before she'd left the U.S. because she wanted him to do exactly what he was doing now—salvage the gold. With it, she could help the poor of her country, send the children to school and to college. Haiti's population lacked the technical skills to extract the mineral wealth from the ground and turn it into infrastructure, schools, homes, and businesses for the local economy. Their mineral rights had been sold to foreign companies who brought in their own consultants and engineers. If Haitians were used at all, they were manual labor, and the meager pay wasn't enough for them to sustain their families, or to achieve the middle-class dream.

The people of Cap-Haïtien had welcomed Joulie back with open arms. She had been their priestess, their link to the spiritual world, Toussaint's trusted advisor, and his fiancée. Toussaint may have been a warlord, but he was well respected, and that respect carried over to Joulie. True, she had to twist some arms and even order men to their deaths for her to obtain power, but she considered it a small sacrifice to put her in a position to do the most good. She could be a *mambo*—a vodou priestess—and provide spiritual guidance for the masses, or she could become a warlord and yield spiritual, political, and military might.

The waiter interrupted her thoughts when he returned with the salads and fruit. She nibbled at the salad, thinking about Ryan. She had been strongly attracted to him from the moment they'd met at the Citadel. Seeing him then had brought back a vision she'd had when she was a seventeen-year-old girl. Joulie took a sip of water, closed her eyes, and concentrated on the dream. It came to her just as vividly as the day she had originally seen it.

JOULIE WAS *a leaf on an oak tree in a hurricane. As the leaf tore free from the tree, a violent twisting, tearing strain ripped through every muscle in her body, causing her to lay spread eagle on the ground and scream. Then her body collapsed into a ball as she fluttered away from the tree. She was floating on the breeze yet falling. The ground came up fast, her body tensed in anticipation of the impact.*

A giant hand reached out. She landed in the palm. The fingers closed slightly, and she nestled into the flesh, feeling safe, warm, and content. The hand released her, and she stood on the ground, gazing up at a man with brown hair. She ran a hand along the man's cheek and stared into his green eyes. She flushed as a deep longing to be with him, to satisfy, and please him, filled her. She knew she must present him with a gift. As her fingertips left the man's face, he smiled and instantly vanished. She had the strong urge to present her body as the gift.

RYAN HAD BEEN the man in the vision. She had given him a cell phone as a present and while she felt a deep longing to be with him in the dream, she wasn't sure it translated to the real world. She had tried to entice him twice and both times she'd been rebuffed. Now she held the power to make his life easy or to complicate his mission. To help him choose, she would give her body to him, the sacrifice for the people whom she wished to help. And to be perfectly honest, as she gazed at him across the dining room, it was no great sacrifice. A flood of desire washed over her when their eyes met.

He crossed the room and took a seat beside her. They exchanged a few pleasantries, and he tucked into the food.

After a few minutes of eating, he asked, "What do they call Haitian food in Haiti?"

Joulie frowned. "What do you mean?"

He smiled at what she assumed was a private joke. "Nothing. Are you living here?"

"Yes, Toussaint's house was damaged by the hurricane."

"Are you rebuilding it?"

"I am, but I prefer this place. It reminds me of my ancestors more than that modern monstrosity." The house had been neglected with Toussaint dead and no one to care for it. It needed more work than she wanted to do, and she had decided to sell the property and live at the hotel. She really did prefer it here. The hotel grounds reminded her of where she had lived before her parents had been killed in a landslide.

Ryan nodded, his mouth full of fruit. He swallowed. "It suits you better." He wiped his mouth with a white linen napkin. "Are you still practicing vodou?"

"Yes. When I could not find you in America and returned to Haiti, I asked the *loa* to bring you back to me." She laid a hand on his and smiled. "I'm so glad they listened."

He nodded and shoved a fork full of salad into his mouth.

Joulie watched as he put away his salad and most of the fruit with blinding speed.

It reminded her of the ravenous street children. "It's okay to chew and swallow, no one is going to steal your food."

"I know," Ryan said with his mouth full. He swallowed. "I haven't broken the habit of eating quickly. It's ingrained in me from the military. I apologize."

"I enjoy a good show with dinner."

He laughed. "Now you're making fun of me."

Joulie smiled and patted his hand. "I would never make fun of you."

Ryan finished his meal and said, "Come on, let's go see whatever it is you wanted to show me."

They walked out of the lobby to where the blue Toyota sat idling near the end of the drive. A valet held the door open for Joulie.

She drove them through the slums. Houses had collapsed walls, and some were missing their roofs. The residents had strung frayed tarps, scraps of cloth, and whatever else they could find over the holes to keep out the rain. Dirty young children played in the streets. One small boy, wearing only a T-shirt, peed while he waved at the SUV. Through open front doors, they could see hard-packed dirt floors with plastic patio chairs. One building had a small crowd gathered around an ancient tube-type television that threatened to collapse the small table it sat on. A soccer match played loudly and men with vacant eyes stared at it with glass beer bottles in their hands. Joulie wasn't immune to the scenes. She had seen, even in the poorest communities, in the United States, a state of wealth that far surpassed what these people would ever have. She glanced over at Ryan, who was staring out the window.

Beyond the city they entered farmland. Fruit trees had been laid flat by the hurricane and their produce lay rotting on the ground. Some trees had already been cut up for firewood. More shacks lay in ruins, destroyed by the fierce winds. Rain had caused landslides to wipe out fields and homes. Without four-wheel drive, the washed-out roads would have been impassible. Everywhere they looked, there was abject poverty, people trying to repair their tin roof shacks with tree limbs, scraps of lumber, and whatever garbage they could find.

Whenever they saw the blue Toyota Rav4, the people waved and called out to Joulie. She waved back, shouted a few words of encouragement, or stopped to listen to them discuss their plights. Always smiling and nodding, she told them she was working to bring them help and encouraged them with prayer. Children raced after the vehicle with their arms outstretched, calling for them to toss out a few coins.

Joulie steered the SUV past long rows of newly planted fruit trees, pointing out the different varieties as they passed. She also showed him rows and rows of small trees planted on barren hillsides and on rocky slopes to combat the deforestation.

She stopped on a hillside overlooking the city and pointed at the bay. This was not the picturesque vision of lush blue Caribbean waters surrounding a charming island. The water here was dark and dirt-stained. Garbage floated in the water and littered the beaches. Plastic jugs, rotting trash, and other debris clogged the river flowing into the bay. Fishermen rowing their boats through the rafts of garbage, leaving trails through which they could see black water. Waves lapped around sunken vessels. Some of the rusty hulls had washed up on shore and men were busy using cutting torches to disassemble them. Old shacks had been torn down along the waterfront, but piles of debris remained. A few were on fire, and men tended them with shovels and rakes. It saddened Joulie to see her country in such disarray.

Yet there was still beauty here. Large green trees grew amongst the houses with their orange and red tile roofs. The massive structure of the centuries-old Our Lady of the Assumption Cathedral towered above the city with its white towers and brown domes. Rugged mountains bordered the city to the west and to the south spread broad, fertile river plains.

This was her home. How could she have ever thought of leaving?

"What is it you want me to see?" Ryan asked.

"All of it. Open your eyes, Ryan. Our country is one of the poorest on earth, yet we have vast resources of gold and oil and the natural beauty loved by tourists."

"You sound like Toussaint."

"There are some things he was right about. We have vast wealth beneath our hills and oceans yet ..."

Ryan broke her silence. "Greg told me Haiti has more oil reserves than Venezuela."

"This is true. We also have twenty billion dollars of gold in a vein that stretches through the mountains into the Dominican Republic. They estimate the gold on their side is worth twice what ours is."

"I had no idea."

"No one does. When outsiders think of Haiti, they picture exactly what you see what your president called 'a third-world shithole.' I cannot disagree with the evidence. But we are just as beautiful as Cuba or the Dominican Republic, yet no one wishes to build luxury resorts or come to a country where they are likely to be murdered. We must change the culture."

Ryan shook his head. "You can't change the world."

"I don't want to change the world. I want to change Haiti." She pointed to the men on the beach tending the smoky fires and cutting scrap. "I pay them to do those jobs. I also pay them to clean the beaches. I've invested in a facility that turns plastic into fuel oil and gasoline. We need to transition away from using wood as our cooking fuel."

"What else are you doing?"

"We planted all those trees. I also want to start a fish farm. Children are going to schools we helped establish with local NGOs and I've made several endowments to local colleges. We have people in Port-au-Prince lobbying for money from the International Monetary Fund and the UN."

"You did all this with the money Toussaint had?"

"Yes."

"I'm impressed."

She engaged the transmission and drove them back to the hotel.

After dinner, and more conversation about the things she was doing to help her country, they strolled the lush grounds. Ryan paused at a stone bench and lit a cigarette. "You had a purpose for that little drive in the country. What do you want?"

She sat on the bench and smoothed her dress over her legs. She leaned back to look up at him. "You're not here for a pleasure cruise. Either you're here to recover Kilroy's weapons or the gold."

"I'm here for myself."

"Then it is easier to ask this of you."

Ryan took a draw on the smoke and put his foot on the bench. He rested his elbow on his knee and leaned into it. The night was humid, and insects chirped and buzzed around them. Her palms were moist, and her heartbeat had elevated with his proximity. Soft music drifted in from one of the nightclubs. She quelled the urge to kiss him.

He sighed. "I have a feeling I'm not going to like this but, go ahead."

"I would like the gold back."

He shook his head. "No."

"Think what it could do for them." She tried not to sound like she was pleading.

"Eighty-twenty."

With a triumphant smile, Joulie said, "I will take eighty." Getting him to concede part of the gold was a giant step. Her plan to tug at his heartstrings was working. She absentmindedly played with a gold pendent on a gold chain she'd worn since Farah, her grandmother, had given it to her. It was her nervous habit. She pulled her hand away, but not without a quick prayer. *Mother, intercede for me with the spirits.*

"Not what I meant," Ryan said. "I have a right to anything I salvage from a sunken vessel. I'm not required to split it with you or anyone else. Besides, I have a crew to pay for. All that gear and the boat weren't cheap."

"What about taxes?"

"What about them?"

"You'll have to report the gold and you will be taxed. Seventy-thirty," she proposed.

Ryan snorted. "If I get the seventy."

"How can you be so callous? Didn't you see those people out there?" She paused and laid one hand on his arm. His skin was warm, and her mind flashed to her vision, the comfort of being in his palm. "You are a good and caring man. I know this about you, Ryan. I know you want to help these people. You help so many with your job, why not share your wealth with those who really need it?"

"What about the money from the Clinton Foundation and all the other charities who've donated a billion-plus dollars toward fixing the problems?"

"The government in Port-au-Prince controls those funds. They take their cut before any money reaches us. I could use the gold as I see fit without their oversight."

"How much of Toussaint's money did you keep for yourself? How much did Wilky Ador's people contribute to the projects?"

The questions annoyed her. "We used it." She scuffed a pebble across the path. "What we had did not go far, but the gold, it would ..."

"The gold will run out too, and then what?"

"We'll make it last by investing in businesses and farms and houses. We'll put those profits into the continued rebuilding of infrastructure and provide clean water and ample food. Right now, the people subsist on what little was left after the hurricane and what's coming in on the container ships. The UN delivers bags of rice, but it isn't enough. Did you see that pile of scrap cars by the container yard?"

He nodded.

"There is a quirk in the law allowing Haitians to import a vehicle packed with whatever they can fit into it. They call them household goods or personal effects. Everything comes stuffed inside those cars, mattresses, bicycles, car parts, canned food, whatever you can think of. The law doesn't say the cars have to run either. It's an informal system of shipping goods for personal use and resale."

"So, start a shipping line."

"It's not that easy. Haiti has been impoverished for centuries."

"You're into vodou, do a little dance and take the Devil's curse off your backs."

"Ryan," she chastised.

"What if I refuse?"

Joulie looked into his wonderful green eyes. "I was hoping I wouldn't have to strong-arm you."

"Strong-arm me?" Smoke streamed out of his mouth as he laughed.

"Yes, there are a lot of people who would like to get their hands on the gold."

"If they knew it was there," he retorted.

"Word spreads quickly when a salvage vessel arrives in our waters. It doesn't matter what you bring up, someone will try to take it from you. I would hate for pirates to board your vessel and steal what you have."

"Is that a threat?"

Joulie shrugged. "It's a suggestion that you cooperate with me. I will give you protection from the pirates and you will give me the gold."

"The only pirate around here is you." Ryan straightened and took a final draw on his cigarette.

She laughed. "I am the descendant of the pirate Jean Lafitte, one who helped defeat the British for American independence."

"He fought in the War of 1812, dear. The British were invaders trying to reclaim what they'd already lost. Much like you."

Joulie waved a dismissive hand. "Regardless, I will become a ruthless pirate to save my people. You may accept my help, or you can expect attacks by armed men. Which do you prefer, to work in peace, or to defend yourself against thieves?"

"I'd rather not have to worry about any of it. So far, we've been fine."

"Because you enjoy my protection." Joulie smiled and spread her hands. "Let's make it sixty-forty."

"Seventy-thirty," Ryan said. "That's close to ten million for you." He stubbed out the cigarette. "Any more is plain extortion."

Joulie stood and cupped his cheek as she had in her vision. "It would be better if it was twelve point five million. Besides, I would hate for word to leak to the U.S. government about a salvage vessel loaded with gold pillaged from Haiti. If they didn't seize it and return it to Haiti, they would tax you on it."

His eyes bored into hers. The green had deepened a shade with his apparent anger, yet he did not pull away from her hand. "You're a ruthless bitch. Even if the government seized it, they would send it to Port-au-Prince, and it would be a loss for both of us."

Softly, she said, "Are you willing to take that chance?"

Ryan's eyes shifted away, and he mumbled, "Fifty-fifty."

Joulie stroked his cheekbone with her thumb. His eyes shifted back to hers. There was no animosity in them now. His reluctance had turned to acceptance. Not because she had threatened him with pirates and taxes, but because the loa had sent him, and the loa were not wrong.

Neither of them said a word as they stood there, the soft music floating over the high stone walls. A mosquito whined about their faces. Ryan broke the stare and his gaze traveled lower, then flicked up and away.

She smiled, skin flushing. He'd just glanced down her dress. His ridged jaw muscles softened.

"Ryan," she whispered, her voice husky with anticipation. "I'm sorry I had to strong-arm you. This means so much to me, to these people." Ryan muffled her "Thank you" by pressing his lips to hers. The kiss started soft and gentle, and as he ran a hand up her back, it turned hard and greedy.

When she pulled away, she said, "I prayed you would do the right thing and the loa have answered my prayers."

Ryan said nothing. He pulled her to him again and kissed her passionately.

This time he pulled away and looked into her blue eyes. She stared right back, a smile on her lips. Her whole body thrummed with excitement. She kissed him quickly and turned out of his grasp. She took his hand and led him up the path to her room.

CHAPTER NINETEEN

J im Kilroy stared through the powerful lenses of the Zeiss binoculars. His distant quarry crouched against the horizon, tall white masts swaying in the slight swell. The pale light of the sunrise bathed the sea, turning the water from black to slate gray. Every minute he stood on the bridge wing of *Northwest Passage*, the ocean took on more of its natural shades of blue. A gentle breeze ruffled his brown hair and wicked away perspiration from his sweat-dampened clothes.

He swept the optics across the horizon, looking for the speedboat which had come and gone from *Peggy Lynn* the previous afternoon. Ryan Weller had left on that boat and not come back.

Kilroy had watched the *Peggy Lynn* run search patterns for the better part of twenty-four hours and when she stopped and put divers in the water, he knew it meant they'd found the *Santo Domingo* and his gold. The payment for all the weapons, gear, and vehicles sunk inside the freighter when she'd been attacked. Items he'd been forced to pay for with his own money when the gold and the guns had sunk. It had nearly sunk him.

Now he was determined to retrieve his gold. It had called them as it called to him. Yes, he could have found the *Santo Domingo*, chartered divers, and recovered the gold on his own. But why bother when one of the largest commercial dive and salvage concerns in the world would be backing Ryan?

Kilroy fancied the gold as a trap, and Ryan Weller had walked right into it. A smile spread across the arms dealer's face as he watched the salvage vessel. A few more days of diving and the whole treasure would be on board the *Peggy Lynn*. Then he'd swoop in and relieve them of *his* gold.

"Beautiful morning," Karen Kilroy said, holding out a cup of coffee.

"It is." He brought the binoculars down, letting them dangle on the strap around his neck, and took the cup from her. He gave her a quick kiss before sipping his coffee. At twenty years his junior, Karen was more than just a buxom, blonde trophy wife. She was his soul mate, and now that she knew about his arms dealing, she was his confidant and co-conspirator.

"Has Ryan come back?"

Kilroy shook his head. "I haven't seen the boat, and Raul says it didn't return during the night."

Karen said, "He's making a deal with Joulie."

"Toussaint's vodou tart? I doubt it."

"Why not? The gold came from Haiti, and she probably wants it back. Perhaps she has the same plan as Toussaint."

"No." He chuckled.

"Maybe she wants to use the gold to help her country."

"That would be like pissing it away. Haiti has always been poor and will always be poor."

"Jim," she reprimanded gently.

"Even Jesus said, 'The poor will be with you always,' and Haiti will always be poor."

"Maybe she could do some real good with the money." Karen cradled her cup in both hands.

Kilroy snorted. "*I* could do some real good with the money."

"How are you going to get it?"

"I'm going to wait until they have it all on the boat over there and then take it at gun point."

A smile passed over Karen's thin lips.

"What?" her husband demanded.

"Do you think Ryan will just let you take the gold?" she scoffed. "He hates you already. You'll have to kill him to keep him from tracking you down and taking the gold back or killing you." She sipped her coffee, then said softly, "Neither option I like."

"What do you suggest?"

"Leverage."

"Leverage," Kilroy repeated thoughtfully. He stepped into the bridge and handed his empty cup to the mate, Raul. "Bring me another cup. I have the bridge until you return."

"Yes, Captain," Raul said, the salute evident in his voice. He disappeared down the ladderwell to the galley.

Kilroy returned to the bridge wing and put the binoculars back to his eyes. He watched a garishly painted Cigarette boat approach *Peggy Lynn*. Even from several miles away, they could hear the low roar of the high-performance racing engines. "The prodigal son returneth."

"What about Joulie?" Karen asked, indicating the speeding boat. "We could kidnap her and keep her until Ryan brings up the gold."

"No," Kilroy said, lowering the binoculars. "She'd have

every member of her gang hunting for her. Besides, I don't think he cares about her enough to save her life."

"This is Ryan Weller we're talking about. He'll try to save her because it's the right thing to do."

"Be that as it may," Kilroy said, "I don't think she's the right girl for the job, especially if she's demanding some or all of the gold." He knew how Ryan operated. He'd used Ryan's sense of fairness and justice to coerce him into delivering the shipment of weapons to Toussaint. And he'd threatened the lives of Greg, Mango, and Ryan's families.

"But," he mused, "there is a woman he would give up the gold for."

Karen's features brightened. "Who?"

Kilroy turned to look at his wife, a smile lifting the corner of his left lip. She still wore the yellow spandex boy shorts and a pink athletic bra from her earlier yoga session. He pictured her doing the downward dog pose and grinned lustfully at her.

Karen cocked her hip and smiled coquettishly.

Raul interrupted them. "Your coffee, sir."

"Thank you," Jim said, taking the cup.

After Raul stepped back into the bridge, Karen said, "Who does he care about?"

Jim sipped the coffee and watched the Cigarette charge back the way it had come. In a soft voice, he said, "Emily Hunt."

CHAPTER TWENTY

Ryan tossed his backpack over *Peggy Lynn*'s rail and began handing up boxes of fresh fruit, vegetables, and canned goods, courtesy of Joulie. Then he climbed out of the Cigarette's cockpit and shoved the sleek boat off with his foot. He hung on the rail, waiting for the Cigarette driver to maneuver the craft with its engines. The man just barely kept it from smacking into the steel hull of the salvage vessel. Ryan shoved the nose away again with his foot. This time, the driver collected his boat and raced away.

When Ryan stepped over the rail, all hands were there to greet him. Stacey's arms were crossed, and she was tapping her foot. Her face carried her normal air of annoyance. Travis stood with his hands in his pockets, feet braced against the chop. Captain Dennis leaned against the bridge hatch with his ever-present coffee cup in hand. Emery and Don sat on the gear bench.

"Well?" Stacey asked.

Ryan lit a cigarette, his first of the morning. "Did you find the other box, Trav?"

"No," Travis said. "I spent twenty minutes looking for it

after you left, and I've already been down this morning while you were doing whatever it was you were doing."

"I was keeping the peace."

"Is that what you're calling it now?" Stacey retorted. Then under her breath, she said, "Probably more like getting a piece."

"What did Joulie have to say?" Dennis asked.

Ryan said, "She's giving us protection while we bring up the gold."

"Protection?" Emery asked, scratching his head under the watch cap. "What for?" His 'for' sounded more like 'fur.'

"There's other people who want the gold, and there's pirates in these waters. Joulie sent out two boats to act as guardians."

Dennis pointed with his coffee cup. "That massive mothership off our starboard side isn't one of them."

Ryan jumped up to the bridge and grabbed a pair of binoculars. He trained them on the ship Dennis had indicated. He recognized *Northwest Passage*.

"How much is this protection costing us?" Travis asked.

Ryan set binoculars back on the bridge console and took a long drag on the cigarette. He didn't want to tell them. "Don, can you overlay what Travis saw on his dives with the schematics of the hold?"

"Already have, and I uploaded it to the DAVD unit for your dive."

"Good, I'll go in a few minutes. Let's prep to dive."

Dennis interrupted them. "There's a high-pressure ridge pushing north. The weather is turning to shit. Waves are going to be four to fives easily, could be more."

"How soon is it going to hit?" Ryan asked.

Dennis glanced at the horizon. "This afternoon."

"I better get in the water."

"If things get too rough," Dennis said, "we'll pull you up and stick you in the chamber."

"And make a run for Cap-Haïtien," Ryan added. "We'll be safe there."

"We will, eh?" Travis asked.

"Yes," Ryan replied. "We've been guaranteed safety."

"Which brings us back to the original question," Stacey said. "How much?"

Ryan walked over to where his drysuit hung on a rack. He began to pull on the thick fleece undergarments which would help keep him warm.

Emery had turned the compressor on and was clearing the umbilical of moisture and checking the topside controls and gas levels.

Travis caught Ryan by the shoulder and spun him around. Leaning in close, he growled, "How much, eh?"

Ryan met his eyes. "Half."

"Half!" Travis exploded. "You're giving her half the gold!"

"Yes."

"I still want my ten percent," Travis blurted. "I don't give a crap how much you give her. I want ten percent of the whole haul."

"You'll get it," Ryan said, shrugging into the drysuit. "Now back off and do your damn job."

Stacey shook her head. "You're an idiot, Ryan."

He stopped and looked at everyone. "I don't want to give it up any more than you guys do. But Joulie is our life-line here. She's providing us with protection and she's going to use her share to help her people."

Stacey gave a short, barking laugh. "You slept with her."

Ryan pulled the suit over his head and checked the neck seal. He held his arms out and Emery tugged the zipper closed. Emery double-checked the seals on the suit and patted Ryan on the shoulder. He whispered, "If I was a young whippersnapper, I'd have slept with her too."

Ryan grinned.

Assured he would get his cut, Travis returned to the business of diving. He brought over the SuperLite neck dam and helmet. "Let's find the gold and get out of here."

"I agree," Ryan said.

Don walked over. "Dennis is right about the weather."

"I know," Ryan said, shrugging into his BCD, and then fastening his weight belt. Travis helped him clamp on the helmet and run through their topside checks. Emery was next to suit up. He would be the standby diver because Travis had already been in the water.

"When you're in the basket, I'll run through Travis's dives with you," Don said. "You can see them on the DAVD."

"Okay." Ryan stepped into the LARS. With the aid of the crane, Travis swung the heavy metal basket up and over the rail and lowered Ryan fifteen feet below the surface. They ran through the in-water checks to ensure the gear was functioning properly.

"Send the basket down after me. I don't want to waste time riding it down." Ryan stepped into the darkness and continued his descent toward the wreck. The water pressure crushed his drysuit, the folds of fabric pinching his skin. He tapped the suit's inflator button, adding just enough air to take away the squeeze. Every thirty-three feet, he passed through another atmosphere, adding 14.7 pounds per square inch of pressure to his body. At three hundred and fifty feet, he would experience one hundred and seventy pounds of pressure. His lungs, the size of deflated basketballs on the surface, would shrink to the size of tennis balls.

Ryan watched the DAVD display and Don talked him through each of Travis's previous dives. He'd covered just under half of the *Santo Domingo*'s hold. Parts of it were left uninvestigated because of the tangle of vehicles. Ryan hoped the gold wasn't under them, but instinct told him it was.

Dennis had positioned *Peggy Lynn* right over the wreck and Ryan landed on the port side of the ship. He climbed over the rail and dropped down the vertical deck, working his way to the hold. He glanced over at the Humvee where he'd positioned their emergency gas.

"Trav, did you mess with the gas supply?"

"No. I was looking for the gold. Why?"

"The hatch is open," Ryan said.

"You must not have latched it, and the current opened it up."

"I latched it."

"Then I have no idea."

"No one else has been down here?"

"Dude, come on," Stacey said. "Who else is stupid enough to go down there?"

Ryan dropped all the way to sea floor and closed the hatch. None of the tanks looked like they'd been disturbed. He turned and looked at the hull. Visibility had tightened since yesterday and he could only make out a portion of the yawning, cavernous hold. The rest of the ship remained shrouded in blues and blacks. He flicked on the powerful helmet-mounted lights and entered the cargo hold.

He retraced some of Travis's steps through the tangle of wrecked vehicles and bent to look at the open box of gold.

"Get moving. You're burning bottom time," Stacey told him.

Ryan ignored her and swept his hand-held light over the bars and paused. There was something wrong. "Don, take a screen shot."

"Gotcha, and ... done," Don said.

Ryan moved aft and began to search the new section. He kept the light on a constant sweep through the hold. The ship creaked and groaned under the stress of the water and the current sweeping around it. Ryan shone the beam along the row of three Humvees suspended above him on the deck. Pausing between breaths, he listened intently to the surrounding sounds. The eeriness that had been with him during the first dive had returned.

"Ten minutes."

"Copy," Ryan replied. He clambered onto an MRAP and stood staring at the rear of the cargo hold. He'd made it to the back and hadn't seen the second strong box. After the strong boxes had been loaded, they were shoved to the side to make way for the unloading process. In the rush to beat the hurricane, the gold hadn't been strapped down.

He pivoted in place, sweeping the light across the hull, deck plating, and vehicles.

"Hold up. What's that?" Don asked in his ear.

Ryan asked, "Where?"

"Back to your left. It looks like a pallet."

Ryan swung back in the direction Don indicated, focusing the light in the nooks and crannies.

"There," Don said.

Ryan trained the light on the spot and then moved toward the indicated pallet. Instead of a strong box, he found crates of Kalashnikovs. Some were open, and the guns had already started to rust even though they were packed in Cosmoline grease, a heavy wax-like substance smeared on the guns to prevent corrosion.

Ryan heard Don sigh deeply before saying, "False alarm."

"It's okay, bro," Ryan said. "Keep watching."

"It's gotta be right in that area according to what you told me."

Ryan resumed his search. The water pressure made his movements sluggish and his steps heavy. Defeat wasn't an option, or a feeling he wore well. He slid off the MRAP into a tight opening between it and another Humvee. He got onto his knees and then laid down. He swept the light into the nooks and crannies. He labored back to his feet and did the same at the next opening.

"Two minutes," Travis called. "Get out of the ship now."

"Copy that," Ryan said. *It's got to be here. The first one was so easy to find.* He struggled through the debris to the opening of the hold.

"Clear," Ryan said. "Where's the basket?"

"Weather's taking a shit," Stacey said. "We pulled the basket. They're going to haul you up with the umbilical."

"Roger that. Ready to go up." The line tightened, and the harness bit into his thighs and chest. A movement to his left caught his eye, and he saw a flash of yellow. He focused on the spot again but didn't see anything. Between the gloom and his steady rise through the water column, whatever had been there was now out of sight.

Not more than fifteen feet off the ocean's bottom, he began to feel the effects of the approaching storm. He was being drawn up and down like a yo-yo, and he knew it would only get worse the closer he got to the surface. He wasn't looking forward to the ten-minute stop at one hundred and seventy-five feet, dangling like a bob on a plumb line. Even the current had picked up, twisting him, and tearing at his gear. He tried to watch his computer and adjust his buoyancy, so he would remain close to his planned depth.

"Give me some slack on the umbilical," he shouted.

"Hold on, whippersnapper."

Ryan's umbilical slackened, and he adjusted his buoyancy. "This isn't working!"

"You got a few more minutes, boy," Emery said. His voice was calm and firm, unlike the normal high-pitched cackle he spouted.

"Roger that," Ryan said. He wanted to say he'd been in worse conditions, but he hadn't. "What's it like up there?"

"Not good, whippersnapper. Soon as we get you through this stop, we're pulling you for the chamber."

"Copy that."

Ryan closed his eyes and tried his breathing exercises. The constant jerking wouldn't let him relax.

Emery's distorted voice said, "Okay, boy, we're bringing you up."

The slack went out of the umbilical and he began to rise. They were reeling him in as fast as they could. Once he reached the surface, he'd have five minutes to get into the chamber before the nitrogen bubbles started expanding and punching their way out of his muscles. Under pressure, the bubbles would slowly leave his tissues, enter the bloodstream, and eventually be exhaled. If he went straight to the surface and didn't get in the chamber, the nitrogen would no longer be under pressure and the expanding bubbles could lodge in his joints, under his skin, and move through his bloodstream to his brain, causing anything from excruciating pain to paralysis, and death.

He swept his gaze around. The visibility was steadily worsening along with the storm.

A gray shape materialized out of the darkness and sped past.

"You better get me out of here, Grandpa. A tiger shark just took a pass at me." The mature fourteen-footer lacked the stripes of youth, but Ryan easily recognized the shark's wedge-shaped head, light-yellow underbelly, and dark-blue upper body. Tigers were known as the garbage eater of the sea because there wasn't much the apex predator wouldn't eat. Ryan didn't want to be on that list. He cranked open the demand valve to vent more bubbles. Sharks normally avoided anything that blew bubbles, which cause cavitation inside the shark's gills and cause it to suffocate.

"Use your bang stick, boy."

"I'd rather you just got me out of the water."

"Hold tight."

The shark cruised in again, tail twitching against the current to hold it in place.

"He's staring at me," Ryan cried, his voice rising an octave.

"Fifty more feet. Don't worry about the shark."

Ryan turned to see the tiger swim by again. He pulled the bang stick out of its holder on his harness and held it out. He wouldn't use it unless it was a last resort.

When they finally pulled him to the water's surface, Ryan could hardly distinguish between it and the rain pouring down. He realized he'd had the easy job, bouncing around on a string, killing time.

As soon as he was on the boat, Ryan began stripping his gear, dumping it at his feet. Time was precious. Travis leaped to him and began unbuckling the helmet before jerking it off. Ryan stepped out of the drysuit on the way to the chamber. By the time he got there, he was naked.

Emery had the small hatch already open and Ryan dove inside. It shut with a solid thunk behind him. Almost immediately, Ryan cleared his ear as the air pressure changed and the tank began recompressing his body back to one hundred and seventy-five feet.

CHAPTER TWENTY-ONE

Outside, the storm raged unabated. Rain rang off the steel tube of the recompression chamber so loudly that Ryan had to cover his ears. He lay on the padded bench in a pair of blue coveralls someone had thrown in on top of a pile of towels. He was dry and as comfortable as he could get. Tossed around inside the steel tube was better than being jerked around at the end of his umbilical while fending off a shark. Still, he had to endure two more hours. They were headed to Billy Parker's place to take on diesel and fresh water and wait out the storm.

Ryan replayed the odd things that had occurred during the dive. There were so many that he didn't know where to start. The hatch lid on the Humvee being open, the shark, whatever had flashed yellow in the distance, the missing strong box, the gold bars being tampered with.

He sat up swiftly, swung his legs off the bench, and moved to grab the communications device. The crown of his head smacked against steel. He was thrown off balance and the pitch of the ship tossed him down like a rag doll.

"Shit, that hurt," he moaned, drawing each word out while trying to rub his ribs and his head at the same time.

"You okay in there?" Stacey asked.

"Yeah," Ryan replied, his voice strained from the pain radiating through his skull. He squeezed his eyes closed and opened them several times. Then he yelled a string of curse words.

"Are you okay, for real?" Stacey asked.

"Did you know it's been scientifically proven that cursing it helps take away pain?"

"Well, you shouldn't be in any pain after that outburst."

"Stacey, can you get Don for me?"

"Sure, hold on."

A minute later, Don came on the line. Ryan peered out the little porthole and saw the mechanic hunched against the rain. "Hey, remember the picture I had you take?"

"Sure do."

"Compare it to what the gold looked like when I first found it. There should be some footage of it."

"Why?"

Ryan shrugged. "Just a hunch."

"Okay."

Ryan lay back down and rubbed his head. He closed his eyes and concentrated on his breathing. Three in, four out. Three in, four out. In a few minutes, he was fast asleep.

He awoke to a pounding on the recompression chamber. Don peered at him through the port hole. Ryan sat up and reached for the communication device.

"I pulled up the photos and compared them," Don said. "You gotta see this."

"What?"

Don shoved a piece of paper against the chamber window. "Look at the way the gold is laying on the ground."

Ryan moved as close to the window as he could and stared at the printed picture.

"Now look at the screen shot you had me take on the last dive." Don pulled away the first picture and stuck a second piece of paper against the window. Fat raindrops marred its surface.

Ryan looked at the paper. "What's off?"

"I emailed the pictures to my friend at DWR. She ran a program that allowed her to look at the placement of everything in the photos to check my Mod 1 Mark 1 eyeball. She confirmed the gold had moved, and one bar was missing."

"Missing?"

"That's what she said," Don said, excitedly. He pulled the picture away and peered through the window. "Did you take another bar?"

"No."

"Seriously?" Stacey asked.

"No, check my gear if you don't believe me. Run all the footage, you can see exactly what I did down there. I didn't move anything."

Don said. "We already did, and Travis went through your gear."

Ryan sat back down. Of course, they didn't trust him. He hadn't done much to engender that trust. The only way a gold bar could be missing was for someone to go down there and take it. There was only one other vessel near enough to them that could facilitate a technical diver, and that was *Northwest Passage*. Whoever Kilroy had sent down to verify that the gold was there had to have done it on a rebreather. He could have followed their trail through the freighter right to the strong box, and taking a brick was the best verification there was. The flash of yellow he'd seen could have been the cover of a rebreather. He racked his brain. *What was the name of the rebreather they called "the yellow box of death?"* The *AP Valves Inspiration!* A man using it could easily make the dive to the *Santo Domingo.* That would explain the open Humvee hatch as well.

More thoughts rattled through Ryan's brain as he lay on the hard pad inside the chamber. He wanted out. He wanted a cigarette. He wanted answers. He closed his eyes and began his breathing exercises. He had to keep the steel walls from closing in.

A change in the engine's pitch interrupted his meditation. The boat slowed, and Ryan guessed they were approaching Billy Parker's docks. He sat up and looked out the porthole. The six-inch round window limited his view to the gear bolted to the stern.

Travis darted by wearing bright, orange, foul weather gear. The boat swung around and came alongside the docks with her bow out to the harbor. Ryan twisted his body to see Travis leap to the dock and wrap the line around a cleat. A moment later, *Peggy Lynn's* diesel engines shut off. The constant vibration of the deck stopped, and the world was silent.

Ryan glanced at his watchforty-five minutes left in the chamber. There was nothing to do but twiddle his thumbs. He hated riding in the Iron Cadillac. Until the weather calmed down, they couldn't dive. Neither could anyone else. He'd set out to destroy Kilroy, and he'd barely escaped with his life. Now, Kilroy was meddling with his gold. There had to be a way to kill two birds with one stone; get the gold and stop Kilroy. His mind drifted back to his time on *Northwest Passage* when Kilroy was ferrying him and Mango to Nicaragua to meet with the *Santo Domingo.*

He studied the problem. His mind was great with spatial shapes. Able to construct a 3D blueprint of Kilroy's ship in his mind, he mentally rotated it in all directions. The most vulnerable spot was the hull and as a Navy explosives expert, that's where he'd been trained to attack, silently and swiftly from the deep.

An idea formed in his head. He'd have to go on a scavenger hunt.

CHAPTER TWENTY-TWO

Emily Hunt dug her paddle deep into the azure blue water off Fort De Soto Park, shooting herself forward. Her body glistened from the heavy exercise of fighting the current running into Bunces Pass and staying up right on her paddle board. Her favorite place to slide into the water was at Arrowhead Picnic Area. From there, she'd work her way around to North Beach. On weekdays, it was a quiet place to hang out and if the tide was right, she could sprint to New Island Fort De Soto and run on the long, white, sand beaches. On the weekends, she avoided the place like the plague. The Fort De Soto beaches would be packed with families. Boaters invaded New Island, backing their pleasure craft up to the sand and partying in the hot sun. She didn't enjoy the drunks and the college kids anymore.

She thought about that as she paddled. She was changing. She no longer belonged to the generation of kids crowding the universities, roasting themselves on the beaches, and guzzling beer by the gallon in the local bars. She'd moved on, or was it just time? In her early thirties, Emily was still lean and fit, with a flat stomach from hours of working out and watching her diet. At five ten, her limbs were long and powerful, perfect for the many outdoor activities she enjoyed. Physically she still fit in, but mentally, she'd matured.

Emily picked up the pace, shoving thoughts of frat boys out of her mind. Her strokes became more rhythmic. She tossed her long, blonde hair, the color of ripe harvest wheat, off her shoulders and continued to dig. She wished she hadn't forgotten her ponytail band. Sweat collected under her thick mane and rolled down her back.

When she was in the cut between Fort De Soto and New Island, she rewarded herself by stepping off her board into the cool water. She let the waves and the tide sweep her along for a few seconds before opening her cornflower blue eyes and surfacing. Her long hair streamed with water as she climbed back on the board. Refreshed, Emily started the reverse trek. The current helped carry her back to where she'd parked her car.

At the picnic area, she shouldered her board and slid it onto the roof rack of the white Ford Focus RS. The hatchback had plenty of space for her gear and plenty of horsepower to let her weave in and out of traffic on the freeways. She drove around to the Gulf side of the island and walked down to the beach to watch the sunset. When the big orange ball was safely below the horizon, she climbed into her car and drove to her apartment. It was a hike across town to get to the park, but it was worth the drive.

Emily secured her paddleboard and paddle in the small storage area and headed inside to take a shower. She came out of the bathroom wearing a pair of black yoga pants and an oversized T-shirt with a kitten playing with a ball of yarn on it. She sat down at the kitchen table with a glass of wine and opened her laptop. She had a few minutes to check emails before going to bed.

As one of Ward and Young's lead insurance investigators, she carried a full caseload and often assisted with several other investigations at the same time. She enjoyed her job and had been instrumental in rewriting corporate guidelines for boat theft investigations.

A knock on the door startled her; she wasn't expecting visitors. Rising from her chair, she reached into her purse and grabbed the can of pepper spray. While she'd been proficiently trained in firearms by the Broward County Sheriff's Office when she'd been a deputy there, she preferred the pepper spray. Blind them and run away. If she had to fight, she knew a few moves and her last boyfriend, Ryan Weller, had improved her fighting skills by teaching her a few more techniques. She had a brief flash of his warning about always being careful as she grabbed the door. Her normal assertion was that he was just paranoid.

For some reason, she heeded the warning bells in her head. She double-checked the chain latch was in place and stepped to the side. She aimed the spray and twisted the doorknob. "Who is it?"

"Hey, lady, I've got a delivery for you," a voice called from the hallway.

"What is it?"

"A package from Amazon."

"I didn't order anything. Go away." She tried to slam the door, but the man's foot blocked it open. She shot the pepper spray through the crack and the man screamed of pain. The foot jerked back. Before she could close the door, someone shoved the man's red face into the crack to hold the door open while he snaked a pair of bolt cutters through to clip the cheap metal chain.

Emily hit the button on the spray again. She got a whiff of the caustic capsaicin and coughed. Years ago, Emily had been dosed with the chemical herself as part of her sheriff's deputy training. She understood the gas's effects on her body and how to react to them. She stepped back to gain some distance, aimed the spray again, and waited for the door to open. The chain snapped, and a burly man swung the door open with so much force that it bounced off the wall. A giant loomed in the doorway, filling it almost to capacity. His face was red from the pepper spray, but it didn't have the same effect on him as the smaller guy who had taken the spray directly to the face. He lay balled up on the hallway floor, rubbing his eyes and crying. Emily aimed her spray can at the giant and mashed the button with her thumb. Nothing happened.

She dropped the pepper spray and ran to the bedroom. Emily snatched open the nightstand drawer and withdrew the Glock pistol she kept there. The giant swatted it away with a flick of his hand before she could even bring the gun up. Pain radiated up her arm like hot wires being shoved under the skin. Her hand and arm below the elbow went numb.

"I don't want to hurt you," Giant said.

Emily brought her knee up hard. He deflected the blow to the groin into his thigh.

"Stop," Giant bellowed with a grimace.

She swung her open hand and caught him on the cheek with a slap that rang off the walls.

The big man grabbed her by the hair and twisted viciously. Emily dropped to her knees, feeling her scalp being torn free. Tears burned at the corners of her eyes and ran down her cheeks to drip off her chin.

"Just stop," Giant said, his voice calmer now that he was in control.

Emily dug her fingernails into the man's arm. "You're hurting me."

"You hurt me first, lady."

"Let go, please," she begged, tasting tears on her lips. "What do you want?"

"I want you to cooperate. If I let go, will you be a good girl?"

"Yes."

"Promise?"

She sobbed in big, heaving gasps. "I promise."

"Good." Giant shoved her to the floor as he let go. "Stay there." The man collected her gun and left the bedroom.

Emily buried her face in her hands and let the tears flow. She was too frightened to move, and she'd learned that staying still would keep her from experiencing more pain.

Her ex-boyfriend, James, had abused her, both physically and verbally, even though she was a sheriff's deputy. He'd left bruises where they couldn't be seen, and he'd constantly undermined her accomplishments. It took her two years of responding to calls of women in similar situations for her to see that she was also a victim of domestic abuse. She'd resigned from her job and run to Tampa. She was done with the abuse and the fear, but the actions of the apartment invaders had put her right back in the middle of those feelings.

Realizing that, she sat up, and wiped her eyes and cheeks with the palms of her hands. She couldn't be a victim again. She had to fight back. She needed a weapon. Fighting technique alone wouldn't help her take down two capable men, especially now that one of them had her gun. She couldn't call for help because her cell phone was in the kitchen beside her computer. She glanced at the nightstand. Her father's old pocketknife was in the drawer. He had given it to her when she'd graduated from the Broward Police Academy, shortly before he'd passed away. While he'd carried it every day, and kept it sharpened and oiled, she hadn't taken such good care of it. A wave of regret and guilt washed over her. She deeply missed him, and the tears started to flow again. In those moments of introspection, while sitting on the floor with her back against the bed, she wondered if her misguided relationships were a replacement for a father who had always seemed larger than life.

Emily ran her hands down the sleek spandex fabric of her pants, thinking she had nowhere to hide the knife even if she took it out of the drawer. Just then, the massive man squeezed himself back into the room.

"Get dressed."

"I am dressed," Emily said defensively.

"Put on some regular clothes, then pack a bag. You're going on a trip."

She went to the closet and pulled out several pairs of pants, shorts, and shirts. At the dresser, she removed panties and bras. She laid them out on the bed as instructed.

Giant grinned as his leering eyes flicked up from the panties and roamed over her body.

"Where are we going?" Emily asked.

"On a trip."

"Ugh," she groaned and picked up a pair of slacks and a shirt. "I'm going to change in the bathroom. Plus, I need to pack my toothbrush and a few other things. My suitcase is under the bed. Will you get it?"

The man slid off the bed and aimed the Glock at her. "Stay where I can see you and no tricks, lady."

"I promise." While she was regaining her swagger, the

threat of being shot kept her in check. She didn't think he would shoot her, but she wasn't going to take that chance.

He knelt on the floor and looked under the bed. While he was down there, Emily quickly changed from her yoga pants to the slacks. She was halfway through pulling the shirt on when Giant came up with the black rolling case.

"Very nice," Giant said, setting the case on the bed, and not taking his eyes off her chest. He grabbed her clothes and tossed them in the bag, fingering her panties before dumping them on top.

Emily buttoned the shirt and stepped to the bathroom, the giant right on her tail. She collected her toilet kit and hairbrushes, then added some feminine hygiene items to the mix. He backed away as she came out and placed everything in her suitcase.

"Are you ready now, lady?"

"My name is Emily."

"Don't make this personal. You're just a package I'm delivering." He picked up the suitcase. "Nice shot with the Mace by the way, you got Victor really good."

Victor was standing in the kitchen, snot running down his nose in long globs. His face was bright red and shiny from tears and the water he'd been using to rinse his eyes. He held the faucet hose with one hand and bent down to rinse his face again. Emily smiled. There was some personal satisfaction at having caused pain to one of her kidnappers.

"Let's go, Vic."

"Damnit, Ronnie, that bitch messed me up."

"You'll get over it. You've had your head under that faucet for ten minutes now. Let's go. We got a flight to catch."

"Yeah, yeah," Vic muttered. He coughed hard, rinsed

his mouth, and spat in the sink. He left the hose out but shut off the water.

Emily looked longingly at her cell phone still laying on the table beside her computer.

"Don't think about it, missy," Vic said, wiping his face with one of her kitchen towels; the good one she used for decoration because it had two flamingos on it. Anger smoldered inside of her.

"Take the suitcase," Ronnie said to Vic. He kept a tight grip on Emily's right arm, just above the elbow, and steered her toward the door. Vic grabbed the suitcase and followed them down the elevator, and out to an old station wagon. Ronnie wedged Emily into the backseat and sat beside her. Vic got behind the wheel. They drove across Old Tampa Bay on Courtney Campbell Causeway, and turned south onto Bayside Bridge, which dumped them off outside the St. Pete-Clearwater Airport.

Emily had a sudden vision of the last time she'd flown out of this airport with Ryan and Chuck Newland. They'd gone to Key West to look for sunken sailboats and she'd found Ryan to be a man who was rough and calloused, but with a kind heart. He reminded her of her dad. Ryan had kept her from drowning and then took her on a roller coaster of emotions as he was lost at sea, found, and infiltrated a Mexican drug lord's compound. After his last mission to arrest Jim Kilroy, she'd ended up with two Homeland Security agents in her apartment as a protection detail because Kilroy had threatened her life. That's when she'd dumped his ass.

Vic stopped the car beside a sleek Jetstream 32 twin-engine turboprop plane.

"Where are we going?" she asked.

Ronnie didn't answer as he maneuvered her out of the

car and up the stairs. He shoved her into a seat and Vic tossed her bag into the plane before the two men retreated to the tarmac. The captain pulled the stairs in and locked the door.

"Where we're going?" she asked the captain.

"Haiti, mon," a muscular man with long dreadlocks and a beard said from the back of the plane.

CHAPTER TWENTY-THREE

I t was well after dark when Ryan returned to the Hotel Roi Christophe. While they were in port, Stacey and Travis had asked about hotel accommodations and Ryan had called Joulie. She booked all of them into the hotel.

Ryan was wet, hungry, and tired when he walked into the dining room. His small crew had lingered over drinks, and Dennis was about to return to *Peggy Lynn*. He'd insisted on spending the nights on his boat. Ryan sat down beside him. "What's the latest on the weather report?"

"Rain and rough seas for the next three days."

"Dang it," Ryan said, shaking his head.

A waiter came by, and Ryan ordered fish and vegetables. He wondered where they were getting the fish from. Haiti's waters were notoriously overfished, and on his dives, he hadn't seen much marine life, save for the shark buzzing his position. He decided not to ask any questions.

"What did you do all day?" Stacey asked.

"I told you, I had some errands to run," Ryan said.

"Your mysterious bullshit is causing a rift in the crew," she said. "First it was the patch, then it was negotiating away half the haul, and now you're running all over the city on errands." She used her fingers to make air quotes around errands.

Ryan glanced around the room. He lowered his voice and leaned forward. "Did Don show you the pictures?"

They all nodded.

"Okay, someone is messing with our take, and I have a feeling it's Jim Kilroy. He owns the mothership that's been hanging out near us. When I was down there, I saw a flash of yellow in the haze. I think it was a guy on a rebreather. It's the only explanation for what's missing."

"Makes sense," Travis said.

"Kilroy is an international arms dealer. He supplied the weapons to the cartel who bombed the Southwest. I went after him a few months ago, and we tangled. I want to finish the job."

"Why's he after the gold?" Dennis asked.

"It was supposed to be payment for the weapons on board the *Santo Domingo*."

"Wait a minute," Stacey said. "This is the same arms dealer you told us you partnered with to deliver the weapons?"

"Yeah." Ryan nodded.

"An international arms dealer, a Haitian vodou priestess, *and* bounty hunters?" Stacey said, shaking her head. "This is just plain weird."

Ryan nodded. "We're going to take care of the arms dealer and the priestess."

"Can I go home now?" Don asked.

"If you want to," Ryan said. "I can get you on a flight tomorrow, but we need you, Don."

Don sat back and picked up his glass. He took a drink and set it down, then twirled it in circles on the table.

"Look," Ryan said, "we've got the advantage. We have all the gear to bring up the gold and we have Joulie's protection to keep Kilroy at bay."

"What happens if we can't find the second strong box?"

"It's there, Travis," Ryan said.

"What did you do on your errands?" Stacey asked.

Ryan shook his head. "I get that you guys don't like secrecy, but some things need to stay a mystery."

"That's an answer I'd expect from an idiot." Stacey sat back and crossed her arms. She blew a strand of fading purple hair out of her face. Her hair was returning to its normal shade of light brown. The rain hadn't done her any favors.

Dennis excused himself and stood. Ryan walked out with him. At the lobby, Dennis asked for a driver to take him to the docks.

"I want to be straight with you, Captain," Ryan said. The rain had turned to a steady drizzle and they stood on the porch steps waiting for the car. "This thing could get messy. I told you that from the beginning. What I didn't expect was for it to become so complicated with Joulie, and now Kilroy showing up."

"I understand," Dennis said. He stood with his hands in the pockets of his khakis. No matter what was happening, he always wore his khakis, white tennis shoes, and red *Peggy Lynn* T-shirt. "I took the risk by coming with you. I wanted another adventure."

"It's shaping up to be one."

"Sounds like adventure follows you around."

"Something like that," Ryan muttered.

Dennis let a moment of silence lapse before saying, "We'll come out all right."

A black sedan pulled around the driveway and stopped

in front of the men. It was slick with rain and its tires and fenders were splattered with mud. The passenger window buzzed down. A grinning black man stuck his head out. "You be da cap'ain?"

"I am."

"Let's be goin'." The driver motioned Dennis into the car.

Ryan bid Dennis good night and returned to the dining room. His meal had been delivered. Only Don was still at the table. Ryan sat down and dug in.

"You sure everything is gonna be all right, boss?" Don asked.

"Everything's fine," Ryan said between bites. "I've got a job for you."

"What's that?"

"Have you ever built an electromagnet?"

"Well, hell, is that all you want?" he asked with a grin.

"Pretty simple, really," Ryan said. "I've got all the components."

"Is that what you were scavenging for?"

"Yep."

"Sure wish you would've taken me along. It's been boring sittin' around the hotel. Did you know I fixed like three toilets since I've been here?"

Ryan shook his head, his mouth full of food. He tended to eat fast, shoveling in quickly. He'd always been like that. Bootcamp and his time in the military had exacerbated the situation, forcing him to eat quickly between evolutions. He swallowed and took a long drink of beer. "I had no idea. Anyway, I've got the stuff in the room. I'll show it to you."

"Cool. I'll start crawlin' the walls if I don't have something to do."

He knew what Don meant. He looked up and saw

Joulie standing in one of the open veranda doors. She smiled at him, whispered something to the waiter, and then walked away. The waiter took a circuitous route to Ryan's table. When he arrived, he bent down and whispered, "The lady would like you to join her in the garden."

"Of course, she does," Ryan said with a shake of his head. "Bring me another beer and take a drink to the lady. Tell her that I'll join her in a few minutes."

The waiter straightened quickly and looked appalled that Ryan hadn't jumped to do Joulie's bidding. Ryan guessed he wasn't used to anyone turning down an invitation from the ruling priestess. The look passed quickly from the man's face, and he returned to the professional he was, replying with a curt nod and a yes.

After the waiter delivered Ryan's beer, Ryan escorted Don up to his room.

Don asked, "What about Joulie?"

"She can wait a few minutes," Ryan replied. He opened the door with his key and led the way to a small desk. Three plastic bags sat on the floor beside it. He took the items from the bags and laid them out for Don to see. When he was through, he explained exactly how he wanted Don to assemble his contraption.

"You sure about that?" Don asked dubiously.

"Yes. It'll work, and we need the speed sensor because radio waves don't transmit well underwater."

Don nodded. "How are you going to get it on Kilroy's boat?"

"That's one of those secrets I'm keeping to myself."

"So, you don't know?"

"I have an idea."

Don shook his head. "Sounds dangerous."

"One more thing. I want you to see if you can scrounge

up some scrap and build this for me." Ryan used a piece of hotel stationary and a pencil to sketch what he had in mind.

Don whistled. "That might be tough. I'll have to take everything to *Peggy Lynn* so I can use the workshop."

"That's fine. Ask Billy Parker for help if you need it. He's pretty well connected." Ryan glanced at his watch. "I better get going. I'll check on you tomorrow."

"Night," Don said, grinning as he placed parts back in the sacks.

Ryan hurried down the flight of stairs and nearly collided with another patron coming up. He excused himself and continued to the garden. The rain had stopped for now, but the weather service said it would begin again around midnight. Joulie was waiting on the same stone bench where she'd negotiated the pants off him. *Literally and figuratively*, he thought.

He paused to light a cigarette, then thought better of it. He stuffed the pack back in his pocket. She patted the bench as he approached, and he sat beside her.

She asked, "How's the salvage coming?"

"We found one of the strong boxes."

"What about the other?"

"The hurricane moved the ship almost a half a mile from where it originally went down. A lot of things got jumbled up inside. We'll find it."

Joulie faced him. "You'd better not lie to me. The loa will tell me if you are lying. They are helping you now. I have prayed to them for guidance."

"I'm not lying," Ryan snapped. "We only get twenty minutes to work on the bottom. We're searching as fast as we can. If it's buried under the vehicles, it'll take some time to get it out."

Joulie put her hand on his arm. It was warm and comforting. "Do your best."

"We have another problem," Ryan said. "Jim Kilroy sent a diver down to the wreck. He messed with our spare gas supply and took a gold bar."

The hand tightened on his arm and Joulie's faced clouded. "I sensed his evil presence."

"I have a plan to fix his wagon," Ryan said.

"What do you mean, *fix his wagon?*" she asked, clearly puzzled.

"It's an old expression for taking care of a problem."

Joulie smiled. "Why isn't Mango with you?"

"He didn't want to come on this trip."

"Why not?"

"He got tired of being my work wife," Ryan said.

"What happened?"

"He went sailing with his real wife."

"That's too bad, I liked Mango."

"I asked him if he wanted to help recover the gold and he said no, well, his wife said no."

"He's a smart man to listen to her."

"Hey, what are you saying?" Ryan put an arm around her shoulders and squeezed her against him. A raindrop fell onto his head and it was quickly accompanied by more. Hand in hand the couple ran up to her suite.

———

IN THE MORNING, rain poured from a slate gray sky and wind whipped through the trees around the hotel. The weather forecast hadn't changed. For Ryan, the storm was moving at a snail's pace. He wanted to get back in the water and finish the job.

He leaned on the iron railing and put his morning cigarette to his lips. He inhaled lustily and let the smoke linger in his lungs before blowing it out.

Joulie came up behind him and wrapped her arms around him. She laid her head on his back and kissed his bare skin. The warmth of her lips and the eagerness of her hands made it hard to concentrate. Her voice was husky. "Come back to bed. Nothing will happen today."

Ryan liked the weight of her against him. He had no illusions about their relationship. She would never leave her country again. Their paths had converged twice and would separate again. They were a comfort to each other, sharing a bed for convenience.

She was right, he would get no work done today. He wondered if Don was on his way to the boat.

She kissed his muscular back again, her long hair tickling his skin. He straightened and flicked his cigarette into an ashtray. She loosened her grip, and he turned to face her. She was naked under her robe. He picked her up and carried her back to bed.

CHAPTER TWENTY-FOUR

Ryan pulled on a clean shirt and khaki pants. He ran a hand through his tousled hair and glanced in the mirror to ensure it was laying properly.

"Let's order room service," Joulie said, patting the sheets with her hand, inviting him back to bed.

"I promised I'd have dinner with the crew. You could join us."

She rolled onto her back.

"You're the head vodou lady around here. You should be able to do whatever you want."

"You're right," Joulie said, sitting up.

Ryan watched her walk into the bathroom. Her ass was a thing of perfection. She was the kind of woman he could settle down with if she wasn't so hell bent on staying in Haiti. He could see himself traveling the world with her. They could buy a sailboat and find a slice of paradise where they could run naked on the beaches. Was the taste of action so deeply ingrained in him that he'd given up on the dream? Had his sailing trip around the world, when he was eighteen, been the end of his carefree life?

He heard the shower turn on. "Go down without me," she called over the roar of water.

Ryan sat on the edge of the bed and worked his feet into his boat shoes. Joulie wasn't going to eat with them. She had to keep her status and position even if everyone at the hotel knew she was boffing the *nèg blan*—white man. They were just using each other for comfort. The rebound. He shook his head to clear away the feelings.

Ryan lit a cigarette on the balcony, walked down the stairs, and along the veranda toward the dining room. Rain continued to drizzle, and the trees still swayed. It was good to have a few moments to himself. Staying under the roof, he crossed to the dining room and paused to finish his smoke before entering. His crew sat at their normal table. Ryan brought the cigarette up as he surveyed the room. His hand stopped halfway to his lips.

Jim Kilroy stared directly at him with an impish smile. To Kilroy's right, a Hispanic man looked up from his meal when Kilroy nudged him. Karen Kilroy turned her blonde head and smiled. It was the other blonde at the table who froze his blood. She did not smile, only stared helplessly at him. He could read the tension in her body, the pleading in her blue eyes. His knees threatened to buckle, and his tongue stuck to the roof of his suddenly dry mouth. Ryan's lips opened and closed like a suffocating fish.

Kilroy stood. "Come join us, Mr. Weller."

Ryan tried to swallow the lump in his throat. He wanted to be callous, he wanted to be suave, he wanted to be more than the fool he felt like right now.

Robotically, Ryan walked past his gaping crew and took a seat opposite Emily. Kilroy waved the waiter over before sitting.

Henri came immediately and said, "The usual, Mr. Weller?"

"*Wi*, Henri," Ryan said.

"I see you've made yourself right at home," Kilroy said, slicing off a piece of his steak.

Ryan couldn't think of a witty retort.

After chewing and swallowing, Kilroy asked, "How goes the search for the gold?"

"I could ask your diver the same thing."

Kilroy paused his cutting and looked up.

"I saw him on the wreck. He took a gold bar."

Kilroy smiled. The silent Hispanic looked both puzzled and surprised. Ryan also saw a gleam of gold fever in his dark eyes.

Henri returned with an ice-cold Prestige. "Anything else, sir?"

"Yeah," Ryan said. "I'll have the steak, medium rare. Jimmy's buying."

"Yes, sir," Henri said before scurrying away.

A foot brushed against Ryan's leg, then it gave three quick taps, three long taps, three quick taps to his calf. S-O-S in Morse code. He took a sip of beer, trying to relieve the dryness in his mouth. After three bursts of code, she stopped. He replied with three long taps, *O*, a long tap, a quick tap, a long tap, *K*. He didn't know if she understood, and he didn't look at her to find out. He couldn't bring himself to look at her pleading blue eyes.

His heart ached. She was a beautiful woman, the girl next door, with her sweetheart smile and classic features. He remembered how she fit against him when they lay cuddled in the V-berth of his sailboat, the softness of her skin like smooth silk whispering against his rough hands. He loved her hearty laugh, and the way she moved with athletic grace. How could he have chosen his job over her? One of her toenails dragged along his ankle.

To distract himself from his thoughts, Ryan tipped his bottle toward the Hispanic and asked Kilroy, "Is this your new bodyguard?"

Kilroy's narcissistic smile creased his tan face. "This is Eduardo Sanchez. He's here at the request of the Aztlán cartel. I'm sure you remember them."

Sanchez nodded, chewing his fish and staring Ryan down.

"You're working together?"

"We have mutual interests. When I'm through with you, Eduardo can have what's left."

Sanchez's lips curled into a sneer under his thick mustache. His heavy eyelids, wavy black hair, and goatee made him a dead ringer for the man Ryan had killed at his apartment in Key Largo.

"How's your mother doing, Karen?" Ryan asked. When he'd first met Karen in New York City, she'd been visiting her mother, who had cervical cancer.

"She passed away."

"I'm sorry to hear that," Ryan said.

"Thank you," Karen said softly.

Turning to Emily, he asked. "Are they treating you all right?"

She nodded. Her foot slid up his pant leg. Her bare toes were cool against his calf. He tried to drink but couldn't swallow. His throat was raw and sore around the lump in it.

"Jim, if you harm a hair on her head—"

"Too late for that, I'm afraid," Jim said. "The boys had to get nasty with her at her apartment. Apparently, she's a fighter. She dosed one of them with pepper spray."

"Good girl," Ryan said.

"Your steak, sir." Henri set the sizzling platter in front of Ryan and backed away. "Another beer?"

"Of course, would you like anything, Emily?" Ryan asked.

She shook her head.

"You sure, a glass of juice, or a shot of tequila. A margarita?" The last suggestion earned him a brief smile.

"A margarita for the lady, Henri, on the rocks with salt."

"*Wi.*"

After Henri stepped away, Ryan picked up his silverware and began cutting his steak. He paused and looked around the table. "I'm sorry, did anyone else want anything?"

"You know exactly what we want," Kilroy said.

"I don't think the waiter can make change for gold bars."

Sanchez spoke for the first time, his thick, Mexican accent hard to translate. "I would like to see your testicles wrapped around your neck and your body dragged through the street by them." He made simultaneous choking and hanging motions with his hands.

"That's rather unpleasant at the dinner table, Eduardo," Kilroy reprimanded.

Sanchez continued to leer at Ryan.

"Better keep your dog on a leash, Jimmy," Ryan said, returning the man's stare.

Kilroy laughed. "That's what I like about you, Ryan. You run toward the action and not away. You're what ..." he waved his knife in the air. "What's the expression they use when a political candidate comes out of nowhere?"

"A dark horse, dear," Karen said, lifting a fork full of salad to her mouth.

"You're my dark horse, Ryan. The long shot to win the

race you're not supposed to win and yet you keep coming out on top. Why is that?"

"Cream rises," Ryan said.

"So do turds," Kilroy said. "But I don't think you're a turd."

Ryan smirked. "Some would say I'm the asshole."

"He's always trying to be clever, isn't he, dear?" Kilroy asked his wife.

Karen blushed.

There was something unnatural and surreal about the whole scene. Ryan had a tough time coming to grips with the polite way he was interacting with the weapons dealer. It was as if Kilroy demanded the politeness. Sanchez was the exception. He was the dog-on-a-chain, ready to bite on command. Ryan was sure there were more goons standing by to leap into action if Kilroy snapped his fingers.

He chewed the steak, and chewed, and chewed. The meat wasn't tough. The difficulty came when swallowing, trying to force it past the lump in his throat. And Emily was so close. He hadn't seen her since he'd left for Belize to chase down Kilroy six months ago. He'd almost gotten into a car and driven to Tampa on several occasions just to see her. She had asked him not to come, and he would just be a stalker if he'd gone. It wouldn't have helped them get back together.

"Did you get my letter?" Ryan asked. He had sent a multiple page tome as an apology and an explanation.

Emily nodded.

"What's the matter, Ms. Hunt," Kilroy asked. "The man asked you a question." He leaned toward Ryan and pointed his fork at Emily. "She's been a mute since she got off the plane."

Henri delivered the margarita. Emily thanked him with

a tight smile. He grinned before departing. She took a sip and then set the drink back on the table. Her hand lingered by the long stem of the glass, gently rubbing it with her fingers. Ryan reached across the table and placed his hand on hers. Emily looked up.

Ryan said, "I'm sorry."

She shook her head. A tear welled at the corner of her left eye and rolled down her cheek.

Ryan withdrew his hand. He started eating again. He couldn't tell what was worse, his responsibility for putting Emily in this situation, or the pain of seeing her in it.

Her toes rested on his foot again. Ryan's pulse rate increased, and a surge of hope swelled through his body.

Kilroy interrupted his thoughts. "When will you dive again?"

"As soon as the weather clears."

"Have you found all of it?"

"No, we still need to locate the second box."

"You better," Kilroy said. He laid his silverware on his plate. "Dessert and a night cap aboard the *Passage*, dear?"

"Yes," Karen agreed.

"Mr. Weller, we must be going now." Kilroy stood and tossed an American one-hundred-dollar bill on the table. "Enjoy your meal."

From the side of a room, a large man approached, took Emily by the arm, and forced her to stand. There was nothing Ryan could do despite Emily's pleading eyes. The enforcer shepherded the group out the veranda doors. Ryan followed them to the small courtyard.

Damian jumped from behind a pillar to block Ryan's way. He had a black pistol in his hand and leveled it at Ryan's chest. The Jamaican lowered his gun and grinned his gold teeth. "Where your Taser be at now, mon?" He jerked his gun back up and yelled, "Bwah!"

Ryan stood stock still, staring at Damian's black eyes. In a voice just loud enough for Damian to hear, he said, "I'm going to put you in the dirt."

"Dat what you tink, mon!" Damian pointed his gun gangster-style at Ryan's head and danced around.

"Let's go, Damian," Kilroy ordered.

"Let me scare da boy some more, Mista Kilroy." He waved the barrel in front of Ryan.

"Enough, Damian, let's go. I need him alive."

"Too bad." Damian leveled the gun and poked Ryan in the chest with the muzzle.

Without thinking, Ryan snatched the gun barrel with his right hand and pushed it to his left. At the same time, he caught Damian's wrist with his left hand and forced it to the right. The violent movements ripped the gun from Damian's hand and snapped his trigger finger inside the guard. He let out a blood-curdling scream as he dropped the pistol and clutched his hand.

"Ya broke me finger, mon!"

"Next time you pull a gun, you better use it." Ryan pointed the gun at Kilroy. "I should have done this a long time ago."

Karen gasped. Kilroy laughed. "You're going to shoot me in cold blood in front of all these witnesses?"

Ryan dropped the magazine, ejected the cartridge from the chamber, and tossed the gun at Damian's feet. To Kilroy, he said, "Next time I see you, I'll have the gold. Stay out of my way until then."

"Smart boy," Kilroy said. He turned his attention to Damian, looking impassively at his hired man still weeping on his knees and holding his broken finger. "Get up and stop blubbering." He shoved Damian in the shoulder with his foot.

Damian climbed slowly to his feet and glared at Ryan. "You dead, boy! You dead!"

"Get in line, asshole," Ryan replied.

The group retreated. Ryan could see tears sliding down Emily's cheeks as she glanced over her shoulder at him.

Ryan called out, "I'm coming for you, Emily."

In a shaky voice, she said her first words of the night, "You better."

.

CHAPTER TWENTY-FIVE

The wind and rain had stopped. The earth seemed to be taking a breather after Mother Nature's fury. Ryan stood on the steps, watching the bright taillights of Kilroy's hired car swing out of the hotel's drive. A moment later they were gone. Ryan took his cigarettes from his pocket and lit one. The nicotine and the routine of smoking helped calm his frazzled nerves. The adrenaline that had surged through his body for the whole encounter had shut off. Suddenly he was weak with exhaustion, and he sagged into a chair.

"So that was Emily?" Stacey asked from his elbow.

"Yeah," Ryan managed to say.

"She seems nice. A lot prettier in person. I can see why you fell for her." Stacey paused, and when Ryan didn't answer, started talking again. "What was that move you put on Damian? That was awesome, what'd you do, like break his finger, or something? Totally cool." She kept mimicking Ryan's hand movements over and over.

"Shut up, Stacey."

"Okay."

She sat beside him for a while. Dennis came over with two beers. He nudged Stacey out of the chair by using a nod of his head to tell her take a hike. Ryan took one of the beers and drained half of it, not realizing how parched and raw his throat was.

"You told me it wouldn't be complicated," Dennis said. "You're entitled to be wrong on occasions. I knew it would be dangerous, and I believe you're a man who could handle himself. I used to be fearless, too, and wanted to make every moment count."

Silence and smoke enveloped them. Lost in his own thoughts, Ryan had barely heard the captain.

After several long minutes, Dennis said, "I've never had to fight for a woman. Peggy never got kidnapped by some pirate." He took a long swig of his bottle. Dennis's voice became so soft that Ryan had to focus on his next words. "If someone took my Peggy, I'd bring hell on earth to them. I'll help you do the same."

"Thanks, Dennis, that means a lot to me."

"We can't dive until the weather clears. Looks like it'll be around for another day or so. Even then the current might still be running strong."

"I'll risk it. We've got the chamber."

Dennis nodded.

"What's the plan? You have Don working on something."

"That's shot to hell. I can't do what I'd planned with Emily on Kilroy's boat."

"Don't throw it out. Something might change."

"Always plan for contingencies."

"You've got a few days. If you want to run something by me, just ask."

"Thanks, Captain."

Dennis stood. "I'm headed back to the boat. I don't trust those security yahoos Parker hired even if he says they're on the police force, especially with your new friends in town. If it was this easy for Kilroy to find you through the coconut telegraph, then who knows what else the natives know about."

"You know where we stored the hardware," Ryan said.

"I've slept with a revolver under my pillow since I was a private in-country. This isn't any different."

Ryan nodded and drained his beer. "You got my shiny trinket under there too?"

"You remember where McGee kept his safe?"

"Yeah." Ryan smiled. The salvage consultant had a safe in the bilge of his houseboat. He kept it covered with water and when he needed it, he activated a secondary pump, which drained the bilge and then pumped water back over it when he was done.

"McDonald got that idea from me. I've been using that old smuggling trick for pert near half a century."

Ryan smiled. "I won't tell."

Dennis squeezed the younger man's shoulder. "We'll get her back."

CHAPTER TWENTY-SIX

Puerto Rico was a country in turmoil. Hurricane Irma had left the island decimated. Seven months after the storms hit, the majority of the island's electrical grid had been rebuilt but it was still subject to blackouts. More work remained, and Dark Water Research was part of those efforts to restore the country to a semblance of what it had been. Within days of the hurricane's passing, DWR ships and equipment were off the coast of the island, providing power and water through on-board systems.

After his trip to meet Ryan in Key West, Greg Olsen wanted to be close to Haiti, and his job as coordinator for DWR's relief efforts in Puerto Rico gave him the perfect cover. It wasn't his favorite job, but he needed something to do after resigning as DWR's president. Greg had chosen to dock the blue-and-white Hatteras across the Mona Passage from Puerto Rico. The Dominican Republic marina, they were staying at, was also closer to Ryan's operation in Haiti.

"Hey, boss, you want me to get you anything while I'm out?" Rick Hayes asked.

"I'm good for now," Greg said. "We'll have lunch at the marina club when you get back."

"Roger that."

Greg watched Rick step over the gunwale and walk up the dock. When Rick reached land, he took off running. Rick made the turn onto the beach and his feet kicked up little rooster tails with each stride. When Rick wasn't tending to his duties on the Hatteras, he was tending a woman. His trips up the beach were always scouting missions to one of the all-inclusive resorts to find his next conquest. The man was only five-feet-six-inches tall, but he constantly joked about his sexual prowess and the size of his manhood. Greg didn't care as long as Rick's affairs didn't interfere with his job.

Rick Hayes was another warrior Greg had worked with during his time in the Navy. He'd met Rick during an operation in Afghanistan. Rick was Army EOD, and they'd been through the same basic service-wide EOD school at Eglin Air Force Base.

While Greg was waiting for Chuck Newland to pick him up, he'd bar-hopped along Duval Street and spotted Rick coming out of Sloppy Joe's. Greg had offered to buy the beer, and they did the scratch-and-sniff dance of who do you know and what had happened since then. Rick was bumming around Key West and Big Pine, flying tourists in a Robinson R44 helicopter. He wasn't thrilled with carting around gray-haired civilians and young kids, and he'd been reprimanded on more than one occasion for flying dangerously according to company policy.

Greg had listened to him grouse about his job, the lousy state of the economy after the hurricane, and the puke-stained civilians he had to tote around. After fifteen minutes of the tirade, Greg had said, "Come work for me."

Now they were in the Caribbean, waiting for Ryan to signal he needed help, or for the DWR crews to require assistance.

The ringing satellite phone cut through the fog of his thoughts as he stared out the window, ignoring the spreadsheets and endless work orders on his computer screen. Reaching for the phone, he wished he were running on the beach with Rick. "Hello, this is Greg."

"Hey, boss," Ryan said.

"You don't sound very happy."

"Killer Roy has Emily on his ship."

Greg straightened. "Tell me what happened?"

"He kidnapped her from her apartment and he's holding her ransom until I give him the gold."

"Did you make the trade?"

"I haven't recovered the gold yet."

"What do you need from me?"

"Some backup. I need Mango with a sniper rifle."

Greg chuckled. "You really want him to say he saved your ass three times?"

"If it means I get Emily back safe and sound, I don't care."

"I'm in Punta Cana. I can be up there in two days."

"What are you doing in Punta Cana?"

"Right now, I'm enjoying the tropical sun while fighting to stay awake as I work my way through budget spreadsheets."

Ryan snorted. "Yeah, right. You're hanging around hoping I'd call you for help."

"Guilty as charged, but I was right." They may have had a running joke about how many times Mango had saved Ryan's life, but Greg felt a burden of debt that he could never repay. Ryan had saved his life by pulling him from a Humvee in the middle of an ambush.

"Teamwork, brother."

Greg smiled. "You remember Rick Hayes?"

"Rick the Dick?"

"That was Rick Gillespie. Rick Hayes is the Army EOD officer we worked with to find Nightcrawler." Nightcrawler was the code designation for a Taliban bomb maker they'd hunted in Afghanistan on their last tour. Rick had determined that Nightcrawler had instigated the ambush on Greg's team.

"Oh, yeah, Short Rick," Ryan said. They'd known three Ricks on that trip, the third being Bald Rick, one of their admin pukes.

"He's with me," Greg said.

"Cool, what's he been up to?"

"Flying helicopters in Key West when he wasn't chasing women."

"Sounds about right. Look, I can't dive until tomorrow when conditions improve. The current is ripping right now. I've got an idea on how to stop Kilroy, but I'm lacking on the details."

"Tell me. Let's work it out," Greg said, grabbing a soda from the fridge. He cracked it open and wheeled into the cockpit while Ryan recounted the events of the past few days and explained his plan.

"First thing I need to do is get a more help," Greg said. "Get the gold up and stall. I'll get there as fast as I can."

"Roger that," Ryan said.

Greg hung up the phone and scratched his jaw. He sat in the sunshine pondering the situation until he'd finished his soda, and then went back inside. He tapped the laptop to wake it up and pulled up a satellite tracking network. He input the name of the vessel he was searching for and was pleased to see *Alamo* was still in Guadeloupe. He made two calls before going down to the bunkroom and retrieving a metal case. With it on his lap, he wheeled out to the cockpit. Then he called Rick and told him to hustle back to the boat.

Two hours later, the two men were in a dark-blue Bell 407GXi helicopter. They skimmed along the clear blue ocean at one hundred and thirty-three knots. The owner, Max Weber, hadn't wanted to fly all the way to Guadeloupe and interrupt his scheduled day of sightseeing tours, but Greg had plied the man with money and promises of further use as a contract transporter for DWR operations in the area. This had brightened Max's otherwise dull day and he agreed to fly them personally. Rick had time in the Bell Jet Ranger, but the 407's avionics suite was distinctly different. He rode in the co-pilot's seat and watched the large LED screens in the dash. Greg sat in the back, beside his wheelchair, which they'd had to take apart to fit into the five-person cabin.

Another two hours and they were bearing down on the split between Grande-Terre and Basse-Terre, the two islands forming Guadeloupe. Max radioed ground control at Pointe-à-Pitre International Airport and they vectored in for a landing. Below them was what people pictured when they dreamed about the Caribbean, lush palms along brown sand beaches lapped by translucent blue water. Boats looked like they floated in air, casting shadows on the sand below. Greg made a mental note to bring Shelly here when they took a vacation, if he could drag her away from work.

"You're going to have to get a cab into town," Max said into the headset. "They won't let me land near the marina."

"Better to ask forgiveness than permission," Rick said.

"It's my bird, and I'm not having her impounded," Max replied, setting the chopper down on the tarmac.

"Fair enough," Rick said.

Rick helped Greg put together the wheelchair and get situated before they went to find a cab. Max stayed to fuel the helicopter for the return trip, which Greg had promised would happen in less than an hour. Rick carried the metal case with them through the surprisingly large airport. In front of the terminal, they hailed a cab. The cabbie stopped the taxi two feet from the curb. The old man jumped out and came around to open the trunk.

"Get in. Get in," he urged.

"Hey, buddy, you need to pull this rig right up to the curb. My boss needs to get in."

"No problem," the cabbie said. "He walk to car."

Rick clenched his fists. Greg's head lolled back, and he rolled his eyes.

"Are you an idiot? Pull the car right up to the curb." Rick pointed.

With a smile, the cabbie said, "No, he can walk like all other old people."

"Look, dumbass," Rick seethed.

Greg punched Rick in the hip to shut him up and said, "I'm a paraplegic. I can't walk. Please, pull a little further away from the curb so I can get down and into the car."

The cabbie looked between Rick and Greg, slammed the trunk, and ran around to the driver's seat. He jumped in and pulled away with a screech of tires. Greg and Rick stared in disbelief at the departing cab.

Another cabbie slid to a stop beside them, its tires squealing as they rubbed the curb. The man gestured for them to get in. Greg opened the front passenger door and tossed his legs into the footwell. Then he slid across to the seat. Rick disassembled the chair, putting the frame in the trunk and the wheels, cushion, and Greg's metal case beside him on the back seat.

"Pointe-à-Pitre Harbor," Greg said.

The man nodded and spoke a few words in Creole, neither of which Greg nor Rick understood. The cabbie pointed at the meter and rubbed his thumb and forefinger together. Greg held up a wad of euros. Dull yellow teeth appeared under the cabbie's dark fleshy lips and he gave them a thumbs up.

On the way through the twisting streets of the island's capital, the cabbie turned on the stereo. Katie Perry blasted from the speakers. The cabbie gave Greg another grin and a thumbs up before tapped the steering wheel in time to the music. Several songs later, and thirty-five euros lighter, Greg and Rick exited the cab and headed for the marina office.

"Does Mango know you're coming?" Rick asked.

"If he knew I was coming, he wouldn't be here," Greg said, giving his wheels another hard push.

"What makes you so sure that he's here?"

"I bugged his boat."

They walked past the marina office and followed the dock toward the glistening steel hull of the forty-four-foot Amazon, *Alamo*. When they came alongside the boat, Greg yelled, "Ahoy, the boat."

Mango Hulsey, clad in nothing but surf shorts, emerged from the main salon. "I'll be a monkey's uncle." He swung his muscular five-foot-ten-inch frame onto the dock and shook Greg's hand. His smile faded to a fearful expression. "What's wrong?"

"You name it," Greg said.

Mango ticked points off on his fingers. "Pirates, sharks, Kilroy, the cartel."

"Kilroy kidnapped Emily."

"That rotten son-of-a-bitch!"

"What's wrong, honey?" Jennifer asked, stepping into the cockpit. She was a head shorter than her husband, with dirty-blonde hair, watery green eyes, and a runner's physique. Her smile turned to a frown when she saw Greg.

"Can I buy you a drink?" Greg asked.

"Sure, I'll drink for free all day long. Come on, Jenn."

"Fine," she muttered. Jennifer locked the salon door, and they headed for the restaurant.

On the way, Mango asked, "Who's the bodyguard?"

"That's Short Rick." Greg hit the highlights of the man's service history.

"I'd ask why they call you Short Rick, but I think I already know."

"And I'll kick your ass if I hear you call me that again," Rick said.

"What's in the case?" Mango asked.

Greg replied, "A present for you."

"Are you trying to bribe me?"

"Nope, just a gift for a friend. Something another friend was working on and thought you might like."

They took seats at a table overlooking the crowded harbor. Rick put the case on the table and slid it across to Mango.

Mango undid the latches and opened the lid. "Whoa! That's awesome." He withdrew a prosthetic leg and held it up. A realistic silicone foot was attached to the tibia shaft. Mango massaged the foot, feeling the titanium bone structure underneath it. Hidden under the aluminum calf cover were miniature robotics, which replicated the movement of calf muscles, the Achilles tendon, and manipulated the foot bones.

Mango slipped off his below-the-knee prosthesis and started to pull on the new one.

"Wait a minute," Greg said. He turned the box and pulled out a rubber compression sleeve designed to fit over Mango's stump. "I was able to get my hands on the last mold of your leg and have it replicated for this one. This sock has electrical sensors sewn into it. They pick up the movement of your thigh and knee muscles and transmit them through the sleeve to receptacles in the prosthetic cup."

After pulling on the new sleeve, Mango tugged on the leg. "It's a little loose."

"It's supposed to be," Greg said, pulling a small hand pump from the box.

Mango fitted the pump to where Greg indicated on the leg and inflated the ballistic nylon air cells around his stump. The tiny imbedded circuits in the air cells mated with the ones on the sleeve.

"There's more adjustments you can make to it," Greg said. "There's a manual in the box."

Mango stood up and began pacing up and down the bar area. "Holy cow, this thing is awesome, bro!"

Jennifer sat with her chin on her hands, watching her husband jump up and down, something which would be perilous at best with his old prosthetic.

"The toes spread out when I land," Mango said. He sat down and flexed his calf and knee muscles, watching the robotics in the leg and foot respond. "This thing is unbelievable."

Jennifer looked over at Greg. "I know you didn't come all this way to give my husband a new leg. What's Ryan gotten himself into now?"

Greg smiled. *There was no fooling her. She's always been shrewd. She and Emily are friends and that's my advan-*

tage. When their drinks arrived, he explained to her about Emily. He felt he had the best shot at getting Mango's help if Jennifer was onboard. "Kilroy wants to trade Emily for the gold," Greg said to finish his monologue.

"When are we leaving?" Jennifer asked.

Greg smiled. "Pack a bag, the helicopter is waiting."

"Are you sure, Jenn?" Mango asked.

Jennifer Hulsey stood. "I'm going to pack. Emily needs our help."

Mango followed her down the dock while Greg and Rick remained at the table, nursing their drinks.

Thirty minutes later, the Hulseys were back at the bar, bags in hand.

"I assume you have toys with you?" Mango said to Greg.

"Accuracy International suit your fancy?"

Mango grinned at the mention of the bolt-action sniper rifle. "It'll be like spooning with an old friend."

"Hey, watch it, mister." Jennifer slugged her husband in the arm.

Greg was another fifty euros lighter by the time they reached the helicopter. The whole trip had been expensive, renting the bird, Mango's new leg, and paying for two weeks of dock space at the marina for *Alamo*. It was all right, he reasoned. As Ryan's benefactor, he was getting a cut of the gold. He rubbed his hands together as the bird took off and headed north.

CHAPTER TWENTY-SEVEN

By the time *Peggy Lynn* arrived over the dive site, *Northwest Passage* was already nearby, and two other cabin cruisers full of Joulie's men circled the area, acting as guards to keep away would-be pirates and gawkers. Ryan Weller was also dressed and ready to dive. The salvage vessel nosed into two-foot waves and Dennis kept the throttles forward just enough to hold them in place over the wreck.

"Send the LARS after I'm down," Ryan said. The dive plan called for him to go straight to the chamber to complete his decompression schedule, and he didn't want to waste his limited bottom time riding the LARS.

"Roger that," Emery said through the helmet radio.

Ryan tugged at the umbilical to give himself some slack and stepped up on the rail. "Ready to dive."

Captain Dennis said, "Dive, dive, dive."

Ryan stepped out into the ocean. He plunged into the water, an explosion of bubbles enveloping him. At fifteen feet, the umbilical stopped him, and he did his in-water checks. With them complete, Emery began paying out line, and Ryan dropped into the haze.

Where's that grinning beast? he wondered, twisting to look for the tiger shark.

His boots settled into the ooze beside the Humvee. The storm hadn't moved it but one of the Humvees that had been chained to the deck was now lying upside down at the entrance to the hold. Ryan maneuvered around it and made his way toward the first spot where Ashlee's algorithm had indicated the gold might be found. After winding his way through the carnage, he found the first spot. The strong box wasn't there.

The next spot was the correct one. Ryan lay flat on his stomach and shone his light under the pile of vehicles. The rusty box was still strapped to a broken pallet, sandwiched between two MRAPs and a Humvee.

"There it is," Ryan said. He stood and played his light along the sweeping curve of the hull and up the deck. There was another Humvee strapped to the deck, twenty feet above him. "What do you think?"

Travis and Dennis huddled around the computer screen, watching the video feed.

"Can we get a winch on the box and drag it out?" Dennis asked.

"Maybe," Ryan replied. "We need to take some weight off it." He turned to look for a place to attach a come-along cable puller. "We can wrap a strap around the bumper of that MRAP."

"Turn back around and shine the light on the other vehicles," Travis ordered.

Ryan complied and ran the cone of light along the tangle of steel.

"We could put a couple of lift bags on that Humvee and

lift the front of it on a pivot," Travis said. "That would free the box and let us drag it out."

"Sounds like a good idea," Ryan said.

"That would work," Dennis agreed.

Ryan made his way back to the first strong box. "We can use another come-along to pull this MRAP over."

"We'll do that first," Travis said. "If I remember right, we can move the MRAP and the first strong box, then we'll have an easier path to the second."

"It'll take two of us to do the work," Ryan said.

"Yes, it will," Dennis agreed. "We need to anchor this tub. I'll have Emery drop a chain. Can you attach it to one of the crane cables?"

"Yeah, send down some cable clamps for an inch-and-a-quarter cable."

"Copy," Dennis said. "The chain will have a lift bag attached to one end. Shoot it when you have everything attached."

"Roger," Ryan replied.

He made his way out of the wreck and heard the muffled sounds of the diesels laboring in the waves. A few minutes later, he heard Emery say, "Coming hot!"

The chain landed in a tangle, fifty feet from the cable Ryan had determined would work best for their situation. It was still attached to the crane's winch drum, and the cable's bitter end had been bolted to the *Santo Domingo*'s deck to keep it from running completely off the drum if the drum brake slipped. He walked over to the chain and found a small kit bag attached to one end. Inside were the cable clamps, wrenches, and a clevis pin. He bent the loose end of the cable around a thimble and crimped it to the main part of the cable with a clamp. Careful to monitor his breathing, Ryan worked steadily. If he started breathing heavily, he might over breathe the gas coming through the lines, causing a buildup of carbon dioxide inside the helmet. If it got bad enough, he could pass out from lack of oxygen.

He used four cable clamps to crimp the loop into place and tightened them with the wrench. Sweat rolled down his forehead and dripped off his eyebrows. Reflexively, he brought his hand up to wipe it away and forgot his head was encased in the helmet. He blinked back the water stinging his eyes.

Ryan attached the chain to the crane cable with the clevis pin. The thimble would prevent the clevis pin from wearing on the cable as it jerked around in time with the motion of the vessel on the surface. When he had the clevis pin screwed into the U-shaped clevis, he slid a cotter pin into the hole to keep the pin from worming its way out, then he walked over to the lift bag. He used his bailout bottle to inject just enough gas to get the chain to rise. He stepped back to avoid being tangled in the chain and cable rode while he tilted his head to watch the bag drag the cable up through the water column. With each foot the bag rose, the air inside it would expand. What had been a tiny balloon at the bottom would be a massive ball at the surface. As the air expanded, the speed of the bag's ascent would also increase. A safety relief valve would prevent the bag from overinflating. Normally, a diver would ascend with the bag to control it, but Ryan didn't have that luxury.

"You'll have to grade this one on speed and distance out of the water," Ryan said.

"Should shoot out about five or six feet," Travis said. "We sent Stacey and Don out in the inflatable to collect the bag before it collapses."

"All right," Ryan said. "Ready to come up."

After his ten-minute stop at one seventy-five, Ryan was

quickly reeled in. He entered the chamber two minutes after he surfaced.

Through the small window, he watched Travis finish gearing up. He'd been Ryan's safety diver and only needed his hat snugged down to the neck ring and topside checks ran. Travis carried an assortment of tools on his belt and gave Ryan the hang-loose hand gesture before jumping over the side. Ryan lay down on the bench, closed his eyes, and started his breathing exercises. Three counts in, pause, four out.

CHAPTER TWENTY-EIGHT

Travis Wisnewski felt the crush of pressure as he dropped through the water column. This was his third dive on the wreck. So far it had been one of the easier salvage jobs he'd worked on. The sea temperatures were moderate, and he didn't require heated or cooled water to be pumped through his suit. Visibility was nearly thirty feet outside the wreck and would expand as the seas moderated. What light that did filter down through the water was augmented by his powerful dive lights. Today, he'd forgone the dry gloves and wore a pair of white cotton with blue latex on the palms and fingers. The rubber made a solid grip on the light switch as he flicked it on.

He stood outside the hull, looking at the sea life slowly attaching itself to the steel. Small, wispy beards of growth swung in the current. A school of black drums hovered nearby. It was nice to see life on the wreck. "Let's do this."

He worked his way to the MRAP hiding the first strong box, climbed another MRAP that the first was leaning on, and began to work a thick nylon strap around the tow hooks on the first truck's rear bumper. He latched the come-along hook to the strap and spooled out the cable as he jumped off the MRAP. He landed with a soft thud on the steel hull and walked toward another MRAP they'd identified as their anchor while studying the video footage.

The come-along's cable didn't stretch all the way to the anchor. Travis dropped the come-along and pulled another strap from his pouch. He stepped forward to secure it to the anchor MRAP. As he started to feed the strap through the truck's bumper hook, he spotted a tie-down chain hanging from a padeye in the hull's deck. He grabbed the chain and put both hooks on the padeye, fed the nylon strap through the chain loop and then stretched the strap between the come-along and the tie-down chain.

"Is that gonna hold?" Dennis asked.

"Guess we'll find out," Travis said, sweeping the camera along the length of the taut cable. He grabbed the come-along handle and began to ratchet it back and forth to crank in the cable. The big troop transporter shifted forward, the bumper sliding on the slick steel. The rear stayed just past vertical, leaning away from Travis. He continued to ratchet the handle back and forth. Slowly, the big vehicle slid forward until the front bumper hit one of the ship's ribs. Blocked from sliding, the MRAP's rear came forward, passed vertical, and fell in slow motion.

Travis sprung back, tugging his umbilical out of the way. A giant cloud of silt billowed up as the MRAP landed on its top.

"Five minutes," Emery said.

"Copy that," Travis replied. He waded into the silt bloom, angling for the strong box.

Through the swirling particulate, his lights found the gleam of gold. He gasped when he saw the pile of bullion spilling out of the strong box. He picked up two bars, weighing them in his hands. "Yeah, baby! This is what we came for."

He knelt and began stacking the gold on the deck outside the box. They would need to right the box and fix the latches before reloading it. He'd held the gold bar Ryan had brought up, but holding these was euphoric. Nothing he'd ever salvaged had given him this kind of an adrenaline rush. The doubts that had plagued him throughout the job, and the arguments with Ryan, washed away in his elation.

"Get out of there, Travis," Emery said.

"I'm coming, Grandpa," he said. Quickly, he shoved two bars into the pockets of his BCD. These were his, payment for services rendered.

Travis spent most of his three hours of deco time sitting in the LARS basket, staring at the two gold bars. At twenty feet, he could easily see Ryan sitting on the rail. He waited until Ryan looked down and stretched his arms over his head, the gold bars held in each hand like a conqueror.

CHAPTER TWENTY-NINE

By late afternoon, the waves had lessened to a foot in height. The weather service was calling for smooth conditions for the next four days. Ryan mounted the steps from the galley followed by Travis, Stacey, Don, Dennis, and Emery. They'd all pitched in to clean up after supper. Ryan walked to the dressing bench and sat down. He started pulling on his drysuit undergarments. Travis did the same. They would dive together with Dennis as the standby.

The men dressed with minimal conversation. They'd already discussed how they would recover the boxes. Stacey and Emery helped clamp their helmets into place and perform topside checks. Each stood, the heavy weight of the gear making the walk to the LARS cumbersome. They stepped into the basket, barely big enough for both, and Dennis raised it with the crane and swung them out over the water. He pressed the lever forward, and the spool began to unwind, dropping the men into the abyss.

It didn't take long for them to reach the bottom. Their lights slashed horizontal beams in the pitch-black water.

Ryan climbed up the basket and removed the hook. He laid the crane cable over his shoulder and they moved into the hull, heading for the second box of gold. As they walked past the stack of gold bricks sitting beside the overturned box, Travis swept his light over them, letting their gleam energize both men.

"Ready to tar paper?" Ryan asked.

"It's *give 'em tar paper*. Get it right, eh?"

Ryan laughed. "I'll wrap, you crank, Yupper."

"Roger that," Travis said, finding a padeye to attach his come-along.

Ryan climbed onto the MRAP and attached his strap to the bumper tow hook. He took the come-along hook Travis held up to him and fastened it to the strap. They cranked the MRAP off the Humvee and left it suspended by the come-along. Ryan grabbed several loose tie-down chains and linked them together to attach the MRAP to the hull. They were able to ease the tension off the come-along. Travis unhooked it from the hull and the strap.

Moving to the Humvee, Ryan took another strap and worked it around the strong box. He had to lie under the Humvee and pass it to Travis, who looped it back to him. Travis passed him the hook of the come-along and he attached it to the strap. Travis hooked the come-along to a nearby MRAP. They extracted lift bags from their work pouches and tied them to the Humvee's front bumper with short pieces of rope. To coordinate the lift, and keep the Humvee level, they slowly added air to the bags.

"Takes a lot of air to lift a Humvee at three hundred and fifty feet," Travis said.

"More than I figured," Ryan replied.

"A little bit more. She's starting to rise."

Ryan pointed at the come-along. "Get ready to crank."

Travis scrambled back to the winch handle and increased the tension on the box. It didn't move.

"A little more," Travis said.

"Copy that." Ryan triggered another burst of air into the lift bag. They'd kept the air in the bags even until now. He didn't want to hop back and forth over the come-along wire to add air to both bags. "I'll add air to the driver's side. If it becomes unbalanced, hopefully it'll tip to the side and take the weight off."

Travis cranked the handle again as he saw the Humvee pivot on the box. "Just a hair more."

Ryan added another burst of air. The Humvee tilted precariously toward the passenger side.

"You gotta balance it out," Travis shouted.

"I know. I know." Ryan stepped over the cable, careful to not get his feet or umbilical tangled in the tight line. He added air to the passenger side lift bag. The frontend rose, stabilizing the Humvee. Ryan bent to look at the box. The strong box lay on its side with the pallet it was strapped to wedged in the undercarriage of the Humvee. "That pallet won't let the box come out."

Travis dropped to his knees to examine the situation. "Give it some more air."

"Screw that. Give me the crane hook."

Travis hauled the hook over to the Humvee and passed it to Ryan, who had wiggled under the Humvee and was lying beside the strong box.

Once he had the hook looped in the cargo strap, Ryan said, "Dennis, get ready to pull."

"Roger."

Ryan moved out of the way and gave the command. It took several seconds for the slack to be pulled in and then the cable jerked taut.

"Pull," Ryan said.

They could hear the wood render and snap as the pallet broke free. The strong box slid out from under the Humvee.

"Hold," Travis said, and the box stopped moving.

"Get the lift bags," Ryan said.

"Five minutes, boys," Emery warned.

While Travis deflated the bags, Ryan removed the rest of the pallet from the strong box and wrapped the box with a strap like a Christmas ribbon around the four sides of a present. He worked three clevis pins into the webbing, one on the front and one on each side of the box. He attached the crane cable to the front and the lift bags to the sides. They filled the bags until the box began to rise.

"Dennis, we gotta move slow. We have the box supported by the lift bags. You're going to pull it out of the hull."

"You got two minutes, Ryan."

"Damnit, Emery, we know."

"I understand," Dennis said. "Just keep talking to me."

Ryan took a breath to calm himself. He understood the time constraints, but he also wanted to get the job done. "Slack in."

Dennis began retracting the cable. The box floated along the ship's hull.

"Emery, pull in some of our umbilical slack, so we don't foul the crane," Travis said.

"Copy."

Ryan continued to narrate their movements for Dennis as they moved the box closer to the hold's entrance. "Pause, we need to lift the box over a rib." They increased the air in the lift bags just enough to clear the rib.

"Slack in," Ryan said.

"We're not going to clear that gap, Ryan," Travis said as they approached a tangle of Humvees and MRAPs.

"Let's go up." They added more air and climbed over the vehicles as the crane dragged the box.

"How much longer?" Emery asked.

"Not much," Ryan said. "Don, run some new deco numbers."

"Roger," Don said.

DWR had sent along one of their new computer programs, allowing them to accurately calculate decompression times and gas blends for any depth and bottom time a diver might accumulate.

They continued working the strong box out of the hold. Once it was clear of the ship, they dropped the strong box into the dirt, deflated the lift bags, and moved the crane cable back to the LARS. Don had the calculations run before they started up. Their extra five minutes of bottom time to extract the box had added another hour of deco.

"Do you want to do it in the chamber or in the water?" Ryan asked Travis.

"It's easier to sleep in the chamber."

"Chamber it is. You heard the man, Emery."

"Will do," Emery said.

They stopped at one seventy-five. Ryan said, "Easier than we thought."

Travis shook his head inside his hat. "We'd have been there a lot longer if you hadn't used the crane cable."

"Sometimes brute force is better than finesse."

"Did you learn that in bomb disposal, eh?"

"No." Ryan grinned. "Construction."

CHAPTER THIRTY

Mango Hulsey rocked forward on the balls of his feet, compensating for the roll of the Hatteras beneath him. He still couldn't believe the flexibility and fit of the new leg. The tiny servo motors accommodated his movements thousands of times a minute as his muscles reacted to changing conditions. As real as the leg felt, it was nothing like the real thing, and occasionally, the phantom pains and feelings from the lost leg still triggered inside his brain.

He still remembered the burning sensation as the Coast Guard's rubber boarding craft pinned his leg to the steel hull of the freighter. Four-foot waves had made the boarding operation difficult, and he'd jumped for the Jacob's ladder, knowing it was a bad idea before he consciously made the decision to leap. His hands had grasped the rope solidly, but his foot slipped, and the boats had collided with his leg acting as the bumper.

The impact had crushed his foot, ankle, and the lower part of his tibia and fibula. They'd medevacked to the Navy base in Bahrain, then flown him to Germany. Surgeons at the massive Landstuhl Regional Medical Center had made the decision to amputate, believing they couldn't save the crushed bones. It still pissed him off that they didn't bother to try, even though he'd seen the X-rays and knew his bones were jelly.

At the time, Mango was serving with the Coast Guard's Maritime Security Response Team. Within the special force, he'd worked in both the Direct Action Section, assaulting and boarding ships, and as a sniper in the Precision Marksman Observer Team. He'd loved his time as a sniper. Once he'd lost his leg, the Coast Guard deemed him unfit to return to combat or to deploy to a ship, and they'd retired him. Mango had filed multiple appeals to the decision but was unable to convince the system to allow him to even return to an administrative role. In the end, he and Jennifer had moved to her hometown, Port Aransas, Texas.

He sprawled out on *Dark Water*'s bridge roof, sliding the Accuracy International AXMC rifle into the crook of his shoulder, his right hand naturally finding the pistol grip. He entwined his left arm in the sling to provide stabilization to the bipod. He breathed out and closed his eyes. The old feeling was back, a tingling at the base of his skull. He ran his tongue across his lips and opened his right eye, peering down the magnifying lenses of the Nightforce scope. This was the moment he lived for. *How could I hide from this?*

Greg had brought an AXMC chambered in Mango's favored round: .338 Lapua. The gun had undergone extensive modifications to the stock, trigger, and barrel. The most obvious was the long black suppressor. Mango worked his elbow into the sling, feeling the gun butt bite deep into the meat of his shoulder, marrying him to composite and steel, and forming an extension of his body. He focused on the rhythm of his heartbeat, his breathing, the shift and roll of the boat beneath him. It was all part of his process, each element adding information to his mind. The drop of the bullet over distance, the effect of the wind, the resistance of humidity, all calculated into the science of a long-distance shot.

Through the scope, he found the white jug they'd dropped earlier. It bobbed in the water two hundred yards off the starboard bow. Mango adjusted his body. He'd been through the gun, tightening scope rings, cleaning components, polishing the burs off the action, checking each bullet before thumbing it into the magazine. Now, it was time to see how the gun performed. It was his opinion that a clean barrel would change the flight characteristics of a bullet. After the first bullet had filled the pits and imperfections of the rifling with lead and copper, the following shots would be more accurate, spinning the bullet in a tighter flight pattern. This was why he was popping a few holes in the jug. He wanted the gun to be slightly fouled, and he wanted to understand the rifle's intricacies. If Emily or Ryan's life depended on his shooting, he needed to know exactly what he was dealing with.

Sweat beaded on his back, the ghostly breeze fanning his face. Even though the ocean was calm, the boat still shifted with the water's movements. He forced himself to concentrate on the tiny white dot swaying in the water. His finger removed the trigger's slack, bringing it against the mechanism which would snap the firing pin. Four pounds of pressure. Squeeze, squeeze, squeeze, BANG. The gun jumped and settled. Mango saw the jug had spun in the water, meaning he'd hit close to one of its edges.

"Hit," Greg said. He was watching the jug through a pair of binoculars. "A click to the left."

Mango made an adjustment to the scope. He settled in

again, concentrating on the jug. The jug didn't move with the next hit.

"Dead center."

Mango's third, fourth, and fifth shots perforated the jug in a circle around the second shot.

"Good shooting, buddy," Rick said, taking the big rifle while Mango slid off the roof and hopped down the ladder to the cockpit. Rick handed the gun down from the bridge to Mango. He took it into the cabin and stowed it in its case.

"Now what?" Jennifer asked when Mango returned from the stateroom.

"We wait for Ryan to contact us," Mango said.

Jennifer shook her head, rolled her eyes, and muttered, "I knew that guy was trouble the moment we met him."

Mango shrugged.

"Don't you stick up for him either." Jennifer leveled an accusatory finger at him. "You two are peas in a pod." Turning to a grinning Rick, she said, "Every one of you special operators are special all right, *touched in the head* special."

Rick laughed. "Come on, pea, let's go hang out in the pod."

They climbed the ladder to the bridge. Mango felt his new foot grip each rung and provide him with a stable purchase. He didn't have to worry about wedging it into the corner of the rung and side rail to prevent him from slipping. On the bridge, Greg had the big boat idling beside the plastic jug used for target practice. Jennifer fished it out with a boat hook and Greg swung the Hatteras toward Cap-Haïtien. He pointed at a cluster of boats on the horizon off the port side. "Looks like Kilroy's boat."

Mango picked up the binoculars and trained them on the vessels. "That's *Northwest Passage*, all right. Looks like two other little boats and a converted trawler with a red hull.

"The converted trawler is *Peggy Lynn*, the salvage boat. The others must be the security boats Joulie put out."

"She's not worried about her own people stealing the gold?" Rick asked.

"Are you kidding?" Greg asked. "*Northwest* and *Peggy* probably have more fire power on them than those other two boats combined. Plus, Joulie would roast them alive if she even thought they were trying to steal the gold."

"She would, too," Mango said.

"This chick must be pretty badass," Rick mused.

"Joulie united two warring factions," Greg said. "The woman knows how to get things done."

Mango took the field glasses down. "Let's hope she agrees to help us out."

CHAPTER THIRTY-ONE

Bubbles rushed up around the two divers as the LARS dropped into the water. Water clarity had improved overnight, and the chop had flattened out into little wavelets. With the improved weather had come heat. The water was cooler than the early morning air by five degrees, but it was still like sinking into bathwater.

Ryan glanced over at Travis, who had beads of sweat lining his upper lip and brow. "Can't wait to hit the thermocline."

"Me, too," Travis agreed.

The few degrees drop in water temperature would feel good. Puddles of sweat sloshed against Ryan's skin where the neck dam had trapped them. He shut off the defogger system now that the face plate had cleared up. His undergarments were wet with perspiration and felt clammy against his skin under the drysuit.

They rode the rest of the way in silence, each man dealing with his diving physiology in his own way. When the LARS settled in the muck on the seabed, they clamored into the *Santo Domingo*.

"Where're you going? The box is over there." Travis pointed.

"I've got something to take care of in the bow. Start on the gold and I'll be there in a few minutes."

Travis put his hands on his hips. "I'm done. We get this gold out of here and I'm on a plane to someplace sane."

"Suit yourself," Ryan said, walking toward the bow. "Just do your job."

He maneuvered himself through the forward hold and into the bow proper. Crushed ribs, mangled struts, and smashed pieces of hull made it hard to discern what had been where. Wilky Ador's two rocket-propelled grenades had done the job Ryan had planned for the EFPs. He traced the detonator wires from the hold door. He had to get down on his belly and work his way under a jagged piece of metal.

"What the hell are you doing, son," Dennis asked, staring at the camera footage being transmitted topside.

"Gotta take care of something." Ryan maneuvered through the debris until he could slip under the forward hold. He kept tugging at his umbilical to ensure it wasn't getting snagged, chafed, or cut.

"You're about out of cord, boy," Emery said.

"Yeah, hold on, Grandpa, I'm almost there." Ryan could see one of the capped sections of pipe he'd used to build the EFPs. With the ship on its side, it now dangled by its det wire from an overhead rib. The other EFP was nowhere to be seen. Ryan shimmied farther into the bowels of the ship. He stretched out his arm. His fingertips brushed against the short section of six-inch round pipe with a cover bolted to its flange. But he couldn't get close enough to grab it. The bailout bottle, strapped to his back, prevented him from sliding deeper into the ship. He dropped his helmet to the deck, face squishing into the rubber oral nasal mask. Closing his eyes, he silently let out a string of curses.

Ryan lifted his head and looked at the bomb. It was critical to his plan. He shoved himself forward; the bailout smacked the deck plating. He'd have to remove it, and that would cost him time. Backing out of the hole, he felt a stab in his thigh. *The bang stick!* He rolled enough to slide the four-foot-long metal rod out of his tool belt and reached out to snag the det wire. He caught the wire with the cotter pin, which held the power head on the pole. He pulled the EFP to him and clipped the detonator wire with a pair of side cuts. He backed out of the hole, dragging his bomb, and made his way to where Travis was methodically stacking bricks.

Ryan laid the EFP beside the stack and pitched in to help. They righted the box and began restacking the nineteen bars back inside.

"Looks like we're missing a couple," Travis said.

"You and I took three up and Kilroy has one. Who knows where the hurricane moved the rest?"

"Neptune's payment," Travis said as he closed the lid. He and Ryan used two straps to wrap the box securely, so the top wouldn't fall open again. They used lift bags and the crane cable to move the box outside the *Santo Domingo* and set it beside its mate.

"Twenty million," Travis said, patting the box.

"Give or take with the missing bars," Ryan said. "Tomorrow, you'll get your payday and you can get out of here."

"I was spouting off, eh." Travis clapped Ryan on the shoulder. "What the hell is that thing?" He pointed at the metal pipe in Ryan's hand.

Ryan set the EFP on top of the strong boxes. "A bomb."

"A what!"

"Trust me," Ryan said, with a grin. "I'm an expert."

CHAPTER THIRTY-TWO

E mily Hunt was in her stateroom on *Northwest Passage*, one of the nicest she'd ever seen on a boat with custom-fitted rose wood panels, a queen-size bed fitted with Egyptian cotton sheets, granite on the bathroom vanity counter, and a tiled shower. Kilroy had given her a tour of the ship and explained how it had once been a crab boat operating in the Bering Sea off the Alaskan coast. After the owners had financial difficulties, they'd put it up for sale. Kilroy purchased it for much less than the asking price by offering them cash, then converted the boat into a luxury exploration vehicle. The luxury didn't comfort Emily or ease her mind. She felt like a trapped rat, sniffing the corners of its box, and peering up walls too slick to climb.

Kilroy had offered her free reign of the ship, but she'd sequestered herself in the small cabin. Her view of the outside world consisted of a porthole. Through the round glass, she could see sunlight reflecting off dazzling azure water, and nothing else. She turned away from the endless view of blue horizon and leaned against the wall.

Slowly, she allowed herself to sink to the polished hardwood floor. Emily hugged her knees to her chest. It had been two days since they'd eaten dinner at the Hotel Roi Christophe, and she'd tapped out an S-O-S on Ryan's leg.

Emily whispered his name and shivered. She was unsure if it was from the blast of frigid air from the air-conditioning vent, or the memory of her former lover. She'd stuffed her feelings deep inside and tried to move on. Here she was again, a pawn in Ryan Weller's life. She hated sitting in this room, waiting for him to rescue her. Yet, she knew he would come. He had told her he was coming. She knew the stubbornness that drove him to a life of action would be the stubbornness that drove him to rescue her, no matter what the stakes.

"Never again," she chastised herself softly. Never again would she be so vulnerable. The gun had been so close, and she'd chosen pepper spray. She'd accused Ryan of being insensitive and paranoid for giving her a snubnosed revolver as a present. Now she saw it as a prudent gift.

After being abused by James, she'd nailed her heart shut to prevent more pain. Ryan had pried it loose. Or she had allowed it. She wasn't sure which.

Emily cursed herself for falling down this rabbit hole again. Since the two men had burst into her apartment, she'd had to force herself to stop playing the what-if and the should-have game multiple times a day. They were the laments of fools. She knew she wasn't a fool, but here she was pining for a man who was clearly not good for her.

A sharp knock on the door quickened her heartbeat. Before she could ask who was there, the door opened, and Jim Kilroy stepped into the room. When he saw her sitting on the floor, he asked, "Are you all right, my dear?"

"Yes." She nodded, wanting to scream, "*No, asshole, you kidnapped me.*"

He stepped over to her and extended his hand. "Come outside, the sunshine will make you feel better."

Emily did not grasp his hand. Instead, she placed hers against the wall, using them to push up and unfold her long body. In bare feet, she stood five-feet-ten inches, two inches taller than Kilroy. She wondered if he felt inferior. In hindsight, it was a problem James had dealt with and one of the many reasons he had for abusing her. Her natural height intimidated shorter men.

Kilroy smiled up at her. "This will soon be over. Your boyfriend will recover my gold."

Rather than continue to correct him on the point that Ryan was not her boyfriend, Emily gave him a patronizing smile.

"Come, join us outside." Kilroy walked to the door and stopped. He turned to face her. "We'll have a toast to celebrate our good fortune. Me, for becoming richer, and you for regaining your freedom."

"A bit premature isn't it?" she asked, following him onto the main deck.

"There's nothing wrong with a celebration."

"I find it is better to celebrate after achieving one's goals."

Kilroy smiled. "A wise decision. Tonight, then, we'll celebrate our good fortune to be alive."

A shiver coursed through Emily's body despite the warmth of the sunshine. *Good fortune to be alive?*

"Mista Kilroy," Damian shouted from the bridge. "Dar's a boat comin'."

Kilroy bounded up the stairs to the bridge, taking them two at a time, hands gripping the railing for support. Emily followed at a slower pace, turning halfway up to see the boat.

"It's the same center console they used to change the guards," Kilroy said, watching the boat approach from the south. It slowed as it came alongside one of the guard boats.

Emily couldn't see what they were doing. She glanced up at Kilroy, who watched intently through binoculars. She turned back to the boat when its engine revved and it sped toward the second guard boat. Idly, she pondered how Kilroy planned to evade the Haiti warlord, and how friendly Ryan was with her.

"It's nothing." Kilroy handed the binoculars back to Damian. "Come, Emily, let's have that drink."

CHAPTER THIRTY-THREE

Ryan Weller lay in the bottom of the center console speeding away from the larger cabin cruiser being used by Joulie's men as a picket boat. He glanced around at the boat's interior. What had once been white fiberglass was now cracked, yellowed, and stained. He could smell old fish guts, rotten chum, and the ripe body odor of men who'd spent all day in the hot equatorial sun.

He'd slipped over the side of *Peggy Lynn*, with his rebreather on, and swam a plotted course to the nearest guard boat. After reaching it, he'd clung to the side of the cruiser until the center console had arrived with the night shift. Blocked from the view of *Northwest Passage*, he'd clambered into the arriving boat while the other men transferred back and forth. He'd taken his gear off once he was in the center console.

"You can get up now, Mista Ryan," the driver called over the noise of the rushing wind created by the boat's thirty-knot speed.

Thankfully, Ryan climbed to his feet and let the wind blow away the stench. He held onto the aluminum tubing supporting the small cover over the console. Behind them, the cluster of boats was no longer visible. To the right, the sun set in a splendid array of yellows, oranges, and reds.

A sailor's delight, Ryan thought.

Forty minutes later, Ryan stepped onto the dock at Billy Parker's small marina. He was busy grabbing gear being handed to him by the young boat driver when he felt a hand on his back, gently pushing him toward the water. He pivoted on his right foot, keeping his weight centered on the boards. His hand shot out and grabbed the wrist of the person who had been pushing him. Instinctively, he jerked backward to throw his assailant into the water. He'd anticipated using his inertia to gain an advantage on the other man, but his movement met with resistance and he found himself hanging precariously over the edge of the dock. He teetered on the balls of his feet, one arm spinning in circles to keep his balance and the other hand still clamped around Greg's wrist.

"Should I let him go?" Greg asked.

"Dump him, bro," Mango said.

Ryan saw his friend was clinging to one of the piers with his other hand, preventing Ryan from catapulting him into the water.

The pressure on Greg's wrist increased as Ryan fought to keep from falling into the water. Boisterous laughter filled the air as the men on the center console watched Ryan flail his loose arm. Greg pulled back in a bicep curl. Ryan's body eased forward and he regained his balance. Greg shoved his arm back straight, and Ryan desperately grabbed for Greg's wrist with his free hand to keep himself from falling into the water. Everyone was laughing now. Greg jerked him back upright.

"You should have dumped him," Rick said.

Ryan let go of Greg's wrist after regaining his balance. "You could have gone in the water."

Greg chuckled. "But I didn't. You're the one who almost went swimming."

"Your gear, Mista Ryan," the boat driver said, still laughing and shaking his head as he set the final items on the dock.

Ignoring the continued chuckles, Ryan told the driver, "Be back here after dark." He wasn't looking forward to the boat ride or the swim back to the *Peggy Lynn*. Weariness had already set in from the long day.

"*Wi.*" The boat driver tossed off the lines and drove away.

"You're going back out tonight?" Greg asked.

"Yeah," Ryan said. "I want to dive early." He stepped around Greg and gave a hug to Mango and to Jennifer. He shook Rick's hand before squatting by his gear.

"Your friend is waiting in the office," Greg said.

Ryan glanced up from wrapping his mask and fins in the harness of the rebreather and saw the blue Toyota RAV4 beside the nondescript marina office building. "I suppose Mango already took her out for drinks." Ryan grinned up at Mango and then glanced at Jennifer.

Jennifer furrowed her brow and crossed her arms. "Is there something you want to tell me, Mango?"

"No, baby," he said, holding up his hands, palms out in defense. "She needed a shoulder to lean on in the Bahamas. Since Ryan was raving drunk, she talked to me. I told you this already."

Jennifer cocked her head a little further and continued giving her husband the evil eye.

Greg said, "Mango was a perfect gentleman. He only has eyes for you."

"He better," she said.

After Ryan stowed his gear in a locker in *Dark Water*'s cockpit, they walked as a group to the small office. Billy Parker held the door open while they filed in. He held up a stack of entrance forms, which Greg had already filled out. "Boy, you sure are filling the government's coffers with all these comin's and goin's."

With seven people in the small office, it was crowded. Joulie said, "We need some privacy, Billy."

"Yeah, yeah, yeah." He waved her off and shuffled over to a small glass front refrigerator. He plucked a bottle of Prestige from it and then went out the front door. "I'll stand guard," he muttered as the door swung closed. They could hear him grumbling to himself as he walked off.

"What's the plan?" Greg asked.

Ryan maneuvered to the fridge and passed out beers to the others before opening his own. He found himself standing beside Joulie. "Our fearless warlord, here, has appropriated half of the gold for herself. If she will graciously allow me to use both strong boxes to negotiate for the release of Miss Hunt, I would be eternally grateful, and I promise to fulfill the requirements of our prearranged agreement."

Joulie Lafitte was a master at manipulating her features. Ryan had witnessed the full range of her skills. She could look at a man with such a genuine desire that he would be forever smitten, and she could make a man want to commit murder for her with a single glance. Even with her mastery of emotional disguise, she was unable to hide the widening of her eyes when Ryan asked to use her gold to rescue Emily.

She stared into Ryan's eyes and said, "You may use my gold to rescue your girlfriend. If you double-cross me, the bounty the Mexicans have on you will look like a pittance compared to what I offer."

He decided her answer was a retort for feeling slighted. *Why wouldn't she*, he thought. *She thinks she's in competition with Emily.*

"You bartered away your gold?" Greg asked.

Not taking his eyes off Joulie, Ryan said, "It had to be done."

"You're going to turn over the gold to Kilroy, and then what?" Mango asked.

Ryan sat on the edge of Billy Parker's desk. He took a swallow of beer to ease the lump in his throat. It was like a pill he couldn't get to go down. His throat had been sore since he'd seen Emily sitting at the table beside Jim Kilroy. "When Mango and I were on the *Santo Domingo*, I built two EFPs to sink it."

Jennifer tapped Mango on his shoulder and asked, "What's an EFP?"

Despite her whisper, everyone in the room heard her.

Ryan said, "It's a bomb."

"Oh," she said, her mouth forming a little circle.

"On our last dive, I pulled one of the EFPs out of the wreck," Ryan said. "I'm going to put it on *Northwest Passage*."

"How?" Rick asked.

"That's the tricky part. I need to convince Kilroy to move his ship to another location. I want us to be in shallow water when we do the transfer. I also need to attach the EFP before we make the swap for Emily."

Greg crossed his arms as he asked, "Did you figure out a way to attach the EFP?"

"I had Don build electromagnets using microwave oven coils and a motorcycle battery. The magnets should be strong enough to hold the EFP in place long enough for the C-4 to shove the penetrator through the hull."

Rick asked, "Would the explosion rip the canister off before the penetrator can form?"

"Maybe," Ryan said. "Even if it does, the steam void should break the hull and sink the ship."

Greg nodded in agreement.

Jennifer again whispered to Mango, "What's a steam void?"

"I'll tell you later," he whispered back, not wanting to miss any of the conversation.

Joulie asked, "My gold will be on Kilroy's ship when it goes down?"

"Unfortunately, yes," Ryan said. "That's why I want to do the transfer in shallow water. We can use scuba gear to recover the strong boxes and not have to worry about long deco stops."

"How are you going to detonate the EFP?" Rick asked.

"Speed sensor?" Ryan said it more like a question.

Greg shook his head and snorted. "No."

"I don't suppose you have an acoustical detonator in your pocket," Ryan asked, half joking.

Greg grinned. "After we talked about this on the phone, I had one flown in from San Juan."

"Good, I'll take it with me back to *Peggy Lynn*. Tomorrow, you're my ride from *Peggy Lynn* to *Northwest Passage*."

"How am I supposed to do that? We'll alert Kilroy that you have help."

"We'll use a scooter and rebreathers."

"Mother trucker," Rick said with a shake of his head. "I always knew you squids were crazy, but why not just take your own scooter down?"

"Number one," Ryan explained, "I don't have one, and

two, I don't want Kilroy to get suspicious because we've not used them during other dives."

"Then what, I drop you off at *Peggy Lynn* and go back to *Dark Water?*" Greg asked.

Ryan nodded. "Mango can use a spotter." Changing the subject, he said to Rick, "I understand you can fly a helicopter."

"Does a bear shit in the woods?" Rick shot back.

"Joulie," Ryan asked, "do you still have Toussaint's helicopter?"

She nodded.

Ryan said, "It's a civilian Huey, the Bell 212."

"I know what it is," Rick replied. "I'm rated for it."

"I have an excellent pilot, David Pinchina," Joulie said. "He flew for the *Gardes-Côtes.*" Her statement drew blank stares. "Forgive me, he was a pilot in the Coast Guard."

"You comfortable being a shooter, Rick?" Ryan asked. "Even you Army boys should be able to hop and pop."

"I'd rather be flying the bird."

Ryan shrugged. "I don't care. You have a shooter, Joulie?"

Joulie folded her arms. "David will fly the helicopter."

"You're the shooter, Rick. Mango, you're going to be overwatch from *Dark Water.* Jennifer, you drive the boat while Greg is gone."

"How are we combining all of these elements?" Greg asked.

Ryan looked around the room and took a deep breath. "Here's how I have it sketched out." For the next hour, they worked through the plan, solidifying it into a plausible scenario.

CHAPTER THIRTY-FOUR

Ryan made the final dive to the wreck of the *Santo Domingo*. The ocean was beautiful, with shafts of sunlight stabbing through the water. There was little current and no waves, perfect for his plans.

He'd ordered Kilroy to move closer to shore to better facilitate the transfer of goods. He had no plans to make another dive to three hundred and fifty feet and spend the long hours of deco inside the chamber. If the transfer got messy, and the gold spilled, he wanted to recover it from shallow water.

His first job was to attach the broken strong box to the crane hook. He stood back and watched eight-and-a-half million dollars rise from the seafloor. The total haul was twenty-two million instead of twenty-five. While the crew reeled in their prize, Ryan moved the spare bailout tanks from the back of the Humvee to the strong box. By the time he had the last one moved, the crane hook was back. He attached the second box and the tanks to the hook before watching it go up.

When he turned around, he saw a school of black drum

hovering near the bridge. He had the sudden memory of standing on the bridge wing with Captain Santiago Guzmán, sipping coffee and smoking cigarettes. The aged Dominican had skin like creased leather and a warm smile for those he liked. Ryan had offered Guzmán a job at DWR, but Guzmán had turned him down. Ryan also remembered how the man's crumpled body looked on the ship's deck, blood pooling beneath him after he'd been gunned down by the attacking Haitians.

Guzmán had made his living on the sea, and he'd been buried by the sea. Ryan brought his hand to his helmet and saluted the old man. The crane cable returned, and he attached it to the LARS basket before stepping in with his bomb.

"Ready to go up."

The basket began its smooth ascent. At one seventy-five, it stopped, just like always. Ryan was usually bored during the decompression stops. This time he had something to do. When he'd come down, he'd brought the custom fabricated housing Don had welded for the EFP. He stripped off his gloves and put them in a bag hanging from the LARS frame. With the tactile use of his fingers, he was able to screw down the clamps that held the pipe into the frame. Then he bolted on the electromagnets, one on each side of the round cage where it would fasten to the hull and then the battery box. Originally, Don had built a speed sensor capable of triggering the bomb when *Northwest Passage* reached four knots. This would ensure Ryan and Emily were out of harm's way when the bomb detonated. If they were in the water at the time of the explosion, they would die from over-expansion injuries. The underwater explosion, or UNDEX, would produce a pressure wave, which was magnified by the density of the water. The wave would pass through the solid parts of their bodies, but when it hit the air-filled organs, the gas in them would be compressed, rupturing lungs, tearing apart internal organs, and hemorrhaging the brain.

This wasn't the movies, where the hero climbed out of the water after being caught in an explosion. Ryan wanted to be as far away from the UNDEX as possible. The detonator Greg had provided would allow him to remotely trigger the blast at a more opportune time and place. He wired it into the EFP's detonator circuit, using the electromagnet's battery to provide it with power. He tested the circuit by switching on the receiver. The tiny LED glowed red. He turned it off, unplugged the wire connecting the transducer to the explosive, and taped it out of the way to prevent an accidental explosion.

There was nothing to do now but wait. He closed his eyes and focused on the mission they'd planned. He relaxed his body and slowed his heart rate with breathing exercises.

With an hour left on his decompression timetable, a dark silhouette emerged from the haze. Greg Olsen, wearing a Dive Rite O2ptima rebreather, drove a motorized scooter up to the LARS and shut it off. He put his arms out to stabilize his body, slipping fingers into the small bungee straps of his swimmer's paddles. He hovered just outside the basket, the scooter dangling from a strap clipped to his BCD.

Ryan extended his thumb and pinkie finger from the closed fist of his right hand in a hang-loose wiggle. Greg returned the gesture before grabbing the LARS basket. He set the scooter on the floor of the LARS. He gave Ryan a hurry-up gesture.

Reaching up to his neck, Ryan unfastened the clamps holding the SuperLite to the neck dam forming the watertight seal against his skin. This was the hard part. He had to shut off the air to take off the helmet. Quickly, he drew in and exhaled several deep breaths, then twisted the knob shut on his air supply. He had already mounted a first and second stage regulator to one of the bailout tanks from the Humvee. It took another minute of fumbling to get the helmet off. When it came free, he hung it on a hook, and stuck the bail-out bottle's regulator in his mouth, blew into it to purge the water, and took a deep breath.

The rubber diaphragm inside the reg sucked open and locked there. No air came out of the hose. He'd forgotten that he'd shut off that tank valve after testing the regulators. Panic bulged Ryan's eyes and his gut muscles spasmed. His nostrils flared as he felt water flow into his nasal passages. He fought for control of his body and mind. They both demanded air. He grabbed the valve wheel on the tank and spun it open. Air blasted out of the purge and he took a deep breath. Water and air flowed into his mouth. He spit out the water and purged the reg again. His second pull was just air.

He dug his spare mask from his drysuit thigh pocket and fitted it over his eyes. With his fingers, he pushed against the top of the mask, looked up at the surface, and exhaled through his nose. The water blew out of the mask and a thought occurred to him as he watched his bubbles rise toward the surface. He twisted on the air supply to his SuperLite hat. The exhaust bubbles would fool watchers into thinking that he was still decompressing on the LARS.

Ryan shed his working BCD and harness before pulling on his rEvo III rebreather, the same one he'd used to escape from the wreck beneath him. Gripping the mouthpiece between his teeth, he opened the breathing loop and took a tentative breath. If the unit had flooded, he didn't want to die from inhaling the caustic gas made when the scrubber material contacted sea water. The rebreather was functioning properly. After a quick check of the computer systems, Ryan hooked two forty-cubic-feet bail-out bottles to D-rings on the rebreather's BCD. Then he hefted the EFP and hooked it to a D-ring on his waist.

He looked over at Greg, still floating beside the LARS with one hand on the basket rail. Greg gave him the finger. Ryan held up both hands in a "what the hell" gesture.

Greg grinned around the thick, black mouthpiece and made a circular motion with his hand. He then indicated with his other hand how Ryan should join him, holding his left hand straight out and bringing the fingers of his right up to his left wrist. Ryan adjusted his buoyancy and became neutral in the water beside the LARS. He gave Greg the OK sign. Greg fastened the scooter to his BCD and zoomed off before circling back. As he passed by the LARS, Ryan grabbed the handle on the butt plate of Greg's BCD.

The scooter's speed increased. Greg made an adjustment to bring them onto the correct heading. Ryan peered over Greg's shoulder at the compass and GPS screen fastened to the top of the scooter. He tucked back in to streamline their bodies as the scooter increased to six miles per hour.

Ryan glanced up from watching the passing coral heads when the scooter slowed. The ripples in the sand looked like corduroy. A quick glance at his watch revealed they'd been motoring for thirty minutes. For the past five, Greg had been flying them just above the sea floor. Through the blue haze, he could see the black hull of *Northwest Passage* swinging at anchor in eighty feet of water.

Greg motioned for Ryan to watch the ship while they skimmed along the bottom. Ryan tapped him when they were underneath the vessel. Greg stopped the scooter, and they dropped to the sand. Nearby, a small coral head was ablaze with color, like a living bouquet. Blue striped grunts and French angelfish huddled under ancient purple sea fans while smaller fish darted in and out of the porous coral.

Ryan allowed a moment of silence for the small creatures that would die when the EFP detonated before slowly swimming toward the surface, staying in the shadow of the boat. He'd be easily spotted in the clear waters. Pausing, he drew the bomb up to hold in his hands. His computer warned of a rapid ascent as he finned to the rear of the ship. He ignored it, knowing he would be near the surface for only a minute or two before recompressing his body.

He positioned the penetrator on the hull beside a prop shaft. The electromagnets made a muffled clink when they attached themselves to *Northwest Passage*. Ryan plugged the acoustical sensor into the battery power. The tiny LED glowed in anticipation. An electronic jolt would detonate the C-4 packed in the pipe and blast out a cone of sheet metal, forming it into a projectile, which would rip straight through the ship's hull and into the engine room. Ryan hoped Kilroy was standing in its path. The combination of the penetrator blowing a hole in the bottom of the ship and the UNDEX explosion would break the ship's back and she'd sink quickly in the super-aerated water.

Satisfied with his handiwork, Ryan descended to where Greg lay in the sand. Greg pointed upward and used hand gestures to indicate Ryan should remain motionless. Ryan rolled over and stared up at the ship. He couldn't see any movement. He glanced at Greg. Greg slowly brought his hand up and tapped his ear. Ryan strained to hear. *Damn, tinnitus.* The constant ringing dampened his hearing over certain frequencies. Then he heard what Greg had heard. The buzzing of motors.

A white hull cut through the blue water, twin outboard propellers leaving twisted white trails of bubbles.

Ryan pointed back in the direction of *Peggy Lynn* and motioned for them to go. Above them, the smaller boat was tying up to the ship, and with everyone distracted, it was the perfect opportunity to motor away. Greg grabbed the scooter. A minute later, they were cruising through the water, following the reverse heading to *Peggy Lynn*.

CHAPTER THIRTY-FIVE

Ryan let go of the scooter as Greg passed the LARS platform. He gave two strong kicks and was back at the basket. With Kilroy out of range, he didn't need to swap back to the hard hat. His rebreather was pumping out almost pure oxygen as he rested on the LARS in fifteen feet of water. He paged through the screens on his dive computer, glancing at the tissue saturation analysis. The bar graph display indicated most of the nitrogen was gone, but it would take several more hours for his body to eliminate all of it.

Ryan gave the umbilical cord four hard jerks to indicate he wanted to ascend. He shut off the gas bubbling from the helmet and waited for the basket to move. Nothing. He waited a few more minutes and the basket still did not move.

"What the hell," he said around his mouthpiece. He added air to his BCD to become neutral and swam under *Peggy Lynn*'s hull to the far side. If there was something wrong, he wanted to have the element of surprise on his side.

He stayed low in the water, his eyes just above the surface. Dennis and Stacey stood on the bridge with Don hunched over the computer screen. Travis and Emery sat in the shade of the awning over the dressing bench and recompression chamber.

Ryan shut his breathing loop and let it fall to his chest. He swam over to the boarding ladder, pulled off his fins, and shoved his hands through their straps. With his gear secure, he climbed the ladder. "Glad to see you guys are paying attention," he said, swinging a leg over the gunwale.

"Calm down, whippersnapper." Emery walked back to where Ryan was now shedding his rebreather. Emery helped him slip it off and carried it forward to the dressing bench. Travis helped Ryan strip off the drysuit.

Ryan couldn't get the black trilaminate material off his body fast enough. Already sweat coursed down his skin. By the time he stepped out of his undergarments, they were dripping wet. He was glad to be in nothing but boardshorts.

Stacey came out of the bridge holding a bottle of water and handed it to Ryan. He drank the whole thing in several long swallows. Between the sweating, the long dive breathing dry air, and the lump in his throat, he was parched. He crushed the water bottle and screwed the top back on. Stacey went to get another bottle.

"How did it go?" Travis asked, hanging the drysuit on a hanger beside his.

Ryan spread out his undergarments to dry. "The bomb is in place."

Dennis stepped out of the bridge onto the narrow walkway. "Greg is back on *Dark Water*.

A determined look creased Ryan's face. "Looks like it's time to saddle up."

Captain Dennis Law led the way down to his cabin

where he'd laid out the twin H&K MP5Ns on his bunk. He and Ryan had loaded the thirty round magazines and test fired the German submachine guns off the stern of the boat while they were underway between Florida and Haiti. Now, their oiled black surfaces gleamed in the dull cabin lights.

"Ready to do this?" Ryan asked.

"Not really. I thought I'd put this life of adventure behind me."

"No, you decided to feel sorry for yourself and quit living."

Dennis's sharp glance told Ryan he'd hit a nerve. Ryan picked up a gun, ensuring the fire selector switch was on *safe*. The N, or Navy model, was developed in 1986 for the U.S. Navy and it had a unique four position switch: *safe*, *semi-automatic*, *three shot burst*, and *full automatic*. Ryan had used one of these weapons multiple times during his naval career. It was a favorite of special operations forces around the world. The last time he'd slung one across his body to do battle was when he'd helped take down Guerrero's pirate ship in the Gulf of Mexico. The gun felt like an old friend in his hand.

"You have an adventurous streak in you, just like I do." Ryan fed a magazine into the receiver and slapped the charging handle down. The bolt snapped forward, loading a 9mm hollow point into the chamber.

"I never had to use a weapon during my career as a salvage diver."

"First time for everything, Captain."

"Yeah," Dennis mumbled, picking up the other MP5.

Ryan stuffed four magazines into the pockets of his cargo shorts. His Walther pistol was snug on his hip in a Kydex holster.

"Suited up and ready to dive on the hook, Captain," Emery shouted from outside.

Ryan said, "This is a simple transfer of gold and a hostage. Once we get her onboard, we take off. When we're a safe distance away, I'll blow the EFP."

Dennis nodded. He turned and walked out of his cabin with Ryan on his heels. Dennis went to the bridge and started the twin diesel engines while Ryan continued to the rear deck. Stacey stood on the gunwale dressed in scuba gear. She had a regulator in her mouth and her mask pulled down over her eyes. She watched Dennis for his signal to dive while clinging to a support line for the crane tower. Her hair was devoid of any purple.

From the bridge, Dennis yelled, "Dive, dive, dive."

Stacey took a giant step off the gunwale. She had one hand over her mask and regulator to keep them in place. She kept her other arm wrapped around her torso. Ryan and Travis watched her level off and swim to the chain rode attaching *Peggy Lynn* to the sunken wreck of the *Santo Domingo*.

Travis moved up on the bow, keeping a close watch on his girlfriend. "She's at the clevis."

Ryan let the gun dangle from his chest harness as he walked up to the bow. Far down, he could see Stacey working on the clevis he'd installed to hold *Peggy Lynn* to the wreck. A few minutes later, she held a fist straight out from her body and used her whole arm to make up and down motions.

"Give her some slack," Travis called.

Dennis eased the boat forward until Travis told him to stop. Stacey pulled the clevis pin loose and the old crane cable dropped to the sea floor. Stacey began ascending along the chain. Dennis cut the engines and let *Peggy Lynn* drift. Travis and Emery dragged the chain and bridle onto the foredeck.

Ten minutes later, Stacey was back on the boat. "Did you see those barracudas?"

"Yeah," Travis said. "They've been hanging out around the anchor line. It's like the storm blew a bunch of life over to the wreck."

They broke down Stacey's gear and stowed it away. Ryan pulled out his satellite phone and dialed Kilroy's number.

"Who's this?" the voice on the other end of the line asked.

"Put Emily on the phone."

"I assure you, Mr. Weller, you don't need proof of life."

"Humor me."

A minute later, he heard Emily say, "Hello?"

Ryan asked, "Are you all right?"

"I'm okay."

"We have the gold. We're coming for you."

"You better have my gold," Kilroy said.

"It's right here. We're on our way now."

"Hurry up." The line went dead.

CHAPTER THIRTY-SIX

G raffiti and old advertisement posters littered the razor wire-topped concrete block wall surrounding Hugo Chavez International Airport. Many of the airport's signs still read Aéroport International de Cap-Haitien. Rick Hayes kept his head on a swivel as they drove down the street running parallel to the wall. The driver, and Joulie Lafitte's pilot, David Pinchina, stopped the old Ford Bronco at a reinforced iron gate. Rick eyeballed four groups of men standing along the sidewalk. One man was sitting with his feet propped up against the wall, back to the street, and returned Rick's stare.

"They're unemployed," David said. He showed his identification to the guard, and the gates swung open. The guard carried an Israeli IMI Galil. Rick recognized it from his time in the Middle East. As soon as the truck was inside the gate, the guards closed it. Rick turned to watch them push a man back into the street.

"They are desperate to leave Haiti. If they could sneak onto an airplane, they would."

"What about you?" Rick asked, turning back to face the windshield.

David shrugged. His big aviator sunglasses reflected the sun and his black skin shone with perspiration under his white pilot shirt with captain epaulets. The rest of his uniform consisted of black slacks and polished dress shoes. The Army had measured Rick at five-feet-three and three-quarters of an inch, and every fraction counted for Rick. David was three inches taller, with a polished black head, and the man was gaunt where Rick was stocky.

"How long have you been flying for Joulie?"

"I flew for *Mesye* Bajeux. Then he died, and now I work for mambo Joulie."

"What's a mambo?"

"A mambo is a vodou priestess."

Rick whipped his head around to stare at David. "She's a what?"

"A vodou priestess." David grinned with uneven rows of stained teeth.

"Like dance around and put a spell on you while sticking a doll with a pin vodou?"

Still smiling, David shook his head. He turned the SUV onto a dirt road and accelerated toward a large, metal building that housed the helicopter. "That is evil, *bokor*. Mambo Joulie is a good priestess."

"How is she as a warlord?" Rick muttered.

"She is very good."

Rick laughed.

David stopped the SUV at the hangar and shut off the engine. They stepped out into the roar of a jetliner taking off. David unlocked a door and the two men stepped inside.

Before Rick's eyes could adjust to the darkness, a heavy

blow struck the side of his head. He raised his hand to touch his temple but found he was falling over. Rick Hayes was unconscious before he hit the ground.

CHAPTER THIRTY-SEVEN

Peggy Lynn approached *Northwest Passage* on *Passage*'s port side, her bow toward the *Passage*'s stern. Travis and Stacey had hung the bumpers and were standing by with the fore-and-aft lines to tie the boats together. Off their starboard stern quarter in the seven o'clock position, *Dark Water*, and her snipers, provided cover.

Ryan stared through the lenses of his wraparound sunglasses at the figures on Kilroy's boat. Emily had a small suitcase at her feet. Her ankles were not bound, but her wrists were behind her back. Ryan surmised her hands were tied. Both Kilroy and Damian wore holstered pistols and Damian held a shotgun. A third man, armed with an AK, kept watch on the bridge wing.

Ryan stood beside the metal strong boxes, one hand on the pistol grip of the MP5. His thumb flicked the selector to *three shot burst*. Moving his left hand from the top of the rusty metal box, he placed it on the forward grip of the sleek black gun. He had the collapsible stock extended and the suppressor screwed on.

Travis and Stacey secured the lines and Ryan stepped to the rail. He had to look up as *Northwest Passage*'s freeboard was three feet higher. "I'll send over one box and then you send over Emily. The second box will follow when she's on my boat."

Kilroy said, "Fair enough."

"Let me shoot him now, Mista Kilroy," Damian said.

"No."

Ryan said, "Swing your crane over and we'll hook up a box."

Out of the corner of his eye, Ryan saw a crewman cross the deck and scale the massive pillar to get to the crane's control station. The crewman swung the crane arm over the side of the ship and lowered the cable. Emery dragged the hook to the first steel box and threaded it into the straps.

The crane operator raised the strong box and swung it aboard *Northwest Passage*. When it was on the deck, Kilroy undid the straps and the operator swung the hook back over *Peggy Lynn*'s stern.

"Moment of truth, Emily," Kilroy said. He pushed the straps off the box, unlatched the clasps, and flipped the lid up. Ryan could see the rush of gold fever cross the man's face. His features physically changed, lifting and tightening. When he turned to look at Ryan, his eyes danced. Ryan had experienced the exact same jubilation when he'd found the first strong box among the carnage inside *Santo Domingo*.

Travis looked forlornly at Ryan. Ryan knew exactly how he felt. The elation of finding the gold and devastation of losing it were powerful warring forces inside their bodies. Kilroy had tossed out the rule book when he'd involved Emily, but he would soon pay the price. The gold would be reclaimed by the rightful salvors, and they would know the elation of gold fever once again.

Ryan motioned for Travis to hold fast and not hook the crane to the second box. Turning to Kilroy, he shouted, "Send her over."

Damian stepped behind Emily, his shotgun dangling on a sling. He seized her wrists and shoved them down, forcing her to bend backward while he nuzzled her neck. Emily gasped.

Ryan jerked the MP5 to his shoulder, cheek welding to the stock, eye squinting through the holographic sight centered on Damian's forehead. "Let her go!"

Damian stared at Ryan while running his tongue along Emily's neck. She shuddered and jerked her hands, trying desperately to get away from the Jamaican. The Jamaican grinned wickedly and snarled, "I not get to have my way with her."

"Emily," Ryan shouted, desperate to control the situation.

She looked up. Her cornflower blue eyes brimmed with tears when they met his.

In a calm voice, Ryan asked, "What did I teach you?"

Recognition lightened her countenance. Steel filled her eyes. Her knee came up, and she slammed her heel down on the inside of Damian's bare foot. He howled with pain and hopped on one foot. Emily spun into him, bringing her knee up hard into his chest. The hand gripping his foot partially deflected the blow. Damian let go of his appendage and swung his arms up to grab Emily.

Ryan was afraid to kill Damian. Kilroy might renege on his deal and not release Emily. An eye for an eye. He was concentrating so hard on Kilroy, Damian, and Emily that he missed Stacey creeping to the rail.

Emily jumped back to avoid Damian's vengeful hands. He clutched at nothing but air, and then he stood bolt upright, twin wires protruded from his chest, linking him to Stacey's stun gun. Damian began to dance to the electricity surging through his body.

"Take that, asshole," Stacey screamed. "You leave her alone!"

Ryan lowered his weapon but kept one hand on the pistol grip, finger straight along the receiver just above the trigger.

Kilroy stood with his hands behind his back, watching Damian writhe on the deck of his ship. Turning to Ryan, he said, "Are you done having fun?"

"If I was having fun, he would have a bullet in his head."

"Touchy, touchy, Mr. Weller. You shouldn't get so emotional."

"Cut her loose and send her over," Ryan demanded.

"No, the gold first."

"We had a deal."

"And I'm changing the terms. You can thank your friend with the Taser."

"I'll light you up too, Jimmy," Stacey yelled.

Kilroy smiled. "Where's your one-legged companion?" he called to Ryan.

"He's not here." Ryan had a sudden suspicion that Kilroy knew their plans and had somehow subverted them by doing something nasty to Mango and the others on *Dark Water*. "Send over the girl," Ryan demanded again.

Stacey moved along *Peggy Lynn*'s railing, grabbed the crane guide wire, and reached a hand across the gap. "Come on, Emily."

"The gold, Mr. Weller!"

"We had a deal." Ryan wanted to just pull the trigger. He wanted to put a bullet into Kilroy's brain and end this useless stalemate. He couldn't count on Dennis; it had been a long time since the captain had fired a gun in combat. If he knew Mango had a clear shot of the guy on the bridge ... *No. Damnit, there's too many of them. If I open fire, they'll shred us.*

CHAPTER THIRTY-EIGHT

Emily listened to Kilroy and Ryan scream back and forth. She'd seen the armed guards Kilroy had posted around his vessel, all of them ready to shoot on command. For twenty-five-million dollars in gold, she knew Kilroy was willing to eliminate Ryan, his crew, and anyone else in his way, including her.

When they'd come for her in her stateroom, Damian had cuffed her hands behind her back with a black plastic zip tie. Emily had made a fist with her right hand and wrapped the fingers of her left around it, tensing the muscles in both arms. The plastic had bit deep into her skin when Damian cinched it tight, but there was a small measure of slack in the plastic ring when she relaxed her muscles, just not enough to keep it from chafing her skin raw. Blood now mixed with sweat around her wrists. Sweat had soaked her shirt from standing in the sun, and her shoulders ached. The glare of the sunlight reflecting off the water caused her to squint.

Kilroy turned to face Ryan, his voice calmer. "Send the gold and I'll release the girl."

Emily backed into the shade of the giant Viking sport-fishing yacht. It blocked the bridge guard's view of her, and she was slightly behind Kilroy who still faced Ryan, discussing the terms of her release. She glanced at Stacey and shook her head, telegraphing to her not to watch what she was about to do. Stacey turned away and loaded another cartridge into the muzzle of her Taser.

In one motion, Emily drew her arms up as high as she could, bent forward, and slammed them down against the base of her spine. The cuffs bit deeper into her skin and more blood ran down her hands. She brought her arms up again, repeatedly slamming them into her hips and pulling her wrists apart at the same time. The third thrust snapped the plastic. She glanced down at her free hands. Blood from multiple lacerations coated her wrists and fingers, and she'd broken two nails. Her heartbeat thundered in her ears. Adrenaline mainlined through her veins.

Without thinking, she took two running steps, lowered her shoulder and slammed Kilroy in the back. She continued past him as he fell. Emily placed a foot on the rail of *Northwest Passage* and launched herself into space.

Time seemed to freeze during her flight, her left leg extended, arms spread for balance. She saw Ryan bring his gun up, heard the muted pop of automatic weapons. Spent casings arched through the air, twinkling as they caught the light. Her foot hit the deck of *Peggy Lynn* and time sped up again. She crumpled, rolling in a ball to slam against the recompression chamber.

A strong set of arms pulled her to her feet and half-dragged, half-carried her behind the shelter of the bridge. The roaring in her ears cleared and everything came back into focus just in time to hear desperate shouting from both ships. "Cease fire! Cease fire!"

CHAPTER THIRTY-NINE

The beat of helicopter rotors drew Rick Hayes from unconsciousness. His left eye had swollen shut and his right eye wasn't much better. The taste of copper was heavy in his mouth. When he ran his tongue around his teeth, two were loose and one was missing. He tried to smile, but the pain was almost unbearable. At least he was alive and in a place that he knew like the back of his hand, the Bell 212.

After being knocked out in the hangar, he'd been awakened by hot water splashing on his face. It tasted salty on his lips, and he wondered if they'd moved him to the ocean. When he opened his eyes, he realized he was being pissed on. His arms and legs were bound, making it difficult to move, yet he rolled away from the stream of urine. "Shit, man, stop," he yelled.

The laughing pisser walked with him, keeping Rick's head under the golden shower.

When the man had finished and zipped himself up, his companions, who were also laughing at Rick, grabbed the bound man and shoved him into a chair. Before Rick could say a word, one of them hit him with a right cross and his head spun again. The stench of ammonia emanating from his piss-soaked clothes and hair helped to revive him.

For the next ten minutes, three men took turns pounding on him while a fourth man asked him questions about Ryan's plan to rescue Emily. Rick gave them just enough information to stop the beating. He knew every man broke under torture. It was a matter of finding the right breaking point. By giving them information, he planned to stay conscious and position himself where he could still help his friends.

For Rick, waking up in the helicopter was like winning the lottery. Through the slit of his right eye, he could see the feet of two of his assailants. He tried to concentrate on what they looked like. He hadn't seen any of them clearly after the first few blows. What he did remember was that they were dark-skinned and spoke with accents. He'd narrowed it down to Central America or Mexico. He closed his eye to think. It didn't matter where they were from, if he had an opening, he would make them pay.

Rick opened his eye again and watched his captors. They weren't paying attention to him. He was lying on his right side on the aircraft's deck, facing the aft cabin wall. To his back were the seats for the pilot and copilot. Being familiar with the layout, he knew the seats slid back and forth on tracks just like the seats in a car.

He rolled back, trying not to groan from the pain emanating from his abused head and torso. His hands met the sharp edges of the co-pilot's U-shaped slide rail. His back hit the seat. Now he could see the men above him. Rick recognized their rifles as CZ 805 BRENs, a gun favored by the Mexican Federal Police. As a gun buff, he prided himself on being able to identify any firearm used in movies or, well, here in real life. *You're stupid*, he chastised himself as he slowly sawed through the thick wrapping of duct tape around his wrists using the sharp edge of the U-shaped slide.

CHAPTER FORTY

Ryan had moved to his left, putting the strong box of gold between himself and the wildly firing gunmen on Kilroy's boat. He aimed the MP5 at the crane operator and pulled the trigger. A ragged trio of holes bloomed in the equipment operator's chest. He dropped his AK and slumped over the rail. Ryan swung his gun toward the man on the bridge wing. Just as he lined up his shot, the man's head snapped back and the window behind him became a Rorschach test pattern of crimson blood and gray brain matter. Ryan could only assume that Mango had joined the fight, sending a .338 boat tail hollow point from his over-watch position.

Ryan trained his MP5 on Kilroy. The arms dealer, while holding his pistol, wasn't firing, which moved him to the bottom of the threat matrix. Even though he was the ringleader, and Ryan wanted to shoot him, Ryan had to take care of the more imminent threats first. He continued to scan for whoever was firing an AK at them while Kilroy shouted for a cease fire.

In the silence following the thunder of automatic fire,

Kilroy said, "You have what you wanted, now send over my gold."

"I don't think so."

"You don't have a choice, Mr. Weller."

"Travis, Stacey, get the lines," Ryan ordered.

"You demanded I keep my end of the bargain, Mr. Weller," Kilroy shouted as he stepped to the rail. "I demand you keep yours. You have the girl."

"Damian broke our deal."

Kilroy raised a handheld VHF radio to his lips. "Now, Mr. Pinchina."

Ryan recognized the name. It took him several seconds to process the information. Everything clicked into place when he heard the helicopter. Joulie's pilot had flipped sides.

"What do we do?" Travis yelled.

"Get the lines," Ryan ordered.

Kilroy countermanded, "Stand fast."

The helicopter's rotor noise increased as it drew closer.

"Ryan," Emily shouted.

He didn't turn to look at her, keeping Kilroy in the center of his holographic sight.

Emily moved up beside Ryan. "Give it to him," she said quietly.

"Swing it," Ryan shouted, knowing that in a matter of minutes, the gold and Kilroy's ship would be at the bottom of the ocean. Kilroy bounded to the crane and used the controls to hoist the gold aboard his vessel.

Just as the box cleared the rail of the salvage boat, Dennis yelled, "Get the ropes."

Travis and Stacey threw off the lines and Dennis eased the salvage vessel away from *Northwest Passage*. He threw the throttles open when they were clear, taking his boat to the west, away from the explosion area. Travis and Ryan watched Kilroy open the box. The gun dealer beamed, his face glowing gold in the reflected light.

Ryan glanced up at the helicopter. He wondered why Pinchina would keep coming when Kilroy had the gold.

"What do you think they want?" Travis asked.

The Bell 212 flashed past the salvage vessel and turned in a long graceful arch, rising through the middle to peak at the end of the turn, then diving toward the starboard side of the boat. It quickly closed the distance and came to a hover off the *Peggy Lynn*'s bow.

A loudspeaker boomed, "This is the Haitian Coast Guard. Shut down your engines and prepare to be boarded."

"You got the wrong guy, asshole," Stacey screamed. She waved the helicopter away and pointed frantically at *Northwest Passage*. "The bad guys are over there."

The helicopter turned sideways, and the cargo door slid open. A man brandished an M60 machine gun. The bandolier of bullets trailed out of the gun's action and draped on the floor. He triggered a burst, sending bullets and spent brass cartridges into the water in front of the boat. Stacey and Emily screamed.

Ryan bounded up the stairs to the bridge. He pulled off his MP5 and handed it to Don who was sitting at the computer terminal.

As he turned to Captain Dennis, Don grinned and said. "Want me to shoot down that helicopter?"

Ryan turned back, a quizzical look on his face.

"What?" Don asked. "I'm a good ole boy from Texas. I like to shoot stuff."

"Maybe later," Ryan said. "Dennis, shut it down."

"What do they want?"

"I don't know, Captain." Ryan pulled the remote for the acoustical detonator from his pocket. "Flip this switch and then press the button. It'll detonate the bomb on Kilroy's boat. Get clear before you blow it though."

Dennis took the detonator, put it in his pocket, and reached for the throttles. *Peggy Lynn* began to slow and dropped off plane, wallowing in the water as the wake, waves, and momentum caught up with her.

Stepping out to the bow, Ryan held up his hands. He had a feeling they were there for him. He braced his feet and stared up at the helicopter, squinting into the thrashing wind and fine mist kicked up by the rotor wash.

The pilot swung the bird around to the port side of the boat and a man pushed a rope ladder out the door. Ryan kept his eyes on Eduardo Sanchez, the cartel member he recognized from Kilroy's table at Hotel Roi Christophe. He now understood the game Kilroy had played. Kilroy had double-dipped, getting the gold for Emily and trading Ryan for the two-million-dollar bounty offered by the Aztlán cartel. Kilroy had asked about Mango to send him to the cartel as well.

"Ryan Weller get in the helicopter," the loudspeaker boomed.

Peggy Lynn had come to a dead stop, and the helicopter crabbed sideways to bring the rope ladder over her bow. After making two attempts to get close to the boat, the pilot found his sweet spot, the rotors just missing the steel poles of the crane tower with little room for error.

Ryan grabbed the dangling rope ladder and gave it a tug. This wasn't the first time he'd boarded a helicopter from a ship. He planted a foot on the ladder and began to ascend. When he was four rungs up, the pilot shifted the chopper away from the salvage vessel. Ryan kept climbing as the ladder swayed. It reminded him of having to climb the rope in gym class. It required intense focus, and his muscles were like jelly from gripping the squirming rope. Besides everyone watching, he had to deal with whipping winds, water spray slicking the ropes and rungs, and the fact there were men waiting to do him harm at the other end of the ladder. He could let go and drop into the water right now, but the M60 gunner would surely have his way with the vessel below. He had to climb. Their survival depended on it.

Two men hauled his quivering body into the helicopter compartment. His arms were lead weights and his hands curved into claws from gripping the rungs. He lay on the cabin floor, breathing deeply despite the foot planted on his back. He rotated his head to look around, taking in the two Mexican men and Rick Hayes. Rick looked bad. He had multiple lacerations on his cheeks and forehead. Twin rivers of blood and snot had flowed from his nose and coated his chin and cheeks. His eyes were puffy sacks of black, blue, and yellow. The left one was swollen shut and the right one was ...

Is he staring at me?

Ryan focused on Rick's right eye. The swelling had almost closed it and the pupil was wide, even with all the light coming in through the open cabin doors. The man clearly had a concussion, yet a slight smile lifted the corner of his lips.

Ryan furrowed his brow in question.

"Get up," the Mexican commanded, screaming into the gale force winds and grabbing the collar of Ryan's shirt. Ryan came to his hands and knees, staring out the port side cabin door. He could see *Northwest Passage* and her long, spreading wake. The helicopter came in close to the ship, and Eduardo jerked Ryan to his feet.

Push the damn button, Dennis! Push. The. Button.

Kilroy stepped onto the bridge wing and waved at the helicopter. Ryan locked eyes with the arms dealer.

Then the sea exploded.

There was the sickening sound of metal shearing and screaming as the penetrator blasted from its tube and tore open *Northwest Passage*'s hull. The sea boiled as the steam void blossomed around the detonation site. When the C-4 detonated, it formed a hot bubble of gas which expanded outward. *Northwest Passage* seemed to give a small hop and Ryan saw the old girl break in the center, her keel shattered. Under the weight of the surrounding water, the pocket of super-heated air collapsed in on itself like a bursting balloon, leaving a void beneath the ship. Gravity pulled the ship down into the void, breaking it further.

Ryan kept his eyes on Kilroy, who had fallen to his knees and was now levering himself upright with the help of the railing. Karen ran onto the bridge wing to help her husband.

A second explosion blew out the ship's stern, sending shards of metal and glass through the air. Kilroy and his wife flew off the catwalk, their bodies tumbling like rag dolls. When they landed in the water facedown, their backs were a mutilated mess from the shrapnel. Kilroy's head was missing a large chunk of skull. Karen began to sink below the surface.

CHAPTER FORTY-ONE

Mango Hulsey watched the scene play out through the tiny lens of the Nightforce scope as he lay sprawled on *Dark Water*'s bridge roof. He focused on the helicopter. The explosion's shock wave interrupted the airflow around the blades and the pilot struggled to maintain control. It dropped rapidly toward the sea and just when Mango thought it would crash, the pilot straightened it out and regained altitude. Then it swung away from Kilroy's boat and headed south, back toward Haiti.

"Jenny, follow that bird!" Mango shouted to his wife. She and Greg were on the bridge. Greg had his Barrett 98B bolt-action sniper rifle with him to act as a spotter and backup shooter.

The big boat didn't hesitate when she pushed the throttles forward and the two massive nineteen-hundred horsepower Caterpillar C32 diesels shoved the big boat up onto plane. Mango slid backward. He braced his foot against the tuna tower and grabbed the front edge of the roof. He glanced to his right to see how close he was to the sweep of the radar antenna positioned in the middle of the bridge's roof.

Mango stared at the laser range finder attached to the rifle. The tiny red numbers told him the bird was a quarter of a mile away and widening the gap. His heart sank with each increase of the numbers.

He turned his head to look for the *Peggy Lynn*. She was steaming toward the sinking hulk of Kilroy's ship. Two other vessels were also speeding toward the wreck to render assistance. They could deal with *Northwest Passage*. He needed to concentrate on not letting the helicopter out of sight.

Mango glanced at the range finder. The bird was a half a mile away on their starboard side. If it got to land, they might never find Ryan again. Mango didn't know who was flying the bird, but it wasn't Short Rick. In the limited time he'd known Rick Hayes, he'd seen the loyalty he had for Greg and Ryan, and to an extent, himself. The man wouldn't betray them.

He snugged his rifle to his shoulder and sighted on the helicopter. He had only seconds to make a shot that would distract the pilot, but not bring down the bird. With luck he could get the pilot to turn the chopper, and he and Greg could shoot the bad guys, giving Ryan a chance to escape.

The helicopter angled to the southwest while Jennifer curved *Dark Water* toward its flight path. Through the scope, he could see the pilot's window and part of the helicopter's windshield. Beneath him, the boat surged on the water, bouncing on the slight waves. He determined the pattern, calculating the timing of the shot. Breathe in, let out, hold, squeeze, BANG!

He wasn't sure if he hit anything. Shooting from a moving platform at a moving target was the hardest shot to make. He had spent years of his life training for this exact scenario, sent thousands of rounds down range to learn how to fire a sniper rifle from a boat, all so he could save Ryan's ass once again. Mango smirked as he racked the bolt and threw another bullet into the chamber. He breathed, aimed, fired. Reload, breathe, aim, fire. Reload, breathe, aim, fire. Maybe just one bullet would find its mark.

Suddenly, the helicopter darted to the left, sweeping around in a tight arc directly toward *Dark Water*.

CHAPTER FORTY-TWO

R yan closed his eyes and took a deep breath. Assess the situation, use what the bad guys are giving you. The words of an old senior chief came floating back to him, "Never believe you're beat, even when the cards are down."

He was free, his hands and feet unrestrained. They'd stripped him of his CRKT tactical folding knife and tossed it onto the floor beside Short Rick's inert form. He'd left his guns with Dennis and Don. Eduardo Sanchez was the leader of this small group. The second Mexican was much bigger. He hefted the M60 with ease. The third sat in the co-pilot's seat, pointing a pistol at David Pinchina, who kept glancing over his shoulder at Ryan with a pleading look on his face. Ryan figured the pilot would be all right once they landed, and he completed the job. He was probably more afraid of the punishment Joulie would give him than what these dudes would do.

The helicopter jerked abruptly, throwing everyone off balance. David swung it hard left and brought it to a hover. Out the door, Ryan could see *Dark Water* charging at them.

Mango lay sprawled on the bridge roof behind his sniper rifle.

Ryan glanced down at Short Rick then searched for his knife with his eyes. It was an orange-handled, Kit Carson-designed tanto blade with a seat belt cutter on the thumb flip and a window breaking point on the butt. It should have been easy to spot on the dark metal surface of the helicopter cabin, but Ryan didn't see it.

The burly Mexican stood with the M60 and maneuvered to the door. He kicked Rick as he braced his feet. Ryan could see Rick's reaction and was glad he couldn't hear the cry of pain.

Just as Burly brought the M60 up to his hip to fire, Rick whipped his arm out, the orange handle of the knife gripped in his fist. He stabbed the blade deep into Burly's thigh. Burly twisted, grabbed at the knife, and dropped the gun. Ryan vaulted up, grabbing an overhead support tube running from the roof to the seat backs like he was going to do a chin up, and swung his legs through the arc. His feet slammed into Burly's back and Burly flew from the helicopter. He twisted in space, screaming as he fell.

Ryan glanced down at Rick and saw the knife was still in the man's hand. The blade dripped with dark blood. How he had held on to it, Ryan didn't know. He turned to face Eduardo, hands still on the support tube.

A fine mist of blood suddenly covered the windshield. The head of the terrorist in the copilot's seat lolled to the side, missing a large piece of skull. Bone, hair, blood, and brain matter coated David Pinchina's face and headset. Pinchina screamed as he tried to wipe away the gore with both hands. The helicopter lurched sideways without the pilot's input on the controls.

The sudden shift of the chopper swung everyone to the

port side. Ryan's feet flew out from under him as he clutched the support bar. Eduardo Sanchez was in the middle of drawing his pistol when he stumbled forward. Ryan wrapped his legs around the man's torso, pinning his arms to his sides. He squeezed, getting his ankles locked together behind the Mexican. Eduardo flailed his body, trying to free himself from the crushing forces of Ryan's thighs.

"David! David!" Ryan screamed despite the rushing wind of the rotor blades and the howling of the two jet engines.

For some reason, the pilot glanced over his shoulder at Ryan, who yelled, "You got this. Don't let us die!"

David looked out the window and realized the gravity of the situation. He grasped the controls, adding power with the throttles and correcting the course of flight with the cyclic and collective. The helicopter tilted to port as David overcorrected. The g-forces keeping Ryan's body parallel to the helicopter's deck were suddenly gone and his torso sagged as he kept a tight grip on the support bar and the wiggling Mexican.

Ryan saw movement beside him. Rick had the Mexican's gun in his hand. They made eye contact and Rick nodded. Ryan unclenched his legs from around Eduardo's waist and let go of the support bar at the same time. He fell to the seats. Eduardo continued to struggle against the forces no longer restraining him. He looked up and saw Rick's outstretched hand. The gun boomed, and Eduardo staggered backward. He grabbed a support bar to keep himself up right. Rick pulled the trigger twice more, then a fourth, and a fifth time. Eduardo's body recoiled from the impact of each bullet.

Lying on the seats, Ryan watched Eduardo try to

remain upright. The will to fight drained out of his body, leaking away like the blood staining the steel deck plates. Then Eduardo let go of the support bar and fell backward out the open door, summersaulting through the air to the sea below.

Rick dropped the pistol, and it clattered to the deck. His head drooped, and he rested his forehead on his outstretched arm. Ryan bent down to check Rick's pulse. It was still beating strong through his carotid artery. He picked up the gun and shoved it into his back pocket. He never liked sticking a gun down the back of his pants. In his experience, the gun always wiggled loose, and he didn't want a Glock wedged in his butt crack where it wasn't easily accessible.

He tapped David on the shoulder and motioned toward *Peggy Lynn*, circling where *Northwest Passage* had gone down. David flew the Bell toward the sportfisher, which had raced away from what could have been a potential helicopter crash site. Ryan turned back to Rick, who was struggling to sit up. He grabbed the man under the armpits and hoisted him into a seat. He strapped the seat belt around Rick's waist and reached up for the headset with microphone boom hanging beside the door. He settled it over his ears and grabbed another one for Rick. It felt good to block out the constant blast of noise.

Ryan keyed the internal communications system, and asked, "What happened, David?"

David responded over the ICS, "We were jumped as soon as we walked into the hangar. They beat *Meyse* Rick to get information. I was left alone because I can fly."

"So can Rick."

"He told me this. They did not know."

"How many other people did you see?"

"Just these three."

"Got any water in here?"

"Look in the cooler behind the seats. I'm not sure if there's any in it. They did not allow me to load anything before takeoff."

Ryan found the small cooler and pulled out two luke-warm waters. He handed one to Rick who stared dumbly at it. Ryan took the cap off for him and Rick managed to dribble some liquid past his split lips. More ran down his chin than into his mouth, the water washing away some of the dried blood.

Ryan turned to look out the open door. The white-and-blue fiberglass and aluminum of *Dark Water* glistened in the sun. He keyed the ICS and said to David, "Get me VHF channel thirty-five." It was the channel DWR traditionally operated on and Ryan knew Greg would be monitoring it.

David paged up through the digital numbers on his radio. "Got it."

Ryan pressed the radio button on his headset. "*Dark Water, Dark Water,* this is Ryan."

"Copy, Ryan," Greg replied.

"We have control of the helicopter and are flying to where *Northwest* went down."

"Copy, we're headed that way too. What's going on up there?"

"Kilroy tried to double dip. Some Aztlán cartel clowns jumped Rick and David at the hanger. They took control of the helicopter and came to pick me up. They beat Rick pretty good. He'll be all right though."

"Copy that."

David brought the helicopter to a hover over the wreck site. *Peggy Lynn* and several other boats were busy picking up flotsam from the wreck. Ryan recognized them as the ones that had acted as Joulie's guard boats. Rafted to *Peggy Lynn* was the Viking sportfisher. Travis and Stacey had commandeered the Yellowfin center console. Stacey was at the helm while Travis used a boat hook to fish debris from the water. The two boats had been in the blocks on *Northwest Passage's* deck when she'd gone down, and Ryan guessed they'd drifted clear when the mothership sank beneath them.

The sea was still churning with air belching from the wreckage, but Ryan could make out *Northwest Passage's* outline through the water. She had broken apart in the middle and lay on her port side. He moved his gaze to the red hull of the salvage vessel. Emily and Don waved at him as he leaned out of the helicopter's open door. It seemed too surreal.

"Get me channel sixteen, David."

The pilot changed channels and said, "Ready for you."

"*Peggy Lynn, Peggy Lynn*, this is helicopter off your starboard side."

"Go ahead, helicopter."

"Any sign of Kilroy?"

"Yes, one of the other boats fished his body out."

"Copy that," Ryan said. "Everyone else all right?"

"Yes, sir," Dennis replied.

"We'll be back in a shortly, we have an injured man who requires medical attention, out."

"Roger that, out."

David slewed the helicopter sideways in a turn and headed for land. Ryan looked over at *Dark Water* speeding toward the scene and saw a man at the top of the tuna tower waving at them with both arms. At the same time, squelch broke on the radio.

"Ryan, this is Jennifer, do you copy?"

"I got you."

"Mango wants you to pick him up."

"Say again."

"Mango says to bring the helicopter over the tower, and he'll climb aboard. He wants to help with security, or something."

"Copy that," Ryan replied. Even over the radio static, Ryan could hear her rolling her eyes. He clicked the ICS and said to David, "Can you bring the bird over the tuna tower, so we can pick that guy up?"

"Sure can. This day just keeps getting better and better. I haven't had this much fun since I was in the United States for training."

Ryan keyed the ICS switch. "Hold a minute before you get over the boat."

David brought the bird to a hover and Ryan removed his headset and stepped out onto the landing skid. He tripped the door latch on the co-pilot's door and shoved it open. He wedged himself in the gap and reached across the lap of the dead man to unbuckle the safety harness. Ryan backed along the skid, pulled the body out of the seat, and let it drop into the pristine water below.

When he climbed back in the cabin, David had edged the helo closer to *Dark Water*. Mango gripped the tower, braced against the rotor wash. He wore a black backpack with two guns strapped to it, muzzles down. The fishing outrigger had been swung away from the tower and Mango had dropped the thick fiberglass radio antennas. *Dark Water* was barely making way on the smooth sea.

"Bring us over the tower, so he can step right on," Ryan said after resettling the headset over his ears.

"Roger that," David said. "Is the rope ladder in?"

"Hold one." Ryan pulled the ladder into the cabin, rolling it to keep it from tangling and making it easier to stow behind the passenger seats.

The helicopter slid sideways over the long nose of the Hatteras and David brought a skid inches from the top of the tuna tower. Ryan extended his hand to Mango, who stepped onto the skid and climbed into the bird.

"He's on," Ryan said.

David raised the collective, and the helicopter rose straight into the air. As they approached one thousand feet, David dipped the chopper's nose and they accelerated toward the airport.

Mango pulled a headset over his ears and keyed the mic. "Did you see the shot that took out the co-pilot?"

Ryan looked up from rummaging through Mango's backpack. "It scared the shit out of David. I thought we were going to crash." He removed a sleek black KRISS Vector CRB rifle.

"Saved your ass again, bro."

Ryan shook his head. "No dice, buddy, you almost wrecked the helicopter. Doesn't count."

The bag also contained a chest rig with magazine pouches. Each pouch held two twenty-five round magazines stuffed with fat, blunt nose forty-five caliber hollow points. Attached to the chest rig was a Spyderco H1 dive knife, a Gerber multitool, a medical blowout kit, and four pistol magazines for a Walther PPQ. Under the rig was the Walther in a Kydex holster and a belt.

"It counts," Mango argued. "If it wasn't for me shooting a hole in the pilot's door, there, he wouldn't have turned back."

Ryan shook his head again. "Nope. Rick and I had this one covered." He fed a belt through the loops of his cargo shorts and the holster. Eduardo's Glock was still in his back pocket. He put it in the backpack.

"What do you mean Rick?" Mango glanced at the man beside him.

"The dude stabbed the machine gunner in the leg just before he could light you guys up. Technically, he saved your ass, bro."

Rick grinned and held up his middle finger. His laugh was more of a cough, but he was smiling. Ryan took gauze from the medical pack, soaked it in water, and wiped Rick's face clean.

Mango gripped his rifle between his knees and checked the action and the magazine. "I'm not admitting to anything."

"This one's on Rick, admit it."

Mango shook his head. "Then you have to admit we both saved your ass."

Ryan snorted in consternation. "David, are you hooked to satellite communications?"

"Yes, sir."

"Can you call Joulie and have her meet us at the airport with a medical team?"

They listened to him make the phone call. She would send a medical team for Rick, but she couldn't make it to the airport. She asked Ryan and Mango to meet her at Billy Parker's dock.

David landed the helicopter ten minutes later. An ambulance sat beside the hangar. The paramedics waited until the rotor blades stopped spinning and then ran over to the bird with a stretcher. Ryan opened the cabin door and stepped out onto the tarmac, the KRISS Vector at low ready. The medical crew didn't even pause at the sight of the firearms, moving quickly around him to get to Rick.

They helped the injured man onto a stretcher and rushed him back to the ambulance.

Mango climbed in after them. He made eye contact with one of the EMTs. "I go where he goes."

David got out of the helicopter and slammed the door. He walked around it, checking out the damage.

"I need to get a ride to the hospital," Ryan said.

David nodded. "If you help me get the helicopter into the hangar, I'll drive you."

"What do we do?" Ryan asked.

"Grab the dolly and we'll move it inside."

When the helicopter was in the hangar, they closed the doors and locked them with a chain and padlock before walking to David's Bronco.

CHAPTER FORTY-THREE

After talking to the doctor about Rick's injuries, Mango and Ryan had headed for the dock. Joulie Lafitte was waiting for them when they arrived. As Mango and Ryan walked down the dock, she had her driver start the Cigarette Top Gun's twin engines. They thundered to life. The idling motors sounded out of time from the lumpy cam shafts the builder had used to achieve the highest horsepower possible.

Mango slung the backpack into the boat and climbed down. Ryan swept his gaze around the marina and out into the bay, still gripping the KRISS Vector. When Mango was seated beside Joulie, Ryan tossed off the lines and stepped into the boat. He leaned his back into the contoured seat and continued to keep watch as the driver idled them away from the dock. Once clear of the no wake zone, the driver threw power to the engines. They raced across the calm bay, avoiding incoming fishing vessels and a large freighter. Weariness set into Ryan's muscles. Joulie, wearing a pair of khaki shorts and a purple top, turned to him, her long hair streaming in the wind. She yelled, "I hear you have my gold."

He shook his head. "It went down with Kilroy's ship."

Joulie said, "My men fished Kilroy's body out of the water."

Ryan looked away, trying to get the image of Kilroy and his wife face down in the water out of his mind.

The boat continued to rocket across the water, rocking side to side as it encountered small waves.

Turning to Mango, Ryan shouted, "When this is over, let's go get some Haitian food."

Mango grinned. "What's that, like Chinese?"

Ryan tapped Joulie on the shoulder. "What do Haitians call Haitian food?"

Joulie narrowed her brow in suspicion.

Still shouting, Ryan said, "In the States, we say we're going to get Mexican or Chinese or Italian. What do Haitians say when they go out to eat?"

She rolled her eyes. "It's called Creole cuisine."

Ryan turned to Mango. "Did you know the national breakfast of Haiti is spaghetti and hot dogs covered in ketchup?"

Mango stuck his tongue out and acted like he was about to vomit.

Joulie punched Mango in the shoulder. "Don't make fun our *espagheti*."

Several minutes later, the driver pulled the throttles back and the big boat slowed. The backend wiggled side to side as the speed came off. Finally, the boat leveled off and settled low in the water as the driver worked the throttles to bring it alongside *Peggy Lynn. Dark Water* was rafted on the opposite side of the salvage vessel. Greg sat in the cockpit enjoying an adult beverage, he held up the bottle in a toast when their eyes met. Ryan wanted a beer himself. It had been a long day, and it wasn't even lunch time.

Travis, Stacey, Emery, Jennifer, and Emily were along the rail as the boats bumped fenders. Travis took the lines and tied them off. The driver shut off the twin engines and silence reigned over the water. Travis extended a hand and helped Joulie climb aboard. Her driver came next, followed by Mango and Ryan. The two former DWR employees went below, stowed their firearms, and grabbed beers on the way back topside.

Dennis came to the bridge door and leaned against it with a cup of coffee in his hand. "We're tied to the wreck. Stacey free dove the anchor rodes for us and the two boats over there." He pointed at the Yellowfin, and the Viking moored to the wreck's stern.

Ryan nodded and drained half his beer.

"How's Rick?" Greg asked.

Ryan hopped over the gunwales, pulled a beer from the cooler, and sat down in the shade of the fly bridge. "He took a pretty good beating, got a couple of broken and bruised ribs, a few loose teeth, and two black eyes. Joulie's people are guarding him at the hospital."

Greg shook his head. "It was my job to keep him safe."

"You suck at your job."

"Thanks, asshole."

"You're welcome."

"Where's my gold?" Joulie asked from *Peggy Lynn*.

Travis said, "If you come over here by the stern, you can see the strong boxes."

Joulie walked over to where Travis stood. Everyone crowded to the stern rail to look at the wreckage below. The strong boxes rested beside *Northwest Passage* on the seabed where they'd tumbled as the boat sank.

"What are you going to do about it?" Joulie asked.

"We were waiting for Ryan to get back," Stacey said. "He's the boss and the one who gets to set the hook."

"Well, boss, get to it," Joulie said.

Ryan sat down again and unlaced his old desert combat boots. He kicked them off and peeled away the socks. His sweaty feet were thankful for the reprieve, and he realized how much he disliked wearing the boots that had seen him through the mountains of Afghanistan. "Drop the hook, Grandpa."

Emery moved to the crane and started the diesel engine. He lowered the hook and cable into the ocean. Travis gave him directions using hand signals to get the hook close to the strong boxes. Ryan opened his gear locker and removed his Dive Rite Transpac and attached a dive tank, then he screwed his regulators to the tank valve. He donned boots and fins and slipped into the Dive Rite harness. After spraying a mixture of baby shampoo and water in his mask, to keep it from fogging, Ryan rinsed it in fresh water and pulled it over his head. He stepped up on the rail, and with a giant stride, he entered the water.

Ryan thrust his arms out in front of him, blading his hands and porpoising his body with strong fin kicks. The depth was close to one hundred feet. He quickly reached the bottom, grabbed the crane hook, and swam it to the closest strong box. After hooking it into the strap system still in place from when they'd craned it from *Peggy Lynn* to *Northwest Passage*, Ryan signaled for the crane to lift the box. Then he floated over to examine the second strong box. Kilroy had opened it to look at the gold. Fortunately, he had shut it before the EFP had detonated. The web of straps was still in place but needed to be adjusted before the crane hook could be set. He tugged them around and looked up at the surface. The crane winch was slow, and the first box was still on its way up.

He glanced at his computer and then turned to the wreck. There was always something to salvage, and Jim Kilroy had lots of toys onboard. Ryan was familiar with the ship's layout from their time spent sailing from Belize to Nicaragua, where they'd met the *Santo Domingo*. Now he steered straight for the dive locker, where he loaded his Transpac D-rings with reels, surface markers, and spear guns. He found a bag and began stuffing BCDs and other gear into it. They would come back for the rest.

Outside the wreck, the crane hook had returned. He attached the strong box and the bag of gear to the hook and signaled Emery to begin lifting. Ryan straddled the crane cable and rode the slowly ascending box up through the water column.

CHAPTER FORTY-FOUR

When Ryan climbed back on the salvage vessel after his three-minute safety stop, everyone had gathered around the strong boxes and each held a bar of gold. Only Captain Dennis remained on the bridge, unaffected by the gold fever. Ryan shed his dive gear and glanced over at Emily, who stood between Joulie and Jennifer. If Emily knew of Joulie's relationship with him, she didn't show it, and he knew Joulie wouldn't volunteer information about their love affair. He didn't want or need them comparing notes. He crossed to the bridge and stepped inside.

Dennis stood with his ubiquitous cup of coffee, staring out the large window. Ryan noticed that the captain now wore a pistol on his belt.

"Ready to repel boarders?"

"One never knows what gold fever will do," Dennis replied.

"Very true," Ryan said. He leaned out the door and called for Joulie to join them on the bridge. She carried a gold bar with her, eyes agleam. She held it out in both hands.

"This is the symbol of my country." She indicated the intricate symbol pressed into the precious metal.

Ryan had looked at it before but hadn't given it much thought. Now he studied it in detail. In the center was a palm tree, at its base, two cannons pointing outward, and six flags—three on each side of the palm—stood at forty-five degrees from the tree's base. The words *L'Union Fait La Force* had been stamped below the nation's emblem.

"What does it say?" Dennis asked.

"Union makes strength," Joulie replied.

Dennis smiled. "Now you can use the gold to help unify your country."

Joulie agreed, "Yes, it will be my pleasure to use this gold to help my people. This is why the loa brought me back to Haiti. They knew I would be needed to distribute this wealth."

Dennis scratched his beard. "When Ryan told us he was giving you half of the gold, I didn't really like the idea. We salvors like to keep what we find. But over the last week you've proved to me how genuine you really are. I know you'll use the money to do good for your country."

"Thank you, Dennis." Joulie kissed him on the cheek.

Her lustrous black hair shined in the late afternoon light. Ryan thought again about how beautiful she was.

The smile on her face disappeared and she abruptly turned businesslike. "Now I will take my gold."

"In the Cigarette?" Dennis asked.

"No, you will bring it to Billy Parker's dock. I will arrange for a truck to meet you there."

"Where are you going to store it?" Ryan asked, crossing his arms, and leaning against the console.

Joulie smiled coyly. "I can't give away all my secrets."

"Fair enough." Ryan moved to the door and lit a cigarette. Looking across the water to the Kilroy's two boats anchored at the far end of the wreck, he said, "I want you to leave one of your crews here to guard those boats."

"*Wi*," Joulie said. "What will you do with them?"

Dennis answered, "We're going to sell them."

"For how much?"

Dennis scratched his beard. "Haven't really thought about it."

"I will buy them from you. You won't have to worry about provenance, and I can sell them quickly."

"Fine with me," Dennis said. "Fine with you, boss?"

Ryan nodded. "Works for me."

Joulie moved closer to Ryan and turned to look at the group of people on the stern and in *Dark Water*'s cockpit. In a near whisper, she asked, "How is your girlfriend?"

Ryan put the cigarette in his mouth and inhaled. Smoke curled around his words. "I haven't had a chance to talk to her."

Emily glanced his way, almost as if she knew they were talking about her. He nodded at her, and she turned back to talk to Jennifer.

"She cares about you. I will pray the loa help you find a way to be together."

"Thanks." He wasn't holding out much hope. She'd broken up with him because of the danger he seemed to constantly put her in. Ryan didn't think she would want to rekindle the relationship after being kidnapped.

Joulie leaned in close and whispered, "What will you do with all of your gold?"

"Divvy it up."

"What if I gave you cash for it?"

Ryan turned to her, eyebrows raised.

"Do you have someone who will convert it to cash without any questions? This much gold flooding onto the market will drive the price down. I'll give you spot price from close of business today."

Ryan leaned into the bridge. "What's spot price of gold, Captain?"

Dennis stepped over to the computer and tapped a few keys to log onto his brokerage account. He read off the current number.

"Figure out a total of what we have for today's price," Ryan said.

Dennis totaled up the weight of twenty-two gold bars and wrote it on a slip of paper. "That's minus the four bars missing."

Joulie frowned. "Why are there some missing?"

"We have three on here, and *La Sirene* kept one as tribute." Ryan said, referring to the Haitian loa of the sea. He pointed to the wreck below them. "Kilroy had a diver who took a bar, too."

"You will retrieve it?"

"Yeah, we'll find it."

Joulie took the paper from Dennis. "Do you intend to keep any of the bars?"

"Two," Ryan said. "Unless you want one, Dennis."

The older man shook his head. "Might make a nice coaster for my coffee mug. Other than that, I've got no use for it."

"Do you have enough cash?" Ryan asked.

Joulie nodded. "It's not a problem."

Ryan wondered where she was going to get eleven million dollars when she'd told him she'd already spent most of her money on infrastructure projects.

"I'll subtract two bars from your total and take three of the bars you have on the ship. It will give you an incentive to find the one Kilroy took."

"Hey, Travis," Ryan shouted and when the man looked, Ryan motioned for him to join them. Travis walked over and leaned against the railing, one foot on the steps to the bridge deck. Ryan stepped down closer to him. "Get one of those gold bars you have in your room and bring it up here."

"What for?" Travis asked with a frown.

"I'm keeping a bar and you're keeping a bar. Joulie is going to give us cash for the rest."

Travis looked past Ryan to the Haitian vodou priestess and whistled softly. "She's got that kind of dough, eh?"

"She says she does."

"I thought you only had one bar."

"I do," Ryan said. "The one she's letting me keep is down in Kilroy's safe."

"That's harsh."

"You cool with taking cash?" Ryan asked.

"You betcha."

"Sure you're not Canadian, eh?" Ryan teased.

"Without a doubt, eh?" Travis grinned.

Ryan gathered everyone around and asked if they would like to be paid in cash or gold. The preferred method was cash. Joulie took her phone from her pocket and walked to *Peggy Lynn*'s bow to have a private conversation.

"What about the bounty?" Greg asked when she was gone.

Ryan shrugged. "I assume it's still in effect. Those guys in the helicopter were Aztlán cartel members."

Joulie walked back to the group, still clutching her phone. "I have arranged for a truck to meet us at the marina to pick up the gold."

"Let's cast off, Captain," Ryan said.

"Aye aye," Dennis said with a salute.

EPILOGUE

Ryan Weller leaned on the white, rust-pitted railing of the salvage vessel *Peggy Lynn*. Beside him was Captain Dennis Law. Both men held cups of steaming coffee, and Ryan had a cigarette between his lips. They were staring down through the crystal-clear water at Travis Wisnewski as he carried items out of the sunken wreck *Northwest Passage*. Don Williams sat in the shade by the recompression chamber. Stacey Coleman and Emery Ducane tended Travis's umbilical, keeping the proper amount of slack as he moved. They didn't need to worry about gas switches or blending. They were pumping regular compressed air to the diver and he would adhere to the standard U.S. Navy dive tables, which gave him twenty minutes of bottom time if they wanted to avoid using the chamber. They were salvaging anything of value they could sell either in Haiti, the Dominican Republic, or back in the States. At the top of the list was the gold bar.

"What's your plans now that this is over?" Ryan asked.

"Can't say that I've thought about it much."

"I talked to Greg when we were in Cap-Haïtien. He

wants to hire us as troubleshooters for DWR, and we might do a few things for Homeland if they ask us nicely."

Dennis nodded and sipped his coffee. "This hasn't been the easiest cruise."

"No, sir, it has not. There were a lot of contributing factors to that, and I was one of them."

"Glad you can admit it."

Ryan chuckled. "I'm not out of the woods yet. I don't think Orozco will be too happy about me killing another one of his henchmen. Greg had our Homeland guy run a facial recog scan, and it came back as one of Orozco's high-level lieutenants."

"At least you won't have to worry about Kilroy double crossing you again."

"Amen," Ryan said.

"Speaking of cartels," Dennis said, scratching his beard. "What about the boatload of drugs we found?"

Ryan stared into the water and sipped his coffee. "There's two schools of thought, one, we turn over the coordinates to the Coast Guard and let them pull them up, and two, we leave them alone. I can use them for leverage with the cartel, if need be."

"And if someone else finds the boat?"

Ryan shrugged. "We'll cross that bridge when we come to it."

They leaned against the rail, each mulling over his own thoughts. Ryan's turned to Emily. He had asked her to stay with him on the boat, even offered to use Kilroy's Viking sportfisher as their waterborne hotel, but she'd rebuffed his offer and took a plane back to Florida. He'd watched her climb the stairs and waved as she stepped through the airplane's door without so much as a glance over her shoulder. His heart had sagged out of his chest again, and he was struggling to return it to a semblance of normalcy.

Joulie had offered a comforting shoulder, and this time he'd taken it, along with her cash. The money weighed as much as ten bricks of gold and took up more room. Ryan had counted out two-point-five mill for Travis, paid Greg for the equipment, and then divided the rest between himself, the crew, Mango, and Rick.

Captain Dennis walked over to Emery and leaned over the rail beside him, watching the bubbles rise to the surface. They talked, but Ryan couldn't hear them above the noisy diesel. A few minutes later, Travis's figure emerged on the LARS basket, water streaming off every inch of his body. He held a gold bar aloft in one hand like Lady Liberty holding her torch.

Emery shut the diesel compressor engine off after Stacey removed Travis's helmet. Ryan leaned against the rail and lit another cigarette, luxuriating in the quiet that had descended on the water. The boat rocked gently in the waves as it swung on the anchor chain. Sunlight sparkled like diamonds on the water. He let out a long sigh and closed his eyes, turning his face to the sun.

"We've talked about it, boss," Captain Dennis Law said.

Ryan opened his eyes. "And?"

"We're all in."

The two men shook hands.

In his best pirate voice, Dennis said, "Now get your scurvy ass in the water and do a day's work."

WHY EOD?

I was first introduced to Navy EOD as a twenty-one-year-old boot camp attendee. I found a flyer on our ship's (that's what we called barracks) bulletin board bearing their insignia, a World War II bomb, nose down in front of crossed lightning bolts on a shield with laurel wreaths curling up from the bottom on both sides. Known as "The Crab," the service badge is issued to members of every military branch after they graduate from the Naval School Explosive Ordnance Disposal at Eglin Air Force Base. The flyer detailed the physical requirements as well as the job description. It fascinated me.

I went on to aviation electronics technician (AT) A-school and then to helicopter squadron HM-14, whose primary job was, and still is, underwater mine countermeasures. This placed me in close contact with EOD, because of their continued work with underwater mines. The squadron deployed to the USS *Bonhomme Richard*, and we had a detachment of EOD guys across from our work center. Those guys were super fit, highly intelligent individuals who always had a kind word and invited me to volunteer. I confess, I liked my job as an AT and had no desire to do all the physical training required. On a deployment to Bahrain, I, again, interacted with the EOD support detachment. They believed they were the best of the best, the elite of the Navy. And rightly so. EOD accounts for less than three percent of all U.S. Navy active duty and reserve sailors. That number gets even more important when we look at the EOD school's fifty- to seventy-percent attrition rate.

When I sat down to write Ryan Weller's character, I wanted him to be something other than a SEAL. Everyone has a SEAL as his/her protagonist. I wanted something different, and EOD traditionally flies under the radar. Especially Navy EOD. They are the only EOD techs service wide who operate both above and below the water and until recently, the only EOD units qualified to deploy with Special Forces.

Until combat operations in Iraq and Afghanistan, not much had been written about the EOD community and the one movie Hollywood had made was highly inaccurate in the depiction of an EOD tech's life and work. I've read all I could get my hands on, especially about who these men and women are, their training, and their time in service. Some of the best knowledge came from technical white papers and war college master's theses. I also talked to men who had served as EOD. They were an invaluable resource. Thanks to everyone who shared their stories with me. I'm always touched and humbled by these brave men and women who place their lives on the line that others might be saved. Thank you for your service.

I tried to get my character right, but this is a work of fiction, and Ryan is infinitely cooler than I'll ever be, partly because I can take all day to think about his dialogue and witty comebacks. Forgive me if I got parts wrong, or I represented something as it shouldn't be.

Check out The EOD Warrior Foundation, a nonprofit organization whose mission is to help EOD warriors, their family members, and the families of fallen EOD warriors. Specific programs include emergency financial relief, college scholarships, hope and wellness retreats, and care of the EOD Memorial located at Eglin AFB, Florida.

www.eodwarriorfoundation.org.

ABOUT THE AUTHOR

Evan Graver has worked in construction, as a security guard, a motorcycle and car technician, a property manager, and in the scuba industry. He served in the U.S. Navy, where he was an aviation electronics technician until they medically retired him following a motorcycle accident which left him paralyzed. He found other avenues of adventure: riding ATVs, downhill skiing, skydiving, and bungee jumping. His passions are scuba diving and writing. He lives in Hollywood, Florida, with his wife and son.

WHAT'S NEXT?

Did you enjoy *Dark Horse*? Please leave a review.

If you would like to follow Ryan Weller's adventures, and learn more about him, visit www.evangraver.com. Sign up for my monthly correspondence and receive the free Ryan Weller Thriller Short Story, *Dark Days*. I send out an update around the 15th of the month about what I'm writing, reading, or listening to. I'll throw in some things happening in my daily life and let you know when the next book is coming out.

 facebook.com/evangraverauthor